Talavera

Book 6 in the Napoleonic Horseman Series

By
Griff Hosker

Talavera

Published by Sword Books Ltd 2019

Copyright ©Griff Hosker First Edition

Chapter 1

I am Major Robert Matthews. I was not born with this name. I am the illegitimate son of a French Count who had been executed during the Terror. My mother was Scottish and the daughter of an aristocrat. I did not have the opportunity to be close to my father who was a cold and distant man but I was sad when he was executed. I had joined the French Chasseurs and served in the French Army until Napoleon Bonaparte abandoned his army in Egypt. That had not been the reason I deserted. I killed a senior officer in a duel and I had had to flee. After a series of adventures and misadventures, I was offered a position in a British Regiment by an Intelligence officer, Colonel Selkirk. My skill with languages and martial skills made me a valuable asset and he used me. I rarely saw my own regiment for I had been loaned to generals such as Sir Arthur Wellesley and Sir John Moore. I was unique amongst officers. I could operate behind enemy lines. The only person in whom I could confide was my servant, Sergeant Sharp. He was a good horseman and, like me, he had skills. I would not have survived as long as I had without his assistance.

Sergeant Sharp and I did not have long with the regiment. We had returned from Corunna in January. I had barely got to know the new troopers and officers of the regiment when the letter from the war office arrived at the barracks at the end of February. The Sergeant Major could not believe how little time I had been granted. Joe Seymour was the best soldier in the regiment, despite his white hairs, and he had seen it all before.

"It is a time of war, Sarn't Major. I learned much with Sir John Moore, not least the threat the French pose. I would rather be fighting them than parading here and preparing to defend England. That is for the Fencibles. We should be in Portugal. We are cavalry and the 11th is one of the finest regiments in the British Army. Perhaps I have been summoned to receive orders for the regiment."

"Perhaps, Major Matthews, but both of us know that it is more likely that you will be sent ahead of us. You have skills the other officers don't." He stroked his chin, "If they do send you then

1

take care, eh, Major? Britain will need lads like you when this war is over."

"Perhaps. Have my gear stored eh, Sarn't Major? In case I am sent on ahead."

"Of course, sir."

I had three horses. All were fine animals. Until I knew the purpose of the summons to Horse Guards, I would ride the one best suited for London, Star. My other two were valuable war horses. I had spent a long time training them. The noise and clamour of London was not for them. Sharp knew how to pack for me and he had a spare horse with our trappings and war gear. Over the last years, we had accumulated a variety of weapons. I even owned a Baker rifle. It had been frowned upon by other cavalry officers. They saw it as the weapon of a common man. I had been called that by many officers and even Sir Arthur Wellesley had thought the same. Not long before he left Spain to travel to England for the inquiry which would exonerate him, he had given me faint praise. He had told Sir John, '*You can trust this one. He may have little breeding but he is a damned fine soldier, honest and brave.*' It was the most generous thing Sir Arthur ever said to me and I had remembered it.

As we headed down the road, Alan Sharp asked me about the letter I had received. "Is it Colonel Selkirk again, sir?"

Each time Colonel Selkirk was involved with us we ended up behind enemy lines risking being shot as a spy. I shrugged, "The letter was from a Colonel Williams. It said I was needed by the Army. However, this has Colonel Selkirk written all over it. We have been asked to bring spare uniforms. We are going abroad again."

"I thought we had been thrown out of the Peninsular, sir."

"No, there are still a couple of regiments in Gibraltar and Sir John Craddock has the remains of the men that landed last year at Lisbon."

Alan Sharp was a good soldier and he knew officers. He shook his head, "With respect, sir, Sir John Craddock is as much use as a one-legged man in an arse kicking contest. He is scared of his own shadow."

I smiled at Sharp's colourful language. I allowed him to be informal when we were alone and his judgement of Sir John was not particularly harsh. He was a natural pessimist. What the army needed was a commander who was an optimist and believed that we could actually win! "Remember to keep your thoughts to yourself in Whitehall, Sergeant. There are a large number of officers who would have your stripes for such comments."

He smiled cheerfully, "Aye, sir, and I dare say that they would add a few stripes to my back. Don't worry, Major Matthews, I can play the game!" We rode in silence for a while and then he asked, "Where will we be staying, sir?"

"I am not certain yet. It may well be that we can stay at my cousin's place. We will speak with Mr Hudson. I think I am still welcome there."

Sharp nodded, "Aye, sir, and it means we will have decent wine too!"

My cousin, Cesar Alpini, lived in Sicily. Thus far he had avoided the attentions of Napoleon but there was a risk that, with his British connections, he might have to flee for his life. His English agent, Mr Hudson, kept a small house for him. It was not far from Queen Anne Square on Wells Street. Mr Hudson had a housekeeper who lived there with her husband. George had been a sailor on one of Matthew Dinsdale's ships. An accident with a block and tackle had cost him the use of his left arm. His accident had been fortuitous and both the Alpini family and George and his wife benefitted.

We rode first to the offices of Mr Hudson. He also acted as my agent and handled the money I received from the goods Mr Fortnum sold for me. My relationship with the Alpini family meant that I benefitted from the sale of their goods. I had helped Matthew Dinsdale to buy a second ship and I had a lucrative income. Had I chosen I could have left the army and lived the life of the idle rich. It was not in my nature. The French revolution had cost me my family, my home and any hope of a title I might have had. Until it was defeated and the monarchy restored, then I would fight. I had money and I never had to worry if I needed to make a purchase.

David Hudson smiled broadly when he saw me. He was my agent but he was also a friend. I think he lived, vicariously, through my adventures. When I was in London, I always made a point of visiting him. We exchanged letters when we could. He knew I had been in Spain. When his clerk admitted me to his office, I saw the furtive glance as he appraised me for wounds.

I smiled, "Do not fear, sir, I am whole. God knows that there are many who will not be."

He beamed, "Major, as ever, it is a joy to see you." He nodded to Alan Sharp, "And you too, Sergeant. The world is treating you well?"

"The world? Not that you would notice, sir. It is full of Frenchmen trying to kill me. Major Matthews, on the other hand, treats me like a gentleman. I am content, sir."

"Go and find Jennings, would you? Ask him for wine, bread and cheese." As a supplier of fine foods and wines to Mr Fortnum's establishment, not to mention half of the great houses in London, Mr Hudson had a fine larder. As Sharp left, Mr Hudson said, "Sit, I pray you." He put another log onto the fire. February and March might not be the coldest of winter months but they were still cold. "Is it your business which brings you here, Major, or the Army?"

"The Army, but I will cast my eye over the books whilst I am here. I fear the war will go on too long for me to be able to buy a home but I would know how I stand in relation to the prospect of purchasing something."

"You have more than enough, sir. Now might be a good time. This war has bankrupted some men and made the fortunes of others." He smiled and spread a hand, "At the moment, I am one of the latter as are you. There are estates which belonged to lords and merchants. You have more than enough for one."

Jennings and Sharp came in with two laden trays. I waited until the wine was poured and we had been cut bread, ham and cheese. This did not feel like England. This was Sicily! The bread was thickly cut and the ham was slightly spiced. They had good ham in Sicily. I could tell that this was from a wild boar. Mr Hudson had good taste. I washed the food down with the rich red Sicilian wine. It was an Alpini wine. I procured it for the mess. The Alpini family was my family. Until I had washed up in Sicily, I had known little about them. I smiled at the memory of my meeting with the Knight of St John on Malta. That meeting had changed my life.

"Then I shall heed your advice about land. If you would be good enough to keep your eyes open for a property. At the moment it is just myself and Sergeant Sharp, but who knows what the future holds?"

Mr Hudson smiled, "Major Matthews, you are a fine young man. There will be many fathers seeking a match for their daughters. With your money, your title and your looks there will be many queuing up for an invitation. Now that you are in London and society you will have many calls upon your time and company." He smiled, "As I say, your situation may change. I will enjoy this challenge. You would like a house with land, would you not? Horses and the like?"

I had not thought about it but he was right. My best horse, Badger, was with the regiment. The stable master would care for him and I did not think I would ride him to war again. I would like him to enjoy retirement. "A good idea, Mr Hudson, but nothing too grand, eh? I am a simple man."

"Leave it with me."

"And, while we are in London, we would like to use the house in Wells Street if that is agreeable to you. I know not how long we will be in London. The letter just asked us to present ourselves to the Military Secretary at the war office."

"St Margaret's Street?"

"I believe so."

Mr Hudson nodded, "They are the newer buildings. Some of the older ones are decidedly damp and full of rats." He laughed, "And I don't just mean the politicians!" We laughed too. The corruption in Parliament was well known. As soldiers, we had suffered from it when suppliers who had bribed politicians to secure contracts delivered rotten food and sub-standard equipment. Sir John Moore had been one of the first to stand against such practices. "And as for Wells Street, of course, George and his wife enjoy playing host. How long will you be in London?"

"As I said, that is out of my hands, Mr Hudson. It will depend upon my meeting."

He waved an airy hand, "No matter. It will give me time to have my clerks prepare a detailed account of your finances. Your investments have done well." He beamed, "I benefit almost as much as you do, Major." As an agent, he earned a percentage of the profits I made.

We chatted, inconsequentially, about London and the changes the war with Napoleon had wrought and then Sergeant Sharp and I headed for Wells Street.

It was dark when we arrived and I felt guilty having tarried so long at Mr Hudson's. Poor George and his wife, Mary, had to race around airing beds and lighting fires. They asked if we wished to have hot food. We declined and, instead, Sergeant Sharp and I headed for the inns and taverns of Oxford Street. This was not the most salubrious part of London. Criminals heading for Tyburn and execution were brought down the thoroughfare and it was filled with low alehouses. Bystanders would spend the morning drinking and then when the poor souls to be executed were brought along the street they would follow, heckling and jeering. They seemed to enjoy the spectacle of men being hanged. It had been the same in Paris during the Terror. The poor from St Giles' Rookery would flock to watch. The Rookery was a tangle of tenements and the homes of the lowest in society. Sometimes they slept eight or ten to a room! Both Alan and I were armed and I did not fear those we might meet. The food would be plain and wholesome and the ale drinkable. The poor liked their ale!

We approached the Lion and the Lamb. I had never heard of it but it faced the road and looked to be clean. I did not mind rough but I would not go somewhere which was lice and flea ridden. As we ducked beneath the low lintel, we entered a dingy and poorly lit room. I would have turned and left had I not seen the welcoming fire and then I saw a familiar face. "Jenkins!"

The one-armed ex-soldier had been at Vimeiro. Jenkins was a rifleman. There was no higher praise than that. He stood and tried to salute with his stump.

I seated myself next to him, "None of that, Jenkins! You survived then?"

"Aye, sir. It was a good sawbones and he took the arm off clean, like, sir. I was luckier than most."

I observed that he had just a gill of beer and an empty plate. He looked thin and emaciated. The entrance of an officer and a sergeant had caused some alarm. Some men thought that we were conscripting. I spied the landlord surreptitiously reach down below the bar. It would be for a club. I smiled. We had handled worse. I nodded towards the bar. "What is the food like, Jenkins?"

"Decent enough for the like of us, sir, but not for an officer like you."

"I will be the judge of that. What would you recommend?"

"The beef and oyster pie is tasty enough and I know the oysters are fresh, I helped to carry them." He gave me a wan smile, "Paid for the ale and a scrap of stale bread."

I nodded to Sharp as I rose. He would watch my back. As I neared the bar, through the fug of smoke from pipes and a smoky fire, I smiled and took out my purse. It jingled for it was full. I had had back pay. "Good evening, landlord. I am Major Matthews of the 11th Light Dragoons." I saw that his hands were hidden and he had a furtive look on his face. "You can take your hands from the club you are fingering. We are not here for conscripts, we are here to enjoy your beef and oyster pie."

He smiled and put his hands back on the bar. His relief was obvious. "Sorry, sir, can't be too careful. We lost lads from around here in Portugal. There is some bad feeling. Would that be two pies then, sir?"

"No, three. I have a guest. And three pints of your best bitter." He nodded. "And don't try to fob me off with watered down slops. I may be an officer but I know ale." I fixed him with a steely stare. It had worked in the Chasseurs and the Light Dragoons. The landlord was no fool. He nodded.

There was, however, one fool. As I went to put the purse away with my left hand, a young lad of nineteen or twenty took what he saw as his chance to become rich. He had a dagger and he lunged towards me. His intent was clear. He thought to hack at the hand which held the purse and, when I dropped it, take it and run. I allowed his dagger to whip towards me and, as I drew back my left hand, I punched him hard in the side of the head with my right. I had learned to fight in the Chasseurs. The light went from his eyes and he crumpled to the floor.

I looked around, "Does he belong to anyone?" I saw two older men, not much older but older than the youth; they looked guilty. I pointed to the prostrate figure. "Take him and leave." They leaned over to pick him up. I patted my sword with my right hand, "And if I even smell you when I leave, I shall use this sword and, believe me, I know how to use a sword."

They nodded, "Sorry, sir. He is young and daft, sir."

As I neared the table, I saw that Alan had a brace of pistols on the table. Ex-rifleman Jenkins shook his head, "Sorry about that, sir. Local thugs."

"Not your fault. Do you live locally?"

"Aye, sir. I lodge in St. Giles Rookery. Ten of us in a room. Most are either matelots or soldiers. We get on and look after each other." I nodded, He went on, "I miss the army. At least we were fed and had respect. Most of the folk who live in London cross the street when they see an old soldier. They think we are all beggars and thieves. They forget that we were fighting for them."

"I know, I know."

The food and ale arrived. I saw that we had a full measure of ale and the food filled the large metal platter. The landlord and serving girl looked at me nervously. "I am sorry about Dick, sir. I should have barred him."

I nodded, "My friend here tells me that you have good food and good ale. You could attract a better clientele. You don't need to pander to such customers. I am here for a few days. If your food is up to muster you will see me again. If I choose then I can spread the word. It is your choice, landlord."

"Thank you, sir. That is very fair."

I saw Jenkins salivating. "Go on Jenkins, dig in. My treat."

"If you are sure, sir."

I nodded and he wolfed down the food. I do not think he had had a decent meal in a long time. The pie was a delicious one. The gravy and the bread were also good. I did not feel like a pudding but I thought Jenkins did. As the platters were taken away and the next round of drinks brought, I said, "Do you do a pudding, landlord?"

He grinned, "Aye sir, the wife does a lovely spotted dick and custard."

"Then bring three and we shall have three pipes, too." Alan looked at me in surprise. We rarely smoked a pipe. I shrugged and he nodded. Alan and I paid lip service to the pudding. It was all that the landlord had said but I had had enough with the pie and bread. Jenkins finished his and then looked at ours. "Finish ours off too, if you wish, Jenkins."

He did so with relish and we had another ale. He looked better already. "Well sir, you have fed me and given me ale." He held up his pipe, "And given me a pipe. "What would you have of me?"

I smiled, "Nothing, save information."

"Whatever I know then I will tell you, sir."

"Then tell me all you know about London." He looked at me as though I had spoken French. "I have spent more time abroad than in London. You know how it is, Jenkins. When you are campaigning abroad local knowledge is important. Who runs this town? Where should we avoid?"

He looked relieved, "Then I am your man, sir."

It proved a useful investment. I learned about the gangs who controlled not only the drinking establishments but also the ordinary merchants of London. Mr Hudson had intimated to me that there was some sort of gang operating around the more popular merchants and ships. Gangs would gather outside and intimidate customers. If money was paid then the streets were kept clear. I also learned about some of the lords and ladies who were powerful in the city. I was not sure if the information would be of much use but I stored it anyway. I had operated as a spy long enough to know that no knowledge was useless.

I ordered another beer for Jenkins and two rums for us. I gave our unsmoked pipes to him. He would enjoy them later. I took out twenty shillings. I could have proffered a guinea but Jenkins would have found it hard to hide and then spend such a large denomination coin. The twenty shillings could be secreted about his person easily. I pushed them across to him.

"What's this for, sir?" He looked a little hurt. "You have paid me with the ale and the food, not to mention the pipes. I don't need charity!"

"And this isn't charity. I want you to work for me."

His face relaxed, "What sort of work, sir?"

"We are staying in Wells Street. I want you to follow us while we are in London. I want to know if anyone takes an interest in us. What do you say?"

"Are you worried about someone then, sir?"

I shrugged, "Let us just say that I have made enough enemies to fear a knife in the night. You are a Londoner and you would blend in. You know who is dangerous and who is not. If you don't recognise the ones who take an interest in us then that means danger for us."

He looked relieved, "I can do that, sir."

I stood, "And it may be that, sometime in the future, I may have a position for you. I have someone looking out for a property for me. When I get one, I shall need a caretaker, someone I can trust."

"That would be perfect sir only…"

"Only what, Jenkins?"

"If you are going off to fight again then…"

I laughed, "They say I am lucky. Let us hope, for all our sakes, that it continues."

"Amen to that, sir!"

Sharp and I were wary when we stepped into the cold night air. We had eaten enough and stayed in the tavern long enough so that our senses were not dulled by drink. We were not followed. We checked on our horses and then went to our rooms. Once in our new chambers, Sergeant Sharp asked, "Do we really need Rafe Jenkins to watch our backs, sir?"

"I hope not but for a few shillings, we know there are a pair of eyes looking out for danger. Don't forget that Boney knows I am still alive. He is a vindictive little man and I would not put it past him to send an assassin. I will be happier when I know who it is will be giving the orders!"

The next day we left for the various errands we had to run. Jenkins thought he had done a good job of hiding himself but I spotted him. Most people would have failed to see him but I was looking for him. We strode towards the river. We had heard people in the streets since before dawn. London was a major city. It was a city of commerce and trade. In offices, men were trading goods and money. The East India Company and the Hudson Bay Trading Company both ran powerful empires. London was at their heart.

There were many other soldiers in London. Since the retreat to Corunna and the disaster that had been the Low Countries, Britain had more soldiers at home than for many years. Some officers would be seeking commissions and others seeking promotion. I might be unique. I had been summoned and that meant someone wanted me. The man who had summoned us was the Military Secretary, a close friend of the Prince Regent as well as the Duke of York, General Sir James Willoughby Gordon. I had never met the man but I had heard of him. His active service had been in Madeira and his last service in a regiment had been fourteen years earlier. When I had mentioned his name to the Colonel, he had dismissed him as a fawning fop. In a way that heartened me for it would be unlikely that I would be given one of my usual dangerous assignments. Strangely, it was Rafe Jenkins who gave us some unexpected information. The mistress of Prince Frederick, Mary Anne Clarke, had been summoned to Parliament. She had admitted to selling, illegally, commissions. I had not heard of this but if it was true then General Sir James Willoughby Gordon's days as Military Secretary were numbered for he was a close ally of the Prince Regent and their fortunes were bound together.

We arrived at his office early. We had been summoned for ten o'clock. While we waited, we went to look across the river towards Lambeth Palace. It was as we turned that my heart sank for I saw, emerging from the building, Colonel Selkirk. That did not bode well. The Colonel always brought with him danger and intrigue. I had had enough of the latter.

Chapter 2

Sergeant Sharp shook his head, "Bloody hell, sir! I hope he was seeing someone else!"

"As do I, Sergeant. Let us not jump to conclusions. This is the War Office and the Colonel is an important man. It may just be a coincidence."

"Aye sir, believe that if you like but I wouldn't bet on it."

To be fair to the Military Secretary, we were not kept waiting for much above a half hour. In my experience that was nothing. He was a large man. He looked florid and I had the impression that he liked both food and wine in equal measure. The fact that I could smell it on his breath confirmed my suspicions.

"Major Matthews, I have heard good things about you. The reports sent back from Sir John Moore extolled your many virtues and Sir Arthur Wellesley has asked for you in person." He picked up a piece of paper. "Here is your commission. You are to be one of Sir Arthur's aides."

I nodded and took the paper, "And where will Sir Arthur be serving, my lord?"

"Why Spain and Portugal, of course." He leaned forward, "This is not common knowledge at the moment. Mr Ponsonby, in the House, is trying to stir up trouble by asking for an enquiry into the wart in Portugal. It will come to nothing. Lord Castlereagh will see to that." Lord Castlereagh was the Secretary of War and the Colonies. More importantly, I had heard that he was a good friend of Sir Arthur Wellesley. "Now that the enquiry has found Sir Arthur innocent, he can be sent back to complete the task he so effectively began. He should never have had to come to England! Sir John would still be alive!"

I thought that was a little unfair. It made Sir John seem inferior to Sir Arthur and he was anything but. I said nothing. This was London and politics played as much a part in life in the War Office as military matters.

"Thank you, sir."

"Sir Arthur will be in residence at his brother's house tomorrow. You know where that is?" Thanks to Rafe Jenkins I did and I nodded. "That gives you a day to yourself." He smiled, "See London!"

I said, drily, "I have seen it before, my lord. Tell me, Sir James, when does Sir Arthur leave for Iberia?"

Worryingly the Military Secretary looked blank. He smiled, "In the fullness of time you will be told. Now if you will excuse me, Major, I have many pressing matters."

We were dismissed. Sergeant Sharp was beaming as we left, "I was wrong, sir. Colonel Selkirk is not involved at all!"

I was not so sure but I did not wish to dishearten my sergeant, "It appears not but we both know that Sir Arthur is a hard taskmaster."

"Aye sir, but he knows one end of a musket from another. We have both seen generals who did not!"

We headed for Mr Hudson's offices. I was aware of our shadow but I doubted that any of the others who thronged the thoroughfares of London would have noticed the man who followed us. I saw a fine carriage outside the agent's house. The liveried coachmen told me that it was a lord. Mr Hudson was busy and so Jennings entertained us while he dealt with the important customer. The lord was an influential man. I could tell that from the way Mr Hudson fawned when the lord and his lady emerged. That was not like Mr Hudson. He was his own man. The lord and lady barely acknowledged our uniforms as they swept out.

When he returned, Mr Hudson looked relieved. "Sorry you had to wait. Jennings, fetch us some refreshments. I need them!" Once in his room, he composed himself. He saw the curiosity upon my face and smiled, "Lord and Lady Ferrers. They have recently arrived in England. He has lands in the colonies. Apparently, he has been selling off his American properties and consolidating his holdings in England. The British are not popular there. He is not only rich, but he is also powerful. He has bought a fine house in Piccadilly. It is not far from the home of the Earl of Coventry. He is holding a ball in a week to which the great and the good will be invited. Your cousin will profit greatly from the business." Jennings brought in the refreshments. "Now then, what can I do for you today?"

"We are at a loose end today and I thought to speak with you further about a property."

His face became animated, "It is strange that you should visit so quickly. Last night I was at my club." I cocked an eye. I had not seen Mr Hudson as a club member. He shrugged, "It is a way to meet men of influence. The club has members who have positions in the city. One of them mentioned that there is a farm which lies not far from Tottenham Court. Bilson's farm lies north of the turnpike. The farm is run down. The last owner drank away the profits and it has been left empty for twenty years or more. The agent was bemoaning the fact that is was too far from the centre of London to attract the right sort of buyer. We could buy it cheaply."

"Would it be possible for us to arrange a visit?"

He nodded, "I am busy today and tomorrow but the day after would be convenient and I could speak with Charles and express your interest."

"And can I afford it, Mr Hudson? It seems to me that if it is run down and derelict then it would take money to rebuild."

"And that is the beauty, my lord. There are many men seeking employment as labourers. The losses in Iberia put many off joining the army and the losses from Trafalgar make the sea less attractive. It is cheaper to rebuild than to refurbish. We could have plans drawn up and as building materials are also at lower prices then you could easily afford it. It would be an investment and a safe one at that. Bricks and mortar are always a sound place to keep your coin." He sounded convincing.

We headed back to Wells Street. I gave a slight nod behind me as we entered the door. Jenkins would know we were done for the day. We went through the house to the stables in the yard and saw to our horses and I asked Mary if she would wash some of our clothes for us. I paid her. She had three serving girls and I daresay she would delegate the task to one of them. I think the two of them enjoyed our company for many of the guests they entertained were not English. Cesar Alpini allowed travellers from his homeland to use it. George and Mary were simple folk and they did not understand what Mary called, 'foreign ways'. I wonder what Mary would have thought if she had known that I was half French!

That evening we found Jenkins waiting for us in the Lion and the Lamb. I saw that he had acquired some better clothes. They looked to be second hand but newer. He was putting my money to good use. I saw no sign of the three men with whom we had had a run in and the landlord rushed over to us as soon as we entered. He recommended the roast beef with Yorkshire pudding and so I ordered it.

"Well Jenkins, how was your day?"

"Interesting sir. You gentlemen were followed from the river. It was an old soldier like me. He looked like a Gordon Highlander. He had the cap you see."

"I didn't notice him."

"No sir, he was good. Not as good as me, sir, he didn't spot me." He laughed. "He thought I was a beggar. When you were in Mr Hudson's I asked him for a light for my pipe. He gave me a plug of baccy."

"And when we returned here?"

"He headed towards Piccadilly. I followed him and he went into a house off Swallow Street. The doorman was an ex-soldier too. He had the look of a sergeant major about him."

"You have done well. Tomorrow we go to the house of Sir Arthur Wellesley, or at least the house he uses. I believe it is his brother's."

"Number One London, eh sir? Easy to find but hard to watch."

"Don't watch us tomorrow. Watch for the Gordon Highlander, eh? When you see him then follow him."

Sir Arthur was a stickler for protocol. He was a snob. Everything had to be just right. We had worn our overalls up to now. For Sir Arthur, we wore our best uniform. I made certain that both of us were well presented as we mounted our horses and rode towards Aspley House. "You have served with Sir Arthur, Sergeant, you will be with what Sir Arthur considers the servants. You know the drill. Keep your eyes and ears open and watch out for Gordon Highlanders."

"Yes, sir." Alan would not be put out by the snub. I shared all information with my sergeant.

The house belonged to Sir Arthur's brother. However, as the temporary home of the most successful English general, it was guarded by servants who could double as soldiers if it was necessary. Our uniforms gained us immediate entry. Of Jenkins, there was not a sign but I was confident that he would secrete himself somewhere safe.

We were taken by a Lieutenant to an antechamber. He wore the uniform of the 33rd, Wellington's old regiment. "If you would wait here, sir, the general is with a visitor."

"Of course, Lieutenant...?"

"Dighton, sir, Lieutenant Dighton." I saw him look at Sergeant Sharp and wonder why I had not left him outside. I did not offer any explanation and he went into the room.

We were left alone and without refreshments. It was a well-decorated and furnished room but it looked to have been furnished by someone who did not share the general's simple taste. The curtains and the cushions were elaborate and floral. Sir Arthur liked things to be plain. While other generals wore uniforms which were festooned with gold, Sir Arthur preferred a plain blue coat and simple cocked hat

The door opened and the Lieutenant came out, "Major, the General will see you now."

When I entered my heart sank. There was Colonel Selkirk smoking a cigar. He beamed at me. Knowing that Sir Arthur liked order he did not speak. This explained his presence at the Miliatary Secretary's! The General did not smile but his usual scowl was missing. I took that to be a good sign. "Major, you survived, well done!" I bowed. "You know Colonel Selkirk, I believe."

I nodded, "Yes sir, we have crossed paths before now."

"Sir, I beg you to sit!" I did as I was ordered. As was his wont the general went directly into the purpose of the meeting. "You are a rough sort of fellow, Matthews, and if I had a daughter I would keep her well away from you, but you know the business of soldiering. I have seconded you from the 11th. You will be one of my aides for the coming campaign." He stood and went to a cloth which covered what I had taken to be a painting. He revealed a map of Spain and Portugal. "We are going back to the Spanish Peninsular. But for those fools, Burrard and Dalrymple, I would not have to go back. Cintra!" He waved a hand as though to exorcise the ghost of that disastrous treaty. "The Colonel is here because he will be serving under me as well. Between you, I want to know as much about the enemy and the land as possible. You are a damned fine scout, Matthews. Selkirk here is as sneaky a Scotsman as I have ever met!"

The Colonel gave a mock bow, "I take that as a compliment, Sir Arthur."

"You have language skills, Matthews, and they will be needed but more than that, you have a good eye for terrain and understand strategy better than most. I want you to copy this map and study it. There are gaps and, when we get to Spain, then you will fill them. There are features here which may stop a column of guns or they may not. That is why I need you. I want a battle and I need to beat the French, decisively! Roliça and Vimeiro were skirmishes, nothing more."

"And Bonaparte, sir, is he still there?"

Sir Arthur looked at Colonel Selkirk who shook his head, "He has left Soult in Portugal and he has gone to Austria." He smiled, "He believes this little adventure is ended! Sir Arthur will be a rude awakening."

"Hrmph, Selkirk, do not get ahead of yourself. Thanks to the debacle in the Low Countries we are seriously short of troops." He looked at me. "We have less than two and half thousand cavalrymen, Matthews."

I looked at Colonel Selkirk, "And the French cavalry?"

"Almost ten thousand." He smiled, "We will be outnumbered four to one in that area."

Sir Arthur shook his head, "Do not worry about the cavalry, Matthews. Unlike you, most of them are better suited to be hunting foxes and shouting '*view halloo.*' No, it will be muskets and bayonets backed by artillery which will decide this war. Our lines against their columns." He looked at me, "You have just a few hours to copy the map. Is there anything else?"

"Horses, sir. Iberia will eat horses. Have we enough mounts?"

"For you and your fellow?"

"Yes, sir. We need local horses."

He rubbed his chin, "A good point. I was not there long enough to judge but you may well be right. What do you think, Selkirk?"

"Damned good idea, sir. I will have one of my chaps go and buy some."

17

I shook my head, "With respect, Colonel, if I am going to ride them then I want to buy them."

"As you wish. Of course, it means sailing before the General and the rest of the army."

"That is not a problem, Colonel."

"Then we sail in two weeks' time from Portsmouth. We are heading for Lisbon. Present yourself there in exactly fourteen days' time." He stood. "And now, Sir Arthur, I should leave. I have much to do."

When he had gone, Sir Arthur shook his head, "Rum fellow, what?" I said nothing. Whatever I said might be wrong. "Some of my other officers have been invited to a ball. Lord Ferrers is holding it. It might be an opportunity for you to get to know them, informally, of course." He scribbled on a piece of paper. "It is in a few days' time. Here is the address and I have added the date. My signature should get you admitted." He smiled, "Of course, you and Selkirk are so cunning I daresay you could inveigle yourself without much trouble, eh? You have until noon. I need the room for a meeting later. If you need anything send your fellow to Dighton." Nodding to me he said, "I shall see you at Lord Ferrers then!"

When he had gone, I called for Sharp. "We have a map to copy." I nodded to the table where there were writing and drawing supplies. "We will both make one. It is always handy to have a spare."

We left before noon. There was less detail on the map than I had expected. Sharp and I would have a great number of gaps to fill. Sir Arthur had thoughtfully provided us with a leather tube for the map. When we reached Wells Street, we changed into our number twos. Our best uniforms had escaped damage from both food and drink. Taking the maps, we left one in the tube and studied the other.

"It is a big country, sir."

"They are two big countries and there are precious few roads. We will need to buy clothes in Lisbon to help us blend in."

"The Froggies are a bit funny about locals, sir. If we get caught, we might get shot."

I nodded, "And that is why we will just get clothes to cover our uniforms."

Sharp nodded, "That is why you wanted Iberian horses eh, sir?"

"Badger is too fine a horse to die in Iberia. I suspect our horses will be ridden hard."

That evening we met with Jenkins. His news was not what I expected. "So, did our friend follow us to Aspley House then?"

"No, sir, that was the funny thing. He didn't. I had to go looking for him. I found him close to the shops in Piccadilly. He was following a woman, sir. She was beautiful. She had a carriage but she seemed to be stopping at lots of shops. She went to that bloke you saw, Mr Hudson. Then she went back to a big house on Piccadilly, number one hundred and six. The Highlander looked to be done for the day. I followed him and he has digs in The Rookery."

That was interesting. Whoever employed this Scot was someone who was not just interested in me. Who was this woman and what connected us? I wondered if Jenkins and the soldier had crossed paths before. "You hadn't seen him before?"

Jenkins laughed, "The Rookery is like a rabbit warren, sir. There are some disreputable types live there, sir. If the law comes, they can leg it as quick as, sir."

I nodded, "Tomorrow we will be going into the country. Our Scottish friend can follow us if he likes. I am unconcerned. Try to find out what you can about him. You know the sort of thing. Say you were looking for a friend from your time in the army. Be careful. If he confronts you then make up a name and a place."

"Don't worry, sir. I have my mates. That money you gave me helped us all out. They will watch my back for me."

Satisfied I added, "And tomorrow evening we may have some news for you which might provide an income. I will say no more but know that I appreciate all that you have done for us, Jenkins."

He grinned, "Sir, for the last three days I have had a full belly. I have supped decent ale and I have had a few pipes of baccy. Add to that the fact that I feel like I have a purpose again and you have made a new man of me, sir. I thought one arm made me useless. It doesn't. There are poor sods, pardon my language, sir, who would swap places with me in a heartbeat save that their hearts don't beat any more. You make the best of life, eh sir?"

As we rode, with Mr Hudson, to Bilson's farm I asked him about the lady Jenkins had mentioned. If he seemed surprised that I knew she had visited him he did not say so. "Ah yes, Mrs Elizabeth Turner; the widow of an East India Company man. Apparently, her husband died during the troubles a couple of years ago when we took Pondicherry from the French. She was young and he was an older man. Her husband was an important chap and quite rich. She took some time to sell their lands and then she returned to England. She arrived just two months ago. She has bought a house on Piccadilly not far from Lord Ferrers. She mentioned his name. I believe they are friends. She wished to buy fine wines, lemons and olives. She intends to host an affair in a month's time." Mr Hudson turned and smiled at me, "She would be a good catch, Major. Very rich and very beautiful. That uniform must draw women like flies."

I shook my head, "My reasons for the interest are nothing to do with my ambitions. Let us say I believe we have a mutual friend. Now that I know her name it will help me when next I meet him."

"Ah," Mr Hudson seemed happy with my response.

I was wondering about the Lord Ferrers' connection. I had learned, long ago, not to ignore coincidences. I had no doubt that a beautiful and rich widow would be invited to a ball such as the one Lord Ferrers was hosting. I would not have had my interest piqued were it not for the fact that the Gordon Highlander had followed her. I had hoped that the employer of the Highlander would have been identified by now. When we had been in Portugal, I had heard a rumour that there were Imperial spies seeking me. It had been inevitable. Robbie Macgregor had disappeared, supposedly dead, but the higher my rank the more prominent I had become. I was now a major. I had been on the staff of Sir Arthur Wellesley and Sir John Moore. I had been present on the battlefield and all it took was one Frenchman to remember me. I feared that the Highlander was in the pay of one such man.

I had never met the Butcher of Lyons, Joseph Fouché, for he had joined Napoleon after the Emperor had returned from Egypt, but I knew his reputation. He was Bonaparte's spymaster and police chief. He was clever and ruthless. If my name was known then my former commander would seek to have harm come to me. Bonaparte was a brilliant soldier but in many other ways, he was a vindictive little man. I would be wary.

The farm, when we found it, was, indeed, run down. There had once been a stone farmhouse, although it had been a small one. The house was dilapidated for the roof had fallen in and there was no glass in the tiny windows. It was surrounded by wooden farm buildings. The one building which looked to still be serviceable was a wooden barn. We dismounted and Mr Hudson said, "I have the agent meeting us here at noon." He pointed to the east, "I thought we could dine in the inn close by the Tottenham Court. It is as near to a rural inn as one finds this close to London. They have passable fare."

I nodded, absent-mindedly. Food was not a concern. I was assessing the land for a potential home and also as a place I could defend. Sir Arthur was right, I did have a military mind. The farm was on a higher piece of land than the road and afforded a good view all around. The fact that the aspect, especially to the south, was not particularly pleasant was irrelevant. Trees and shrubs could be planted. There was a large pond. I walked over to it and saw that there were fish in it. I knew, from what my father had said, that in times past lords and monks liked to have fish ponds to provide fish in winter. This looked to be one such. I wondered if there had once been a grander house here. I saw humps and bumps around the remaining buildings which suggested something beneath the surface.

"There are just four acres with the farm, Major. That means it would not be viable as a farm. It struck me that it would make a good home for you. There is a wood for hunting," he pointed to the north and I spied the wood, "and the pasture would suit a gentleman who likes horses. I believe the farm was what they called a mixed farm but as it has been many years since the land was tilled nature has reclaimed it."

I nodded again. My mind was racing. I did not know the cost of the land or the rebuilding but I was excited. I had not had a home before. My mother and I were little more than servants living in the chateau. Since that time, I had been a soldier living in barracks, in digs or, more normally, sleeping in fields. I liked the idea of having a home. I walked over to the remains of the house. The door was no longer on its hinges. As I pushed it open and went inside the first thing to strike me was the thickness of the walls. Despite its diminutive size, they were substantial. Despite that everything else was in disrepair. There had been a staircase to the upper floor but when I viewed it I knew it would fall the moment someone stepped upon it. The house would be demolished and I wasted no time in further inspection of the inside. Instead, I went outside and began to examine the ground. I saw both Mr Hudson and Alan watching me. We had had rain and the ground was soft. I knelt to look along the land. I saw something which intrigued me. The humps and bumps were in straight lines. I took my sword out and slid it into the soil. It did not go far before I felt resistance. I kept walking and inserting my sword until I was able to sink it halfway along the sword's length. Satisfied, I stood.

"This will do Mr Hudson." After cleaning my sword on a discarded scrap of material from what might have been a curtain at one time, I sheathed it. "The question is, "Can I afford it?"

"The owners are asking for one hundred and fifty pounds. I believe if we offer one hundred, we shall have it."

"And the rebuilding?"

"That depends what you wish to build. The grander the house the more expensive."

"Mr Hudson, I am a simple man. I want something solid. I would have a house of, perhaps, five rooms on the ground floor and four bedrooms. A smaller dwelling for servants and a stable block. And," I swept my hand around in a circle, "a wall connecting them."

Mr Hudson laughed, "You would build a castle?"

"Not a castle but a home with a wall and one gate which can be barred and it is not such a fanciful idea, Mr Hudson." I pointed to the marks I had made with my sword. "The line I marked marks the foundations of a bigger building. I have spoken to engineers and know that a building may fall but if there are good foundations then they can be reused. Could I afford the building I have described?"

"Easily, Major Matthews!"

"Good! When the house is demolished, I would have the ground cleared first to reveal the foundations. The house and walls will use those foundations."

"Then I will have a friend of mine, who is an architect, draw up the plans."

The agent arrived an hour later. During that time, we had found the other foundations. Whatever had been here was larger than the farm which had replaced it. Had a family fallen on hard times? I was guessing a manor house of some description. I allowed Mr Hudson to negotiate. I played the part of a bored officer and adopted a disinterested attitude. The result was that the agent ended up persuading me to buy it. We managed to get it for just ninety-six guineas. We retired to the Dog and Gun by the Tottenham Court to seal the deal. After the agent left us I went over my plans with Mr Hudson.

"Time is of the essence, Mr Hudson. Sharp and I will be heading for Spain soon. I want all in place before then. I would have the ground cleared and the first dwelling to be built would be the servants' quarters."

He looked surprised, "May I ask why Major?"

"I have a man in mind to be caretaker. He is an old soldier and he can supervise the builders. I do not doubt that you will find me a reliable person but it is in the nature of man to be less than diligent if they are unsupervised. You cannot be here to watch and so I will provide the man. You will pay him weekly wages. When the first dwelling is finished then he will live there."

"Rafe Jenkins, sir?"

"Aye, Alan, and if he has a mind to bring some of his comrades to live while it is being built then I shall not mind. If they are all old soldiers then who better to watch the men build?"

When I told Jenkins the news, I thought he would burst into tears. To cover my embarrassment I said, "Now, Jenkins you will be working for me." I gave him half a guinea. "You need to dress accordingly so you must buy yourself good clothes. Mr Hudson has arranged a meeting the day after tomorrow. Tomorrow you get yourself some clothes and any other gear you might need. I want you there when we meet the builders. You have to look the part."

"Aye, sir but what about your watcher?"

"Do not worry about him. We will keep him busy. Tomorrow Sergeant Sharp and I will be making purchases for our next foreign foray. I do not mind wearing out his shoe leather."

Chapter 3

The days before the party flew by. There were not enough hours in the day. Sharp and I did not use our horses in the busy London streets. Instead, we walked everywhere. As I told Rafe, if there was a watcher then he would earn his money. My previous experience in Spain and Portugal had prepared me for the coming campaign and I made certain that we would have all that we needed from England before we left. I acquired as much ammunition for our pair of Baker Rifles as we could manage. We bought spare flints for all our weapons. We were already well furnished with stiletto daggers, knives and, of course, our swords. Mr Hudson's friend had visited Bilson's Farm and confirmed that what I had found were, indeed, the foundations of an earlier dwelling and he sketched out a plan which met with my approval. For a relatively small fee, he would draw them up for the builder.

The builders were sound chaps. Jenkins had managed to buy himself decent clothes. They were not new but they were well made and he had had his hair washed and trimmed too. He had a short sword hanging from his belt. He later told us it was a memento from Portugal. I showed the rough plan to Harry Harper. At first, the builder was sceptical about my plans but when he had one of his navvies dig where I pointed and he saw the foundations his attitude changed.

"Well Major Matthews, this will save some work and cost, that is certain."

"Now you are sure you understand how this will work Mr Harper? You will see Mr Hudson for monies but Mr Jenkins here will supervise your work. You will be building his home first. It is he who will be site foreman."

He looked at Rafe and nodded. My caretaker might only have one arm but old soldiers who were not lying dead drunk in a gutter had steel in their eyes. "Aye, no bother, sir. My dad was a soldier who served in the colonies. I will do a good job for you, sir."

And then Sharp helped to prepare me for the party. I did not like such functions but I knew that my position on the staff of Sir Arthur meant I had to attend. As Sharp was helping me to dress I decided that whilst I would attend, I would stay for the minimum amount of time. I would meet with my fellow officers, I would smile. I would drink sparingly and then slip away as soon as I could.

I knew which house it was as soon as I turned on to the fashionable street which was Piccadilly. Fine carriages disgorged richly dressed women and their husbands. Officers pranced up on expensive hunters. They were taken away to stables in the rear. I had my piece of paper from Sir Arthur. It felt inadequate somehow. I hoped there would be no embarrassment when I tried to enter.

The doormen looked like ex-soldiers. They were dressed in fine livery but they had the hands of fighters and their faces displayed the marks of punches, blows and beatings. These were not pretty doormen, these were guards. One of them must have recognised me for he nodded and gave a gap-toothed smile, "Good evening Major Matthews."

I smiled back, I was relieved. "Sorry, I don't remember your name."

"No reason why you should have, sir. I recognised you straight away. You were one of the officers your troopers rated." He suddenly realised what he had said, "No offence."

"None taken."

I stepped inside and saw that Lord Ferrers had spent a fortune on his home. A liveried footman glided up to me with a tray of drinks, "Wine sir?"

I took one. I would nurse it. I sipped it and found it to be a good one. I sniffed at it and. holding it up to the light, smiled; it was Alpini and had been supplied by Mr Hudson.

I had not arrived early and the affair was already in full swing. I heard music from a ballroom. There would be dancing. I doubted that Sir Arthur would be found there. If this was summer then he would have been in the garden. As it was February the garden would be too cold and he would be somewhere quiet. I needed to show my face to the General and then leave. I headed for the library. I knew it would be at the rear of the house and close by the garden. That was the way they did things in this sort of house. Even Wells Street had a small library and double doors leading to the small garden and patio.

I passed rooms with ladies sat around tables, their heads almost touching they huddled together to gossip and tittle-tattle. In other rooms, couples spoke. It was an enormous house. I also spied Colonel James Selkirk. He did not see me for he was speaking to a dark-haired woman. She was beautiful. Her skin showed that it had been touched by the sun and that meant she was not English. I did not wish to speak to the spymaster and so I scurried by him. As I did so, I was engulfed by the woman's perfume. I felt drawn to it like a sailor to a siren! The fug of smoke I spied ahead led me to the library. I wondered how many books would actually be read. Certainly, they would all reek of tobacco.

I entered and saw Sir Arthur. He was surrounded by senior officers. There was one sharp-eyed man in civilian dress. I did not recognise him but, if he was with Sir Arthur, then he was important. The lowest rank I saw was a colonel of the 23rd Light Dragoons. I had been spied, for as I appeared in the doorway, all faces turned towards me. I could not wait for a quieter moment and so I stepped forward, clicked my heels and gave a slight bow.

"Sirs!"

Sir Arthur rarely smiled but the hint of one played around his lips, "Gentlemen, as you know this is a somewhat clandestine gathering. Parliament still dallies." I saw him glance at the civilian. "I think it is appropriate, therefore, that you meet Major Matthews. Although he will serve on my staff and when we fight will lead men, his main purpose is to discover where the French are to be found and how to winkle them from their positions. Major Matthews here is adept in such matters." I gave another bow. He went around the men and gestured as he said each name, "Sir John Murray, General Rowland Hill, Sir Edward Pakenham, Brigadier Stapleton Cotton, Brigadier Henry Fane, Colonel Hawker and Lord Castlereagh, the Secretary of War."

I was in august company. Lord Castlereagh said, "I understand, Major, that you are fluent in many languages. In fact, you speak French like a native."

I was intrigued as to how the Secretary of War had come by such information. I wondered just how indiscreet Colonel Selkirk had been. "Yes, my lord, I appear to have been blessed with a gift for tongues."

Colonel Hawker, the Light Dragoon, smiled. I could see that he was in his cups, "And I hear that you are a damned fine cavalryman!" He nodded to the Brigadier next to him. "Henry here knows a thing or two about cavalrymen."

I saw the flicker of annoyance on Sir Arthur's face. He did not like such informality. He was more comfortable with titles.

The Brigadier nodded, "I saw you in Spain. The retreat was a shambles, but you did fine work and Sir Edward spoke highly of you." He referred to Sir Edward Paget who had held off the advancing French.

Lord Castlereagh had a commanding voice, "Let us hope that this time it is the French who do the retreating." There were the appropriate nods all around. These officers were not defeated officers and they must, like me, have been chosen by Sir Arthur.

That led to a general conversation about the best way to defeat the French. I was forgotten. I sipped my wine and I listened. What I heard heartened me. These men had been specially selected by Sir Arthur. He was using this gathering to speak to them informally. That the Secretary of War was present guaranteed that we would be going to war.

I was on the periphery and I suddenly heard a voice in my ear. It was Lord Castlereagh. "A word, if you please, Major Matthews."

You did not refuse such an invite, "Of course, my lord."

He gestured towards the garden. There was no one there for it was a chilly evening, "I feel the need for fresh air. Do you need your cloak?"

"No, sir. The road to Corunna hardened me."

"Quite." He led me outside. "I spoke with Colonel Selkirk and I have asked the question of others. You have been less than truthful, Major."

"Sir?"

"Do not be coy with me. Your real name is Macgregor and your father was Count of Breteuil. Do you deny it?"

"No, my lord."

"What is more interesting is that you served with Bonaparte as one of his guards." I nodded. There was little point in denying it. I wondered if I was about to lose my commission. "Tell me, what is his weakness?"

I was relieved. Lord Castlereagh was just seeking information to help Britain defeat the man the newspapers called, the Monster. "That he has no weakness or, at least, he believes he has no weakness. He sees enemies as a challenge and he is clever enough to see a way to defeat all those who come against him. More importantly the men he leads believe that too."

"Enigmatic, Major; Colonel Selkirk was right. There is more to you than a horseman who can speak many languages. What you are saying is that he has such confidence in himself that it borders on the overconfident?"

I nodded, "Yes, my lord. He uses men as though they mean nothing to him. He is driven to winning at all costs. As he wins more than he loses his men see him as invincible. Men fight better for a leader they believe will win. That kept our army together on the road to Corunna for Sir John Moore was another such successful general. Of course, if Napoleon is not on the battlefield then his leaders are less successful."

"You knew them?"

"Some of them. Bessières, Murat, Lannes."

He looked reflective and then gestured with his head. The back of Sir Arthur was in the window. "And Sir Arthur? Is he the man to defeat him?"

"Sir, that is unfair."

"Whatever is said here is private."

He was a politician and I did not believe it for one moment but he was, technically, my superior. "Yes, my lord, he and Sir John Moore could both have defeated Bonaparte. Sir John's untimely death was a sad loss."

"Yet we have his equal. Thank you, Major. I appreciate your candour and your honesty. Britain is lucky to have you. I hope you stay alive for we need men like you." I was about to go when he leaned in, "Be careful, Major. There are rumours that Fouché knows of you. He is a dangerous man even for someone like yourself."

"Thank you for the warning, my lord." That was the second such warning. I would heed it.

I held the door open for him and, nodding to Sir Arthur, passed through the library and headed back into the maelstrom that was the party. I knew now that I had specifically been invited to meet with Lord Castlereagh. That was patently obvious and now that I had met him, I could leave. As I stepped into the hallway, I drained my glass and placed it on one of the tables strategically sited along the corridor. Turning, I found myself face to face with the beauty who had been speaking with Colonel Selkirk. Now that I was closer, I could see that my first impressions had been wrong. She was not in her early twenties but her later twenties. That did not make her any less attractive. I saw, in her eyes, experience and she gauged me without any fear. She did not see me as a superior. This was a woman who knew her own mind.

She put her hand on mine, "Surely you are not leaving, Major? I was so looking forward to speaking with you. I have heard your name before and I do so admire a dashing officer. You are no man playing at war, you are a warrior!"

"I am sorry madam, you have the advantage of me. Have we met before?"

"You have good manners and I like that. No Major, I am Mrs Elizabeth Turner. I believe we both know Mr Hudson."

Now I understood. This was the Pondicherry widow. What I did not understand was why she had been speaking with Colonel Selkirk. The old spymaster did not seem to me the type to flirt with widows, no matter how attractive. I suddenly realised that I was staring at her and her hand was still upon mine. I confess that I was aroused by her. I took her hand and kissed, "Apologies, Mrs Turner. I am a soldier and meeting beautiful ladies is not a normal occurrence, I am forgetting my manners. How are you finding England?"

She laughed, a tinkling laugh which sounded like water cascading over rocks, "You are a gentleman! England is cold. I spent the last few years in India. I grew used to the climate there. England is also expensive. In Pondicherry, I could have had ten servants for each one I employ here. However, it appears that there are compensations." She leaned in, "One is meeting handsome and single officers!" I must have flushed for she laughed, "Oh, I have shocked you!" Lowering her voice, she confided, "My husband was twenty years my senior. I was a wife who could draw admiring glances. There was little love in the marriage. I endured his meetings and his boring friends and my reward is a pot of money for me to enjoy. Now I am the equal of any man and I act as a man does. If a man finds a woman attractive, he pursues her. You, Major, are the most handsome man in the room. Even the scar on your face adds to that. I fear that I have taken you by surprise."

Just then Lady Ferrers appeared and took Mrs Turner's hand, "Elizabeth, Lord Castlereagh is here and you said you wished to meet him."

Mrs Turner flashed an angry look at her hostess and then quickly covered it. "Of course." She had a purse around her wrist and she took from it a card. "Here is my card, Major. I would appreciate you calling upon me tomorrow if that is convenient. We have not had enough time to talk and this is not the place." Lady Ferrers returned the look of anger at the insult. I bobbed my head and took the card. Her fingers squeezed mine as she handed it to me. "Shall we say eleven?"

"Eleven it is, Mrs Turner."

"Elizabeth, please. Mrs Turner has too many unpleasant memories for me."

As I left, I felt flattered but also a little worried. I had been taken unawares and I had had little opportunity to take charge. As a cavalryman I was used to making quick decisions but I felt as though I was out of my depth with the redoubtable widow. I had been ambushed. I think my worry saved my life for it made my mind work. Jenkins and Sharp had the night off. It was dark as I left the grand house but I did not have far to travel. I was passing houses which belonged to the great and the good. There were doormen outside. Most were ex-soldiers and sailors. They saluted and greeted me as I passed them. The problem came when I turned off the main thoroughfare.

I headed up Swallow Street. The houses on that particular street were still the homes of the relatively well to do but they had no doormen and the road was quiet. Those who lived within would not venture forth at this hour. I was wary. Not because I feared an attack but because I could not explain Mrs Turner's behaviour. It had been almost outrageous. I knew that she was a widow but widows did not act the way she had. My senses were tingling. The one glass of wine I had consumed had little effect on my reactions. I had been brought up French! I could drink a bottle and still not be unduly affected by it. I headed towards King Street and Carnaby market. In all honesty, I do not think it would have mattered which road I took for I was followed. I spotted the man behind me as I turned off Lower Swallow Street. I walked with my hand on my sword hilt but I also had a dagger tucked into the top of my boot.

Knowing that I was being followed, I looked ahead. I had to cross King Street to get to the open area which held, during the day, Carnaby Market. I would cross that. It was the largest open space until I reached Oxford Street. Argyll Street was narrow and there I would be trapped. Someone had counted on me becoming drunk. My early departure might just have put them off. The two men who rose from the shadows of the stalls of Carnaby Market must have raced ahead to cut me off. I wondered if there were others.

I drew my sword and shouted, "If you are footpads, I must warn you that I am an officer and I am armed. I know how to use my weapon!"

One of the men ahead of me held a club and a dagger. He leered, "It makes no never mind to us. We were told to slit your throat and we shall! You are worth a pretty penny to us!"

This was not an accidental meeting nor was it simple robbery. This was murder. There was a watch but that was in the city. Public buildings would be guarded but a man took his life in his hands when he ventured forth at night. I was alone and I knew that there were three of them; two ahead and at least one behind. There might be more. I had to act. I feigned a stumble and grabbed my dagger. When I rose, I ran like a greyhound from the traps. I took them by surprise.

The one with the dagger and the club reacted first and I ran towards him. I had the light cavalry sabre. It was intended for slashing. It was longer than both of their weapons. I was light on my feet. I was aware of feet pounding behind me and another thug with a short sword and what looked like a knuckle duster rushed at me from my right. As the club swung at me, I accelerated to be inside the head of the clumsy yet lethal weapon. Holding my sword to the right, ready to fend off the short sword, I ripped my dagger towards the club man's throat. As I felt the club strike my shoulder I connected with his throat and blood spurted. I pushed his body away as I whirled to face the swordsman. I was just in time to block his sword with my own. I saw his knuckleduster come towards my face as my follower thundered towards me. I rammed my dagger at his hand and the blade went straight through his palm. He screamed and that would wake the neighbourhood. I smashed him in the face with the hilt of my sabre and turned.

The last man had halted. When he shouted, "Jem, Davy, where are you?" I knew that there were two other men! I took my chance and, leaping over the dead man and the unconscious one, I ran as fast as I could for Oxford Street. I gained ten paces on the one following me. Oxford Street, however, was a dangerous place at the best of times. When I reached it, I did not pause but ran straight across the busy thoroughfare. Had a horse or a carriage been coming down the street then I would have been a dead man. Fortune favours the brave or, perhaps, the foolhardy. I made it across and then sprinted across the open area that was Oxford Market. I did not turn. That invited disaster but I heard more feet pounding after me. There was a large open area off Titchfield Street and that was the saving of me. Without an obstacle to slow me I began to open a lead. The men who chased me smoked pipes, drank too much and were unfit. I was not. As luck would have it the door of the house next to my lodgings opened and our neighbour looked in horror as I pounded towards him pursued by three thugs. The man shouted loudly for help, "Thieves! Vagabonds!"

Sharp opened the door. He stood on the steps with a pistol in his hand and he raised it. I was not afraid for I knew he was a deadly shot but the ones chasing me feared the worst and they turned.

I was out of breath. I bent double trying to get my breath back. "What happened, sir?"

I waved a hand and I turned. The three men had fled. I stood and gasped. "I was attacked on the way back from the party. I think Boney has sent assassins here. It was a mistake to stop Jenkins following us."

"Let's get inside, sir."

With the door locked and a brandy in my hand, I felt safer. Mary was mortified, "Oh sir, what is the world coming to when a gentleman cannot walk home without the fear of robbery."

"Aye sir, there are bad uns around! London is not the place it was. Full of villains sir!"

I smiled, "I am safe now, George, and none the worse for wear. I am just grateful that there is no blood spattered on my uniform."

After George and Mary had left us, I told Alan all that had occurred. Like me, he could not understand Mrs Turner and her actions.

He shrugged, "If she is a widow woman who was married to an older man, perhaps she is ready for something exciting, sir. You must admit that you are dashing and a Major." He added, "And she was talking to Colonel Selkirk. Perhaps he rejected her. Unless she was a French spy, he wouldn't give her the time of day!"

I laughed, "So, Sharp, I am to be compared to a shrivelled-up Scotsman?"

"No sir, it is just…" He saw I was teasing him and he smiled.

"We need to be careful from now on. Neither of us leaves alone and tomorrow we summon Jenkins. Perhaps we employ some of his pals." I swallowed the brandy. "And I have a meeting with the widow at eleven. Perhaps the encounter may shed light on tonight."

My uniform needed work for the attack and scuffle had resulted in some spoiling of my uniform. It would clean. I tossed and turned all night. The fact that the widow had upset my train of thought had undoubtedly saved my life. If it was not for the confusion she had caused me, my mind would not have been as alert. I would have strolled through the streets of London just grateful that I had escaped a dull party. My mind was also filled with the coming campaign. The General was placing a great deal upon my shoulders. I was just pleased that the 23rd would be there for they had served in Portugal before.

I rose and, while I breakfasted, Alan sought Jenkins. They joined me in the dining room. He was shocked that robbers had been brazen enough to attack me. As I forked a piece of bacon I pointed south, "Go to Carnaby Market. They will be setting up for the day. If these were just common robbers then the stall holders and the authorities will have had a body to move. If there was no body then these weren't ordinary brigands."

Jenkins stood, "I'll go, sir, but I can tell you that these are not the usual footpads. I'll wager there was no body and they probably cleaned the blood away too. From what you say these were professional killers. They sound like ex-soldiers. There are hundreds in the city and not all of them seek honest employment. When a man has learned to kill there is a great temptation to continue to do so."

After he had gone Sharp said, "He is right, sir. What was it you told me one said? *'We were told to slit your throat.'* That sounds like orders and payment. If Lord Castlereagh was right then this might be men hired by Fouché."

That disturbing thought had kept me awake. Sharp was just confirming my fears.

When Jenkins returned it was to confirm that there was no sign of a struggle. "I will get a couple of lads to keep an eye on you, sir."

It would have been arrogant foolishness to refuse. I took a handful of coins and pushed them towards Jenkins. "They will need payment and I will feel better if they are paid."

Sharp came with me when I called upon Mrs Elizabeth Turner. We were expected. The doorman was Indian. He wore a turban and had a long, curved sword at his side. He looked like he could handle himself. When he admitted us, I noticed an accent. I had spoken to men from the Indian sub-continent before and it was not that. The accent was French. He asked me to wait and I said, "Merci."

He replied, "D'accord." I saw the flash of irritation upon his face. He had slipped up. I know not why but I took comfort from the fact I had tripped him up.

Mrs Turner was dressed beautifully. Her dress was cut to accentuate her figure and to give enough of a hint of her breasts to arouse. She smiled, "Major!" She held out her hand for me to kiss, "I cannot Major you all the time. What is your Christian name?"

I kissed the back of her hand, aware that she was, once more, squeezing my fingers, "Robert, but my friends call me Robbie." It was as I said it that I realised how few friends I actually had!

"Robbie," she seemed to roll the name around her mouth as though tasting it, "such a lovely name and it suits you. If you would leave your man here, we will go to the drawing room for refreshments."

Nodding to Sharp, he would keep an ear out, the widow led me to the drawing room. There was a table and four chairs but she took my hand to lead me to a chaise-longue. She patted the cushion for me to sit. Another male servant, also Indian, entered with a trolley upon which were delicacies. There was also a pot of tea. She turned, "You like green tea? I grew addicted to it in the east. I do not like the milky brown tea which those on this island seem to drink by the gallon."

"Of course."

The servant poured and handed us our cups. Mrs Turner dismissed him. "Help yourself to these delicacies. My chef came with me from India. They may be a little too spicy for you."

Politeness dictated that I had to try one. They were spicy but I had served in Egypt. I had had hotter. "They are delicious. Your servants, they are all from your husband's estates?"

She gave a slight frown and then smiled, "Yes, why do you ask?"

"Your doorman speaks French."

She nodded, "Not a surprise. We lived close to Pondicherry. That was a French colony until recently. I speak French myself."

"Ah, I just wondered."

"You are an interesting man, Robbie. Why are you still single?" I almost spat out the tea I had just swallowed. She laughed and took my cup from me. She placed it on the trolley and said, "Robbie, forgive me. You are unused to someone, especially a woman, who speaks her mind. I know that women are supposed to wait upon gentlemen. That was how I was until recently." She took my hand in hers. She leaned toward me. Her perfume was intoxicating and her hands were soft. "I had a dull and boring life because I allowed a man to choose me. When my husband died, I swore that I would take my life back. I would be in control and I would make my own decisions."

36

Suddenly, she cupped my chin and pulled my mouth towards hers. She kissed me. Putting her other hand behind my head she pulled me down so that I was lying on the chaise-longue. Her tongue darted out into my mouth. I could not help myself I found myself becoming aroused. She stroked her long fingers down my cheek. Her nails left a mark. She moved her mouth around to my ear, she nibbled my lobe and said, huskily, "My body is yours, Robbie. Take me."

As much as I wanted to this was all too hasty. I put my arm around her back and in one deft move lifted her so that she was on my lap supported by my arm. I leaned forward and kissed her, briefly. I had to take charge, "Elizabeth, nothing would give me greater pleasure but I cannot sully your name. My sergeant waits outside. What will people say? This is England."

She laughed, "And your Duke of York is about to lose his post because of a mistress. Do not worry about my name. It is my name and I do not need to worry about what gossiping women think. I told you, Robbie, I am my own woman." She pulled my head down and kissed me harder than before. Her teeth fastened on to my bottom lip and nipped. Pulling away she stood, "However, I hear what you are saying. Would you feel happier if you returned when it is dark and there are no prying eyes?"

I nodded, "I think so."

She smiled coquettishly, "And I can anticipate the pleasure which is to come. I am ready for you now. I burn with desire but this will just add to the fire. She threw her arms around my neck and gave one last kiss. She pressed herself into my body. As she broke away, she laughed, "And I can tell that you are ready for me too. Tonight, my love, I will take you to a world you can only dream about."

Chapter 4

I waited until we were back in our rooms before I spoke with Sharp. He shook his head, "I wouldn't go back, sir. This does not sound right."

"I know but I think there is more to this woman than just someone who gets me into her bed. She mentioned the Duke of York and his mistress. I think that is a slip she made. She seems to know a great deal about current affairs for someone recently arrived in England. Her servants speak French. I don't think she came from British India. I think she is French. She asked to speak with Lord Castlereagh. I think she is a spy."

"That is a huge leap, sir. How do you come to that conclusion?"

"The furniture for one thing. It was not English and it did not look Indian. Indian furniture is made from different wood. I grew up in France, Alan. I know what French furniture looks like. Everything, from the trolley to the chaise-longue, looked French."

"Then tell Colonel Selkirk or Sir Arthur."

"As you said, Sharp, this is a huge leap. I need more evidence. I will go back tonight. You and Jenkins can try to get information about the servants. You can speak French. If they converse in French then they might let something slip. Change into civilian clothes and go to the tradesman's entrance. Try to get work. I will be with the widow and I am certain that her bodyguard will be close by. They won't recognise you."

Sharp seemed mollified by my answer. "Right sir. I will go and see Jenkins."

I had some civilian clothes with me. I often used civilian dress when I operated in enemy territory. This felt like enemy territory. It meant I would not be able to use my sword and so I put a dagger in each of my boots. I did not think I would need a weapon but it paid to be careful.

While I waited, I studied the maps of the Peninsula. By the time we left, I would not need them for they would be in my head. I guessed that we would be landing in Lisbon. There was still a garrison there. That meant we had three choices, south to Spain or east, across the mountains to Spain. As the Portuguese were the ones we had abandoned, I guessed it would be the third option, north to Oporto and the Douro. The French could just squat there and we would not be able to advance. I remembered it from the retreat.

Sharp returned a few hours later. "Rafe has begun to scout out the servants, sir. He seems quite excited. He reckons the servants don't go in the taverns around here but they do shop at Carnaby Market. He is going to follow them around there."

"He doesn't speak French."

"He says he doesn't need to. They will have to speak English to get what they need and he knows the stallholders. They are a good source of intelligence."

Satisfied the two of us pored over the maps together. I pointed out where there might be possibilities and Sharp did his best to find fault. It was a good system. I found myself becoming quite excited as I prepared for the evening. I would have been lying to myself if I didn't say I relished the thought of a liaison with the beautiful Mrs Turner. However, I was no fool. If she was a French spy then she was using me. It made sense. She had been at the ball and knew that I was one of Sir Arthur's aides. I was an easier target than the more senior officers. She would try to get information from me about the coming campaign. When she made her move, I would have evidence and I would summon Colonel Selkirk. The only thing which prevented me from doing so was the thought that I might be wrong and she was just an amorous woman looking for some excitement after a dull marriage. I did not wish to look the fool.

I went alone for Sharp and Jenkins would be at the rear of the house. I felt as I had when I had been acting as a spy for Colonel Selkirk. London seemed like a foreign land. I walked warily and nervously. The turbaned bodyguard opened the door and he took my cloak. I noticed that I had seen no women in the house. I assumed there must be some and I wondered if they were Indian too. This time Elizabeth Turner had not bothered to disguise her intentions. She was dressed in a silk dressing gown and beneath it, she wore a silk nightdress. She giggled coquettishly, "I thought it would be quicker to remove these items." She waved an imperious hand at her servant. "Go. You are done with for the night." I realised that might upset my plans. He would recognise

Sharp. I had no time for thought as she reached up and, grabbing my cravat, pulled me down upon her. She kissed me and I could taste rich kir royale upon her lips. The open champagne bottle had a silver spoon in the neck. Her kiss was long and passionate. Once more I found myself becoming aroused. I fought against it.

She pushed me away and shook her head, "You are not yet ready. Half of the pleasure of the act is the anticipation!" She stood and poured me a glass of champagne. I noticed that she did not top her own up. She handed it to me, "So, Robbie," she rolled my name around her mouth as though savouring it. She sipped some more of the kir coloured drink. She had, I noticed, the eyes of a vixen. Her rouged lips and cheeks, added to the red of the kir made it look as though she had just savaged an animal. She ran a long fingernail down the back of my hand, "You are going to Portugal soon?"

Now I had it. This was the evidence I needed. I decided to play her and feign stupidity, "Yes, Elizabeth. I fear our liaison will be brief."

She laughed, "It will be brief but memorable. You sail in two weeks?"

That was another mistake. If she was English, she would have said a fortnight. Her English was impeccable but the idioms we used were not embedded in her conversation. "Something like that."

"And you enjoy riding ahead of the army? You like to be alone?"

Another mistake. That I was a cavalry officer going to Portugal and Spain was one thing but to actually know my role was something different. "No man likes to be alone, my lady, but we do what we do for our country."

She nodded, "I can understand that. There is nothing more important than serving our country and doing all that we can to defeat her enemies." She sipped some more wine and ran a finger along her lip to wipe up the surplus. She put her finger in my mouth for me to lick off the wine. She giggled and put the finger in her own mouth. "You are good at your job?"

"I believe so. I am still alive."

She dropped her hand and began to stroke the inside of my thigh. "I can see that. Come," She stood and lifted me to my feet. She kissed me again. "I am ready and I pray that you are too."

She took my hand and led me up the opulent curved staircase. There was no sign of anyone else in the house. We could have been alone. She raced up the stairs. She was eager. She dragged me into a bedroom lit by red candles. The room had been perfumed and the bed lay inviting. The sheets looked to be silk. As we entered, she threw off her gown. Her nightdress was cut low to reveal her breasts. The flesh coloured material revealed a perfectly formed body beneath the silk. She kissed me and began to take off my jacket. I fumbled with the fastenings on my shirt. I was becoming bewitched by this enchantress.

Then I remembered the daggers in my boots. I disengaged her and leaned into her ear. I nibbled it. "This will be far quicker if I take off my boots. As far as I know, there is no romantic way to remove boots and breeches."

She gave a soft sigh, "You may be right."

As I sat on the bed to remove my boots and breeches, she stood before me and slowly lifted the shift over her head. She did it like a magician revealing a trick and then dropped it. She smiled, "What do you think, Robbie?"

"I think I should have worn shoes!"

She ran to the bed and lay upon it. That allowed me to remove my boots and hide my daggers beneath my jacket. I pulled off my breeches and shirt. That was as far as I got. Elizabeth dragged me on to the bed and completed my undressing. The rest was down to nature. Afterwards, as we lay there, she nibbled my ear and whispered, almost sadly, "Such a waste."

I turned, "Such a waste? What is a waste?"

She sighed and shook her head, "That you have to leave for Portugal so soon." She rose and slipped on her gown. "I must go to …" she giggled. "You know."

She slipped through a door into a room off her bedroom. I guessed it was a bathroom of some sort. I had had just the one glass of champagne and I was alert. I sensed a movement behind me. I rolled and the servant's sabre sliced down to where my head had been and ruined the silk sheets. In that instant, I knew that she was not just a spy. She had been sent to have me killed! I picked up the shirt and threw it at the man. I was naked and a man did not fight well naked. I ran around the bed as he threw the shirt from his head and lunged at me. He thought I was going for the door and he stepped back. That allowed me to pick up my boots and throw one at him. He thought I was resorting to hurling anything at him. While I wrapped my jacket around my left hand, I picked up the two daggers. I held the longer one in my right hand and the shorter in my left. It was too dimly lit for him to see clearly and he lunged at me again. I blocked the sword with my jacket. The sword was sharp and, ripping through the material, it raked across my hand. The dagger in my right hand ripped up under his ribs. He gave a scream and a shout like a bull elephant. I used my left hand to whip the other dagger across his neck.

As he fell, I smelled perfume. I turned to see Elizabeth, now dressed, with a long stiletto in her hand. She said, "Such a shame!" She lunged at me. I brought my left hand around but I was too slow and she was deceptively quick. I deflected the blade but it just succeeded in stabbing me in the left side. Even as she raised her hand for the mortal strike, I heard feet pounding up the stairs and heard Sharp's voice, "Major! Major!"

I quickly turned but she stabbed at me again. My reflexes took over and I blocked it with my dagger but the knife sliced across my right hand and the blade fell. The footsteps were closer now and she turned and fled.

Sergeant Sharp stood in the doorway with a pistol and a sword. "Sir!"

I pointed to the door through which my would-be killer had fled, "After her. She is a spy!"

There were other people in the house and I put my breeches back on. I had just pulled on my boots when Sharp came back and shook his head, "Gone sir. There was another set of stairs on the other side. I heard a horse galloping away. She had planned her escape, sir. Here let me look at those wounds." He nodded to the silk sheets. They were cut and bloodied. "They are ruined, sir."

I nodded to the dead Indian, "If he had had his way then I would have been in the same condition."

Sharp knew his business and he bandaged my side and hand. I would need a doctor but we both knew that stopping the bleeding was the most important thing. I was wincing as he tightened the bandage when the door opened and I heard a familiar voice, "Robbie, laddie! You do get in the most amazing scrapes." It was Colonel Selkirk. "I take it the bitch has gone?"

"You knew about her?"

"That she was a spy?" He nodded. "I had my suspicions but I was hoping to turn her and have her work for us. I suspect that option will now be denied us." He pointed to the bandage. "There is a doctor in Dover Street." He took out a card. "Give him this and tell him to charge it to me. Then I will see you tomorrow morning in that tavern on Oxford Street."

I looked up at him, "You know about that?"

"The Gordon Highlander your man spotted, Angus, he is one of my fellows. I must confess your one-armed rifleman is his equal. I could use him. Now you had better cut along. My chaps and I have some clearing up to do and some searching. Who knows, the Widow Turner might have left something incriminating behind although she is clever and I doubt it."

The doctor was not happy about being woken but the card from Colonel Selkirk assuaged his irritation. "I thought, when I saw the wounds, that this was the result of some drunken brawl. This card tells me otherwise. You have been lucky, young man. It was a sharp knife and a clean blade. There should be no ill effects. I will have to stitch the two cuts. Would you like something to dull your senses?"

"No, doctor, stitch away."

He nodded, "A soldier then."

The doctor was careful and he was good. Even so, my side and the back of my hand ached. The stitches would be removed before I boarded my ship. Once in our room, I had a large glass of brandy.

We had said goodbye to Jenkins and his friends at the door. I had given them money for ale. Sharp explained what had happened and how close I had come to death. "We did as you asked, sir, and went to the tradesman's entrance for work. The Indian chap was positively unpleasant. We argued for a bit and then we heard a shout and a scream. It didn't sound like you but it sounded like trouble. When the Indian chap pulled a knife, I smacked him one and we ran in. There were four or five of them. I stuck one with my sword and left Jenkins and the lads to sort the rest out. The house appeared empty." He grinned, "I guessed you would be upstairs. The door was open and, well, you know the rest. The doctor and the Colonel were right, sir. You were lucky!"

I nodded, "I was stupid too. I knew there was something wrong but I was also flattered that such a beauty would take me to her bed. That was an expensive night. Let us hope we have seen the last of the Black Widow!"

Chapter 5

The next day we met with Colonel Selkirk. We found him to be in a less critical mood when he entered the inn with the Gordon Highlander. The colonel actually smiled! The huge highlander grinned at us and then went back outside. Colonel Selkirk nodded as he waved over the innkeeper, "You impressed Angus as did your lads. That is not an easy thing to do."

The innkeeper approached deferentially and said, "Sir?"

"Ale all round and have you any decent food?"

The man looked at me and I nodded, "The pies are good!"

"Your best pies then." The innkeeper left. "I may have been a little harsh with you, Matthews. This woman was cunning. We now see the web she spun. I took her for someone who was taking advantage of a dead husband. It seems she had her husband murdered. She is a French lady. Her father was executed in the Revolution and she was brought up as a patriot. She was young and impressionable. Fouché took her under his wing. She is his protégée." He shook his head, "She is a zealot who, as it happens, has a great appetite for sex. I think that might have saved you. If she had done her job properly then she would have killed you when you were naked and vulnerable. Luckily for you, she is like the Black Widow spider and copulates before murder! A lesson to us all." The ale arrived. "We can forget her. She is now known. She may have been attempting to kill Lord Castlereagh. It was a lucky escape. She went for you first. It is a harsh reality but your death would not harm the country as much as that of Lord Castlereagh. She failed. We know her face and it is a face and a body which are not easily forgotten, eh Matthews? Did she get any information from you?"

"No sir, although she knew that we were leaving for Portugal."

He nodded, seemingly satisfied, "Now we can look to Portugal and Spain." He raised his tankard and drank deeply. "Good ale. I shall have to remember this place. So, you have your maps?" I nodded, "The four of us leave in seven days' time."

"Isn't that earlier than the Duke said, sir?"

"It is and the Black Widow is the reason we leave. It will take her time to return to Paris but she may have other means to send a message to her master. As you said, she knew when you were leaving. We need to be one move ahead in this deadly game of chess. We need to get to Portugal sooner, rather than later. Finish your business with the house and Mr Hudson and be in Portsmouth six days from now. We will be travelling on the *'Black Prince'*."

Sharp was intrigued, "Sir, was the woman a magician? I mean I ran after her and followed her down the staircase. I was just behind her! She just vanished!"

"We have learned much. It takes time for a ship to reach India and return. We held off approaching her as we needed more information. It is here now and things are much clearer. I received the package two days ago but I wished to study it." That was as close to an admission of guilt as we would get. "She is a clever woman. We believe she had a horse ready and bags packed. She planned on moving once she had disposed of you. She had an assignation with Lord Castlereagh today. Needless to say, she will not be keeping it and I have informed his lordship of the incident. His lordship is grateful to the two of us. That is a card we will save for later in the game, eh Matthews?" He drank some of the ale. I could never play this game as well as the Colonel. Everything he did was calculated. "The servants we questioned were loyal but, after much persuasion, they told us what we needed to know. She has a network of contacts in England. There are Bonapartist sympathisers. We will make arrests. She will get home; it will take her time that is all." He smiled and it was a cruel smile. "Fouché and Bonaparte are not the only ones with spies."

The food arrived, "I hope it is to your liking, sir."

The Colonel nodded, "Don't worry, if it is not you will be the first to know of it!"

I ate in silence. I felt like a fool. I had let my body get the better of my mind. Even now I desired the woman who had tried to kill me. The Colonel was right, she was good.

"This is a good pie. I shall use this place again." He pointed a fork at me, "Stay close to home, Robbie. The witch might be gone but there are still hired killers. Jenkins and his mates are no match for them."

"Don't worry, sir, I have learned a lesson."

He laughed, "Aye, don't think with your dick!"

He had put it crudely but he was right. I would not make the same mistake twice.

We had much to do to prepare for the journey to Spain. Although the regiment would have been informed of my secondment, I was honour bound to write to them and tell them myself. I would send our horses back from Portsmouth once we no longer needed them. That done we had much work to do with the proposed dwelling. Three days before we were due to embark, we visited the building site and discovered that part of what would, eventually, be the servant's quarters was built.

Harry Harper had done well. "We can have a roof on tomorrow, sir. Mr Jenkins can move in if he likes. It will be rough and ready but I would be happier with someone on site at all times. There are some thieves around here. We have had some tools stolen already."

Rafe was happy enough to move in. "Trust me, Major, this is ten times better than The Rookery." He pointed to the woods, "There are plenty of rabbits over there. Me and the lads will live well."

"The lads, Rafe?"

"Aye, sir, with your permission, the lads who share the room in The Rookery would like to come here. It won't cost you anything, sir. It will be cheaper to live here. There is no rent and they can hire out to farmers in the season. We have little enough without wasting it on ridiculous rent for a rat and flea infested slum."

I smiled, "I am more than happy for them to share your home, Rafe. That is what it will be, your home. When I return to England and this is finished then we can look to making this my home. I know not yet what it will look like but I daresay I will need servants other than you. This arrangement suits me admirably."

We headed back to London and we called in to speak with Mr Hudson. Leaving Sharp and Jenkins to sup tea with Jennings, I sat and conferred with Mr Hudson. "I am sorry about the Widow

Turner, Major Matthews. If I had known what she had planned..."

"Water under the bridge, Mr Hudson. She deceived me as well. Did the company lose money with the affair?"

He shook his head, "No sir. We had not delivered the wine and food she had ordered. She even forgot to recover her money."

I nodded. Colonel Selkirk had told me that the house had merely been rented. The owner had fine furnishings as recompense but there had been damage in the fracas. The widow had disappeared but she left a trail of destruction behind her.

"And my finances can cope during my absence?"

"Oh yes, Major Matthews. Mr Harper is doing a good job. Some of these builders milk the work but he is working hard and you are not being robbed. I believe he sees it as his patriotic duty. You are a soldier and serving Britain. I will ensure that Mr Jenkins continues to be paid."

"If you see aught which needs changing then you have my permission. I will be in no position to send or receive letters. After today the next time you see me will be when I return from abroad."

"You can leave all in my hands, sir."

When we headed for Portsmouth I was in a happier frame of mind. My wound had healed and I felt less foolish about the encounter. I had managed to put the widow and my embarrassing behaviour behind me. I still found its images creeping into my mind and I would shiver and berate myself for my foolishness. When I did so I would see Sharp smile. He knew me better than any man alive. I was lucky to have him as my sergeant. We stayed in the 'George Inn'. It was an old inn and overlooked the harbour. It was popular with officers going to sea. Since Trafalgar, the French fleet had been confined to the West Indies and the Mediterranean. Britannia truly ruled the waves and the officers with whom we dined were in an ebullient mood. I paid a man to take our horses back to the regimental barracks. It was a fortunate happenstance for he had a mother who lived there and needed to visit her for she was sick. Then we waited with our chests and our war gear for the ship which would take us to Portugal.

The Colonel arrived the next day. He had the Gordon Highlander, Angus, with him. Unlike Sharp, the man wore no uniform save a highlander hat and I guessed that he was not a serving soldier. That evening, as I dined with the Colonel, he told me Angus' story.

"Angus was a sergeant major in the 92nd Foot in Egypt. He had a falling out with an officer. You know the type, Matthews, green as grass, no chin and full of daddy's money. It was at Lake Mareotis and the 90th and the 92nd had been ordered to attack the Maroba redoubt. The young officer lost his nerve and wouldn't attack. Angus led his men. After the battle, he reported the matter to the Colonel." He shook his head and threw the stub of his cigar into the fire, "He was an idiot! He took the side of the young officer and Angus was dismissed. Worse he had him whipped as a punishment for suggesting that the officer had been a coward. No regiment will take on a man who has been whipped. They see them as troublemakers. I found him in Naples." He grinned, "A little like you eh? I took him on."

I nodded, "But Colonel, he wears the Gordon Highlander cap."

He lit another cigar, "Aye, that was his father's. It is a harmless affectation although I confess it marks him as an ex-soldier. Still, he is damned handy with his fists and he is quite happy to go into places which are, shall we say, less than friendly; a bit like your Sharp."

The *'Black Prince'* sailed into port the next day. The captain, Jonathan Teer, was more like a pirate than an officer in the Royal Navy. He had been promoted to Lieutenant Commander although he still sailed his little sloop. He greeted me like an old friend. "My lucky charm is back!" He tapped his epaulettes, "A promotion and much of it is down to you, I think. You bring us luck!"

"Yet you still sail this little sloop."

"Robbie, it suits me. If I had a larger ship then I would be tied to the fleet's apron strings. This way I get to poke around little bays and coves. We drop spies behind the lines and I get to cut out enough French ships to keep my crew happy." Prize money from captured enemy ships was the lifeblood of small ships.

"'*Prince*' has enough firepower to beat anything our size and she has the legs to run if we meet a bigger boy!"

Colonel Selkirk said, "And when do we sail, Lieutenant Commander Teer?"

"On the morning tide, Colonel. We have supplies to take on. Lisbon is not well supplied. We need powder and shot as well as hard tack and pork. We also need fresh water. If you will excuse me, I shall see to those matters. Mr Hyde will take you to your cabins."

Mr Hyde was the new Midshipman. He was about twelve years of age. He was better off with Jonathan than in many ships. My friend was a fair man. In a larger man of war, a three-decker, there would be many such midshipmen and bullying was rife. Here the boy would have a chance to learn. "If you would follow me, sirs."

With Angus and Sharp carrying our chests we descended into the Stygian gloom that was the bowels of the sloop. I knew that our quarters would be cramped. As I expected, we had been given two officers' cabins. I guessed that the officers would double up while we were aboard. There were two hammocks slung in each cabin. The chests would fit underneath and that was the extent of the room we had. Sharp and I had known what to expect. I think the Colonel expected more. I heard a crack and a curse as he banged his head on the beams. Sharp and I had learned the hard way. We walked like hunchbacks while aboard.

When we left Portsmouth, the wind was pleasantly fresh. It came from the north-west and was, perforce, cold. I was wrapped in my cloak. I had learned, long ago, the value of a good cloak. Mine was oiled. It would keep off rain. I stood, with Sharp, at the bows as we edged from the anchorage and passed the forts which guarded the entrance to the home of the British Fleet. The Colonel was still abed but I liked to watch the sea.

"Back into it, eh sir?"

I nodded and said nothing. It was less than three months since we had left Spain. The taste of the retreat still felt like a defeat. Sir John had worked miracles to take us off and we were lucky to have served such a good officer. We had lost so many horses that Sir Arthur would have limited cavalrymen at his disposal. I would need to bear that in mind when I sought paths and trails through

Portugal. It would be the light infantry which would be of the most use. The 60th Rifles, who would serve with us, would be spread out amongst the regiments. Fifty-one men to each brigade was not a great number but they would be with the two light companies and they would decimate the tirailleurs and voltigeurs who would screen the French. I knew Sir Arthur. He would need me to find ridges with dead ground. He used dead ground to hide his men. He liked to preserve his own men and let the enemy bleed. He knew that the firepower of a British Brigade could stop any French column.

That evening we dined with the captain. Once we had cleared the land the little sloop flew. Johnathan was certain that we would have a swift passage. The Colonel quizzed him about the situation in Portugal. "Is Lisbon threatened, Lieutenant Commander?"

"No, sir. The French appear to have met more resistance on their way south. My last mission, before I came to pick you up, was to sail to the Douro. Marshal Soult was fortifying the north bank of the river. He has more than two hundred guns facing the south." He laughed, "They had not got them in position and they wasted plenty of shot and powder trying to hit us." He became more serious. "If we try to force the crossing, sir, then I fear we will lose many men. Trying to hit a lively little sloop is one thing but slow-moving troop transports is quite another."

Lighting another cigar, the Colonel said, "And that will be the remit of the Major here. He is the burglar who will pick the lock of the Douro."

The next day Sharp and I took a map on deck. Jonathan added detail to it. He knew the Douro. "There are a couple of bridges in Oporto. They are well guarded. You will have to go many miles upstream to find a bridge which is unguarded. The Portuguese use ferries. They were all being taken to the north bank. I suppose if you have engineers then they could build them."

I shook my head, "Under fire from two hundred guns? Sir Arthur has precious few troops as it is. No, the Colonel is right." I jabbed a finger well upstream. "I shall have to find a way."

"Rather you than me, Robbie!"

Lisbon was busy. Jonathan had to negotiate large East Indiamen as well as the smaller boats which seemed to fly around the anchorage. We docked next to a two-decker, the *'Lion'*.

While our chests and bags were taken ashore, we said our farewells. I had discovered, on the voyage over, that Jonathan was operating along the coast of Portugal and Spain. In essence, he was a privateer. He would cut out any French ship which came close to him. It was still easier for the French to send supplies for their army from the Atlantic and Mediterranean ports rather than risk overland and the guerrillas of Spain. The odds were that we would cross paths again.

Our first night would be spent at the British Embassy. The ambassador was not at home. He had been ill and was now in England recuperating. He would return to Portugal with Sir Arthur. Colonel Selkirk took advantage of the absence of a superior to virtually take over the embassy. As one of Britain's oldest allies, the building was substantial and the Colonel took the best of rooms. He did so by pointing out that he was preparing for Sir Arthur.

"And now we need horses! Come let us take the ambassador's carriage. We can save our legs."

Of course, the carriage meant people assumed we were with the embassy and we were not hindered. We had to travel five miles north of Lisbon before we found stables with horses for purchase. I knew we were lucky. There was a hiatus. No one was on the offensive. Winter had just finished and the French had halted at the Douro. They had defences on the Vouga River but that was as far south as they had come. The Colonel had the money for the horses but I would choose them. He would have had any old nag so long as it could carry him! I wanted at least five horses for the sergeant and myself. The Colonel rolled his eyes when I told him.

"Sir, we are not riding to hounds. This will not be a little jaunt for a couple of hours and then back to a stable. We might ride forty or fifty miles in a day. If we do that over a week we either kill our horse or ride a spare. Five is the minimum. In a perfect world, it would be seven or eight."

He accepted my opinion and we negotiated. French cavalry rode smaller horses than the British. Some were little bigger than ponies. We preferred horses which were fifteen hands high. The horses which came from England would be that size. The man was keen to do business with us. I think he anticipated that we would recommend him and he would make more money from those who came along later. I chose six horses which were fourteen hands high. All of them were locally bred horses. Their coats were not as glossy as ours in England but they looked hardy. They would be able to survive on a poor diet. We had been going to buy just five for us but the sixth was just twelve hands high and the horse breeder let us have her for a song. The Colonel and Angus bought two horses which looked as though they had been left over from the retreat. They had had regimental numbers. The horse breeder had tried to remove them but I knew that they were dragoon horses. We tied them to the back of the carriage and headed to Lisbon.

When the Colonel and Angus went off into the streets of Lisbon, I did not ask why. Sharp and I stabled the horses and then headed off to buy four saddles. The Colonel was unconcerned about the quality. To him the horse and saddle were functional. Alan and I would be in the saddle for much longer periods. I bought good ones.

That evening the embassy chef outdid himself. I think he thought the Colonel was more important than he actually was. Colonel Selkirk did not disillusion him. Angus did not join us. The Colonel had sent him off to gather intelligence in the poorer parts of the town. The fact that the Scotsman did not speak Portuguese did not seem to bother the Colonel. "Angus has a way with him. There are many who speak English in this part of the world." He gestured with his fork, "Good food eh, Robbie? We should make the most of it. Rations for us soon, eh?"

"Yes, sir."

"And you are itching to get on with the job I am guessing?"

"When Sir Arthur arrives, he will be like a whirling Dervish, sir. We both know that. I need to get to the Vouga as soon as possible. I intend to leave in the morning. Sharp and I will get some lodgings further north. The general will be here by the middle of April?"

"Closer to the end."

"Then I will be back here by the fifteenth."

He put his knife and fork down and leaned back. He sipped the wine. It was a good one. "Your dedication does you credit, Robbie, but don't stick your neck out too far." He gestured at the scar on the back of my hand. "Those two most recent wounds are a reminder of your mortality!"

"I know, sir. The encounter with the Black Widow was a wake-up call for me. Fouché now knows where I will be. I expect another attempt on my life. That is why the countryside is the safest place for me. Towns are where there is danger. I will be happier the sooner we leave Lisbon."

"And where will you go first?"

"The rumours are that there are French on the Vouga River. That is one hundred and forty miles north of here. We get as close to the French as we can and work as far north as possible. I know what the general needs. I just have to find it for him!"

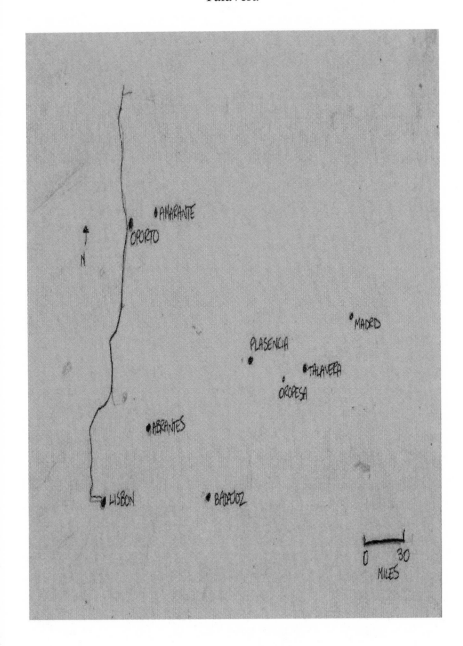

Chapter 6

This was not England. There were few roads and, as we headed north, I realised that Sir Arthur would have trouble just moving around the country, let alone fighting. The few roads we found were poorly maintained and memories of the retreat came flooding back. The only consolation was that, as the English, we were welcomed. The French wanted to convert everyone to their way of life. The English just wanted to be rid of the French. We had no wish to rule another country. Parliament could barely rule England!

We stayed that first night, in the town of Torres Vedras. We had left Lisbon early and ridden hard, arriving in the early afternoon. There was a castle and substantial city walls. Had I been Soult I would have moved at least as far south as here for it would have taken a huge army to shift him. That he had not was a mistake. It was the only large town north of Lisbon and south of Oporto. Coimbra was on the coast but Torres Vedras was a rock. The French would beat themselves against it if Sir Arthur could garrison it.

We were both wearing uniforms but as we had buff facings on our blue uniforms, we were not garish like some of the hussars. That helped us to blend in. Neither of us were wearing our Tarleton helmets. Sharp had a forage cap and I had a cocked hat. Our heavy cloaks disguised us still further. The Portuguese knew we were English and we were welcomed. When Junot had retreated, after the treaty of Cintra, he had sacked the churches and monasteries. It had not gone down well and there was much anti-French feeling. So long as our troops behaved themselves then there was hope. A disgruntled, not to say belligerent local populace was the last thing an attacker needed. We left three of our horses in a local stable and paid for them to be fed and cared for. We pared down what we would need. Our pistols, swords, Baker rifles and a blanket were each essential as well as a water bottle. All else was a luxury.

We stayed a couple of days in Torres Vedra while we gathered intelligence and improved the maps we had. This would be somewhere that Sir Arthur could use. When we left we found a more desolate road and an emptier landscape. The road north twisted and turned through rough and inhospitable terrain. I reflected that this would be a good place to stop a French advance. I marked it on the map. We could have ridden faster had I not made frequent stops to annotate the map and to write in my notebook. We passed through tiny hamlets. Torres Vedras appeared to be the largest place we had seen since Lisbon. Looking at the map the next place of any size that we might see would be on the Douro! We stayed in poor inns but that did not bother us. The road took us close to the sea. There were many rivers but all of them were either bridged or had fords. We made good progress.

We were just twenty miles from the Vouga River and the small town of Fermelâ when we found trouble. Oliveira was a tiny village of, perhaps, twenty souls. There was no inn and so we had paid a local farmer to sleep in his barn. We ate with the family. It was simple fare but tasty and washed down with rough red wine. His son had been watching sheep on the hillside and he raced in excitedly as we ate. I could not keep up with his Portuguese. His father forced him to slow down. He managed to calm himself and told us that he had seen French horsemen. They were north of us and appeared to be scouting. He was an observant youth and had taken careful note of their uniforms, horses and weapons. From his description, they were Chasseurs à Cheval. I guessed from his words that they were the 5th for they had yellow cuffs. Showing him the map was of little use, he could not understand it, but I managed to get a good description of the place he had seen them.

That night as we lay in the barn, we spoke of what the news meant. "This was a stroke of luck, Sergeant. We might have ridden on north tomorrow, blissfully unaware that there were French ahead of us. We go slowly. We thought they had vedettes only on the Vouga. If they have Chasseurs à Cheval then that means they are there in force."

"We go armed and ready then, sir?"

"Yes. We load the Bakers and keep a brace of pistols ready."

He nodded as he took out the rifles. "I knew we should have brought the saddle holsters with us."

"Hindsight is always perfect, Alan. Ask yourself what would we have left behind to bring them?"

"Aye, sir. You are right. Perhaps we might relieve some Frenchmen of them."

The saddles we had were not cavalry saddles. They were Spanish and had a pommel. They were perfect for the Baker's sling. We had loaded them the correct way which meant that it was highly unlikely that the ball would fall out. Once we were in action, of course, it would be different. We would ram them down any way we could. They were a secret advantage we held. Most cavalrymen used a short carbine. The range was relatively short and the effect of the Paget Carbine unpredictable. The Baker could send a lead ball three hundred yards and the gun was accurate enough to hit the target! I hoped we would not have to use them but it was a comfort knowing that we could hit the enemy well beyond the range of anything save an artillery piece.

The dilemma with the country through which we travelled was the fact that there were many trees along the side of the road and the roads twisted and turned. The vineyards and cultivated land lay north of us on the Douro. I wondered if the Romans had ever been in this part of the world! Thus it was that we came upon the four Chasseurs so suddenly that we had no time to use our Baker rifles. Our horse's hooves masked the sound of the Frenchmen speaking. We turned a bend and they were there just thirty paces from us. It was a Brigadier, what we called a corporal and three troopers. Sharp dropped the reins of the spare horse and his hand went to the pistol in his belt. I smiled and was about to speak when the Brigadier shouted, "Get them! They are…"

He got no further for my hand had drawn my pistol and I had fired it at him. It was not a service pistol. It had been made by one of the finest gunsmiths in London. When we had loaded the pistols, we had used perfectly spherical balls. It hit him in the chest and threw him from his saddle. Sharp's pistol hit a trooper in the face. Pieces of skull and brain came from the back of his head. I spurred my horse. I had called this one, Donna. I was already drawing my sword. The trooper before me panicked. His uniform was covered in the brains of his comrade. I was merciful. I slashed him across the neck. We could afford no prisoners. I gave him a quick death. The last man put his heels to his horse and galloped back towards the Vouga. The Baker barked as Sharp reacted the quickest. The last trooper fell from his horse. His body bounced along the road held by one stirrup.

Unsure if there were more, I levelled my Baker and scanned the road. "Sharp, go and fetch back the last trooper and his horse."

There appeared to be no one else. I did not hear the sound of hooves disappearing in the distance. I slung my Baker on the pommel and dismounted. I tied Donna and the spare horse to a tree and then gathered the other three horses. They were typical French light cavalry horses. They were much smaller than our horses. It was why I had been able to kill the trooper so easily, I had been able to slash downwards. I went to the dead Chasseurs. They were the 5th. The shepherd boy had good eyes. They had no papers on them. Their carbines were in their saddles and they had no pistols. Sharp came back with the dead trooper draped over the saddle. I pointed to a slope to the west of the road. It was rocky and covered with weedy shrubs. "Take the feet." Sharp took the feet and I the head. We swung the body of the corporal and threw it toward the slope. It hit undergrowth and rolled down before stopping against a tree. We could not see it. We repeated the same thing with the other three. We could not see their bodies. Their sergeant would assume they had been ambushed by guerrillas. Villagers would suffer but there was little I could do about that.

Stringing the small horses behind our spare we headed down the road. I had seen a small side road and we would take that. We needed to find a camp and make a base so that we could explore the area around the river. There were Chasseurs who were present. Who else was there? We had planned on risking the few vedettes on the Vouga. Now it seemed it was defended in force. That changed everything. Before Sir Arthur could tackle the bridges over the Douro, we would have to deal with the Vouga!

The side road dipped and then climbed. There was a burned-out house a mile or so from the main road. I had a cocked pistol ready but the burned-out house looked to be abandoned. There were holes made by musket balls in the wall. I could picture the scene. There had been a skirmish here. Men had defended the house. The door and frame were no longer there. I assumed whoever had been attacking had brought up a small three pounder and blasted their way in. I hoped that the dead had been buried but I would not risk entering. That way I could assume that the victors had treated the defenders well. As I waved Sharp to follow me down the road, I realised that I was a hypocrite. We had just callously thrown four bodies down a slope. Was I any better?

The house would have provided shelter but I needed somewhere closer to the river. The road turned into a track and then a trail but it kept winding down the gentle, wooded slope. Ahead I could smell woodsmoke. There were men ahead. Were they on this side of the river or the far side? When we came to the stream which bubbled down the hillside, I stopped. I handed Donna's reins to Sharp and gestured that I would scout. I slipped the Baker from the pommel and cocked it. I took off my cocked hat and cloak. At a distance, my blue uniform might be taken for that of a French soldier.

I watched my footing as I made my way down to the river. I knew there was water ahead for I could hear it. Recent rains had made the slope a little more treacherous than it might otherwise have been. I was quiet. It was one of the things which had made me so valuable when I had served in the French army. I heard voices ahead and I heard splashing. Even before I saw them, I knew what I would find. These were soldiers washing their clothes. I moved even more slowly and edged my way through the trees and scrubby undergrowth. I had long since left the path Sharp and I had been following. I had to find a way through the undergrowth. I did not mind for it hid me from view. The noise of voices grew and then I spied my first Frenchmen. Two of them were beating their shirts against a rock. I dropped to all fours and wormed my way a little closer to the water. I found a fallen log. It was jammed at an unnatural angle and I had a clear view under it.

The river was not wide, perhaps forty paces and there were small mudbanks showing that it could be forded. I made a mental note of that. I counted just twenty men by the riverside. There were more in tents beyond the treeline in the fields. They were line infantry. I guessed this was an under-strength company. That would make it about a hundred and ten men. I saw that they had defences. They had felled trees to make crude barriers behind which they could take shelter. I picked out some words as they bantered and joked, as soldiers do. The men were happy that they were not advancing but, as with all troops, bemoaning the fact that there was no town nearby. I had seen enough and I made my way back to Sharp. As I neared him, I realised that we could, after all, use the deserted house. I needed to investigate the river further west. I knew that it would be wider there. The slope down which I had just clambered was too steep for all but light infantry. An assault across the river there would be a disaster. I needed to find somewhere we could attack and for that, I needed a place where horse artillery could be deployed. If Soult had placed two hundred guns along the Douro then it was unlikely that he would have many to spare for the Vouga. He was using his Chasseurs and, probably, a battalion of line infantry, to act as a screen. It would give him advance warning and he could rush troops to the Vouga to throw back an attacker.

I uncocked my Baker and slung it on the saddle. Mounting, I gestured for Sharp to head back up the trail. I would not risk speaking until we were well away from the river. If the French voices could travel then so could ours. When we reached the wrecked dwelling, I entered the house first. There was no smell of death. The place had been ransacked but there were no bodies. We would have a roof.

As much as I wanted something hot to eat, I would not risk a fire. We ate cold rations. As I washed down the food with water from my canteen I said, "Tonight we take just two horses with muffled hooves, we can hobble the rest, and we head down to the river. There will either be a bridge or a ford. Daylight is too dangerous. Let us see what we can see, eh?"

We left after dark. Once we were on the road I stopped frequently to listen for signs of danger. There were none. The men we had killed would be missed but they would not search for them until daylight. I had a plan for that. I would lead them away from us. First, we had to discover the strength of their defences. The slope was a gentler one than the one I had had to negotiate. The trees had been cleared from the side of the road and I reined in. I could see the pinpricks of fires ahead and I was aware that we might be seen. I dismounted, as did Sharp, and we tied our horses to two scrubby bushes. We picked our way down the side of the road. By keeping to the side were almost invisible. The bushes and trees made us hard to see. Once again, I could hear voices. This time it was the sentries ahead and it proved that there was a bridge. I could hear the feet of the sentries as they clumped along it. The French had cleared the banks of the river to give a clear line of sight but there were still a couple of fences which would afford concealment. We crept closer and hid behind one. I was hatless and I risked peering over the top.

There were just two sentries and they were in the middle of the bridge peering into the black waters. The bridge looked wide enough for four horses to ride across it abreast. I could see that the vedettes on the other side had a campfire and there were six men seated around it. They were also, by their uniforms, line infantry. There was, in addition, a three-pounder cannon. I could not be certain of the calibre but that was the normal gun a battalion might have. It was light enough to be manhandled by a couple of men and, loaded with grapeshot, could decimate an attacker. It was useless against other artillery. There was neither the sound nor the smell of horses. The Chasseurs were further from the river. That was to be expected for horses needed grazing and they took up a lot of space, add to that the smell then it was obvious they would be away from the battalion of infantry.

We headed back to the house. We went to the captured Chasseur's horses. One of the French saddles was covered in blood. We saddled one horse with the bloody saddle and, after taking the cloth from Donna's hooves, I led the French horseback to the road. I crossed as quickly and quietly as I could. After using my sword to cut and hack at the bushes and branches of the foliage close to the western edge of the road I then headed down a small road which led towards the sea. I rode for no more than half a mile. I found a tree and twisted the reins of the French horse around it. The horse had been fed and watered. It could reach the grass and would not come to harm. When the French sought their men, they would find the horse and look to the west.

When I returned to the farmhouse, I was exhausted. I unsaddled Donna and Sharp and I risked sleep without a sentry. We were lucky because no one came to seek us. The next morning, I added to the map we had brought. Sharp and I then headed back to the road. We went on foot and we secreted ourselves in the undergrowth. We would watch the road. We saw little traffic. That was not a surprise. North of the river was

French territory and south was Portugal and the allied army. Who would travel such a road? It was mid-morning when we heard the hooves of the Chasseurs. There were ten of them. This time they were led by a very young looking sous-lieutenant and a grizzled old sergeant.

One of the sharp-eyed troopers shouted, "Sir, there are broken branches." He leapt from his horse and ran to peer at the ground. He saw the hoof marks I had left. "There were horses, sir, and they headed west."

"Well done, Trooper La Forge. The rest of you, draw your weapons. Let us be more careful than Brigadier Lejeune and his men."

The sergeant said, "That is unfair, sir. We don't know yet what happened to them. The Brigadier was a good soldier."

"Then why did he not return? Come, we are wasting time!"

I saw the sergeant look over in our direction. He could not see us, we were too well hidden and his eye line was above us but he was a veteran. The young officer had made a mistake. He should have investigated both sides of the road. The patrol headed west.

An hour later they returned with the horse. "They were ambushed and their bodies disposed of. The colonel will take reprisals against those who live in this area."

The sergeant was nothing if not persistent. "Sir, our men were good soldiers. We found but one horse. What happened to the rest? Where are their bodies, sir?"

"They have probably eaten the horses and we know what guerrillas do to men they capture and kill. It is probably as well we have not found their bodies. We return to camp!"

We had seen all that we needed to see. The Vouga was defended. There was at least one battalion of infantry there as well as a regiment of horsemen. They had artillery. I did not think it would slow down Sir Arthur but it would stop us from venturing further north. Until I could scout the Douro then we had done all that we could. We headed, slowly, back to Lisbon. I sold the French horses to the stables which looked after our horses but I kept the saddles. We were in profit!

We reached Lisbon on the fourteenth. There was still no sign of Sir Arthur but transports had begun to disgorge his troops. Until the ambassador returned, we had free rein and we stayed in the embassy. I told the Colonel what we had discovered. "Soult has made a mistake. Too cautious that one. If Boney was in command, he would have taken Lisbon and then we would have had the devil's own job to shift him! Thank God he is giving the Austrians hell."

"He is beating them?"

The Colonel laughed, "He is destroying them. Their generals are still fighting as though it is fifty years ago. Even the French have a faster rate of fire than the Austrians." He lit a cigar. "When we rode east, Angus and I discovered that the Spanish and Portuguese are harassing the French lines of communication. It might explain Soult's reluctance to overextend himself. It will please Sir Arthur!"

Now that we had time to spare, Sharp and I dressed in our best and strode to the Royal Palace. We had helped to facilitate the escape of the Portuguese Royal family to Brazil. A Portuguese noblewoman, Donna Maria d'Alvarez, had helped us. She had said she would guard the palace until the King and Queen returned. The gate was open but I saw a man standing nearby. He had a musket. As we approached, he began to lower the gun to aim it at us. Then I heard a familiar voice bark in Portuguese. The man raised his gun immediately.

Donna Maria had a wide-brimmed hat and she had garden scissors in her hand, "Roberto! You are back! When I saw the ships arriving, I hoped you would be amongst them. And you, too, sergeant." She nodded to the man with the musket, "You must excuse Giorgio. He is new. He is a bodyguard. We had people trying to steal from the palace. Giorgio discourages them. He is a good man but he is still getting used to my ways."

Alan bowed and she hugged me, "I wondered if you had survived Coruña." She laughed, "Of course you would survive. It is in your nature. Come, let us go into the palace and take refreshments."

Donna Maria and her staff were living in the servants' quarters. She was a redoubtable lady. We enjoyed some fine Portuguese wine, it was a rosé and delicious. The Portuguese made rosé wines which compared well with those of Provence. We shared stories. The French threat had been just that, a threat although Donna Maria was adamant that she would not have left even had the French come. I believed her. We told her of the retreat. She was sad to hear of the death of Sir John. It had been reported but my eye witness account clearly upset her. I did not say we had been up country but she worked out that I would be doing what I did best. "This time Roberto, you and your general must drive the French from this land. They are savages!" She put her hand to her mouth, "What am I saying? You are half French!"

"And what you say is true. It is not the ordinary people. It is those who lead them who are the problem!"

When we left, late in the afternoon, I felt much better for Donna Maria showed us the real reason we were here. Britain had no desire to rule Portugal. The French did. It was as simple as that!

Chapter 7

When the General arrived, on the 22nd of April, then our relatively leisurely life ended. We were in the centre of a vortex! He wanted everything done yesterday. He seemed to be able to juggle social and diplomatic commitments whilst also ensuring that the army knew his plans. The first day saw the Colonel and me closeted for three hours with him while we gave him our assessment of the situation. We told him everything and, save for making an occasional notation, he just nodded.

"You have both done well. It will take me a week or so to organize my men and for all the troops to land."

Colonel Selkirk said, "I will take myself off, sir, and see if I can find any intelligence from the south, eh?"

"Good idea. And you, Matthews, take yourself back to Torres Vedras. The place intrigues me. I will send a troop of cavalry to join you just as soon as they have their legs. I want you to return to the Vouga. This time you can scout aggressively. Probe for weaknesses."

"Yes, sir."

I would be pleased to be out of Lisbon. The already crowded streets were impassable as infantry, cavalry and artillery negotiated its streets as they made their way north to Coimbra where the General was mustering his allied army for the push north. Sharp and I left as soon as we could. My only unnecessary delay was to bid farewell to Donna d'Alvarez. She was a practical woman and she gave me the names of some contacts who lived north of the Douro. I knew that they would be more than useful. Sharp and I headed north.

As this was the third time we had stayed in Torres Vedras we were given good rooms in the inn we had previously used and paid a lower rate in the stable. When I mentioned that Sir Arthur would be heading north with an English and German army, we were feted. We were served the best food and the best wine. We were greeted with smiles of welcome. An English army meant profit for all. With little between the Douro and Torres Vedras, it meant the town would be richer!

"This is the life, eh sir. When do you think the Light Dragoons will get here?"

"It normally takes a good three or four days for horses to get their land legs. I would say four days. Any sooner and it will be a reckless officer who brings his troop." I wondered how many would be in the troop. It was unlikely to be the full complement of ninety officers and men. We would be lucky if it was fifty. That would still be better than just Sharp and me.

In the end, Captain Rogers and his forty-nine men arrived late in the afternoon a week later. Their horses had been ridden hard. I saw the look on the troop sergeant's face and knew that he was not happy. I had arranged rooms for the men for one night. I had estimated at sixty. We were drinking wine in the main square when they arrived. They saw my uniform and reined in. The Captain dismounted, "Captain Charles Rogers, D Troop, 23rd Light Dragoons reporting for duty, sir. I take it you are Major Matthews?"

I nodded to the horses, "Yes I am but there was no need to rush. This is not England, Captain, there will be no remounts." I turned, "Sergeant Sharp would you show the troop sergeant the stables?"

"Sir!"

This was a test. If the Captain went with his men then it would show me that he was a good officer. Instead, he said, "Lieutenant Minchin, go with the troop. Hargreaves, take my horse!"

He sat in the seat vacated by Sergeant Sharp and grinned, "What is the wine like then, sir?"

That was not the first question I expected from his lips but I would give him the benefit of the doubt, "Fairly decent." I raised a finger and the waiter nodded. He brought over another glass and poured the captain a glass.

"I was honoured to be chosen by the Colonel for this assignment. I have been itching to strike back at Bonaparte."

My heart began to sink. Captain Rogers was in a brand-new uniform. It showed no wear whatsoever. It looked like a best uniform and veterans rode in their oldest. This was a new officer. "When did you buy your commission, Captain?"

"Six months ago! I was most miffed to have missed the earlier battles, still, better late than never." He looked around the square. "The Colonel said we would be operating further north?"

I nodded, "I hope you have brought tents and supplies."

He looked crestfallen, "I assumed we would commandeer houses, sir."

"Portugal is an ally. There are few villages and towns north of here." I smiled, "Still, your chaps can probably make hovels eh?"

"Hovels, sir?"

"Improvised shelters using wood, branches and brushwood."

Just then Sergeant Sharp returned with the Lieutenant. "Sir, I shall just take the lads to their digs. They rode hard today." He looked meaningfully at me, "They didn't stop for food."

Captain Rogers said, "We were keen to get here, don't you know!"

"Carry on, Sergeant. I flipped him a couple of gold coins. See that they are fed eh?"

Grinning, Alan said, "Yes sir, thank you, sir."

I looked up at the Lieutenant. He was older than his captain. "Sit down, Lieutenant." I waved over the waiter who brought another glass.

"Thank you, sir."

"Another bottle of wine and another chair."

"Yes, Major Matthews."

"They seem to know you, sir." In contrast to the Captain, the Lieutenant looked like a veteran. His uniform was faded. It was almost pale blue. His boots were scuffed and I could see that they needed to be resoled. His sword was standard issue. The Captain had an engraved one which would have cost a small fortune.

I nodded, "This is the third time we have stayed here." The Lieutenant sipped his wine. "Have you served before, Lieutenant Minchin?"

"Yes sir, I was in Egypt. I was in the 26th before it was renumbered, sir."

I nodded. Egypt had killed my horse, Killer. "Damned hot country and no good for horses."

He smiled, "Yes sir. Were you there? Which regiment?"

It was my turn to be enigmatic, "I was unattached. If the troop has experience then that will help." I began to see why Colonel

Hawker had sent the troop. The Officer might be a novice but his men were not."

Although I spoke to both of them the Lieutenant understood that my words were addressed to him, "I take it you are well provisioned with ammunition."

The Lieutenant looked at Captain Rogers who smiled, "Thanks to Geoffrey here, we are. He and Sergeant Fenwick insisted on having spare flints and plenty of powder and ball. I told him we would not need them. We are cavalry! The charge is what we do best, eh Major?"

"If you wanted to charge, Captain, then you should have joined the Dragoons or Dragoon Guards. We are the eyes and ears of the army. You will use your carbine more than you use your sabre."

"But I have not brought a carbine, I thought…"

I shook my head, "Hopefully we can take one from a Chasseur." The Lieutenant looked up, "There is at least one cavalry regiment on the Vouga. The 5th Chasseurs."

Captain Rogers' eyes widened, "You have met them already?"

I nodded, "Sergeant Sharp and I had a run in with four of them. Luckily, we also carry a brace of pistols. We managed to take their horses. Speaking of which, have you any spare mounts?"

"I have a second hunter, sir, but we have none for the troop."

"Surely you have animals to carry your supplies?"

The Captain was silenced, I think it was the embarrassment and Lieutenant Minchin shook his head, "They are with the regiment, sir. We have neither pots nor food to cook in them."

This would be harder than I thought. I would have to buy back the three French horses and another three. I was lucky that the general had given me money before I left Lisbon. "Then we will have to go and buy some when Sergeant Sharp returns."

Alan arrived back a short while later. His face was a picture. I guessed Troop Sergeant Fenwick had shared the dilemma of the novice Captain with him. "When we have finished the wine, Sharp, we will need to buy horses and cooking utensils as well as supplies."

"I took the liberty, sir, of speaking with Manuel at the stables. He has ten horses for us. He said he would sell them at a fair price."

I knew what that meant. He would take his profit first.

It became clear that the Captain had paid his £2682. 10 shillings to get his captaincy and not bothered to find out what else he needed to do. The buying of commissions was outdated in a modern war. The Lieutenant had not been as well connected as the Captain. He would have to wait for a battlefield commission to be promoted. When we had bought everything and had it delivered to the stables we ate. I explained, as we ate, what we would be doing.

"Our main aim is to find out the full strength of the men opposing us. I know there is at least one battalion of line infantry backing up the cavalry. There is at least one cannon too. French spies will have already told them that we are coming. Once we leave here we will need to be wary. I will use your experienced men as scouts. We will be riding hard each day. My sergeant and I have done this before. We will be riding at the head of the column. Captain, I want you in the middle."

"It is my troop, sir!"

I decided that being brutal was the only answer to the Captain's naïvety. "You bought the commission, Captain, not the troop. I will be giving the orders and the sooner you realise that the better. This is not a game. French Chasseurs are good! Damned good. Luckily our troopers, when well led, are better. Look upon your time with me as an extended training period. Lieutenant, you have been with the troop the longest. I want your best sergeant and Corporal with me."

"That would be Sergeant Fenwick."

I shook my head, "The Troop Sergeant, no. I want him at the rear. He will be the most experienced man in the troop. If we get cut down then we will need his experience at the rear."

"Then it would be Sergeant Parkinson and Corporal Groves, sir."

"Good. Standing orders are that when trouble strikes the men draw carbines. I hope that they are proficient in their use."

The Captain said nothing. He was in his cups already. All my words had depressed him. He had seen this as a great and glorious opportunity to show how brave he was. The Lieutenant said, "Like the curate's egg sir, good in parts."

"Then pair up the experienced with the novice. This is all about the quick and the dead."

The Captain looked up, "The quick and the dead, sir?"

"If you are not quick then the odds are that you will be dead!"

He went to bed drunk and unhappy!

The next two days were hard. I not only had to watch for the French but also had to train the Captain. He had become an officer just for the uniform and the position. Lieutenant Minchin was loyal and he did not speak out of turn but from his omissions and looks I gathered that Colonel Hawker had sent the Captain to me as a kill or cure. Parkinson and Groves, on the other hand, were perfect. They reminded me of men with whom I had served in the Chasseurs and some of the 11th. I recognised that they were both quick and reacted promptly to the messages I was sending them. The first halt we had I examined their carbines. They were perfectly maintained. The flints were good and they each had a ball already loaded.

Sergeant Parkinson nodded towards the Baker rifle, "Unusual sir, for an officer to own such a gun. Especially a cavalry officer."

"I learned long ago, Sergeant Parkinson, that the further away I could kill an enemy the better my chance of survival. This is a very accurate weapon."

"Slow to load though, sir."

I shook my head, "In the retreat to Corunna I watched the 60th. They just rammed the ball down when time was pressing. Even half loaded they are still accurate. The other secret is to have a good partner. While I reload Sergeant Sharp fires his weapon."

Parkinson nodded and then lowered his voice, "Sergeant Sharp told me that you were promoted from the ranks. Is that right, sir?"

I didn't tell him that it had been the French army. I nodded, "Would you like to be an officer, Parkinson?"

The involuntary sideways glance at Captain Rogers spoke volumes, "I think I might make a good leader, sir."

I nodded, "The trouble is to become an officer on a battlefield normally means doing something so stupid that it might result in your death! Stay safe, Sergeant, and stay a sergeant. You will live longer."

He grinned, "Aye sir. That is good advice."

As we neared the river, I became alert. I rode with my Baker across my saddle. I remembered our encounter with the Chasseurs. As it happened, we did meet them. We were closer to the river this time. By my estimate, we were just ten miles from the river. However, on this occasion, we had a little more warning. As we dropped through a pass a flock of pigeons took flight from the wood ahead. I reined in immediately. Sergeant Sharp and I had our Baker rifles in hand and aimed down the road in a flash. Parkinson and Groves were a heartbeat behind.

Some of the troop showed their inexperience. They continued to ride even though we had stopped. They spread untidily across the sides of the road. I had no time to worry about that. I saw the leading Chasseur. There were four of them ahead of a column of forty men. I guessed forty even though I could only see ten or so. They galloped towards us.

Sergeant Sharp shouted, "Carbines at the ready!"

Both the Chasseurs and our men knew how inaccurate were the carbines both armies used. They were a short-range weapon. They were better than a pistol but at a range longer than forty yards it was a lottery if you hit. The Baker, on the other hand, was deadly. I did not need to order Sharp to fire. He knew what to do. I did not aim at the leading Chasseurs. I saw a sergeant, four men back, urging his men on. He was a hundred and ten paces away and must have felt himself safe. I let out my breath and I fired. Smoke erupted from the end of my weapon and then I heard the crack. I could almost see the ball as it struck the Sergeant in the chest. It punched him from his saddle. A heartbeat later and the Corporal next to him fell as Sharp's ball burst his head open like a ripe plum. The four leading riders were oblivious to what had happened behind them but the officer, who had been behind the two dead men, held up his hand to halt the rest of the column. Perhaps he saw that we outnumbered him or, more likely, he thought we were all armed with the Baker rifle.

Parkinson and Groves opened fire together. Another four carbines barked. Two of the Chasseurs fell. The other two glanced at each other and then tried to wheel their horses around. More carbines fired. The two men were hit but did not fall. I slipped my rifle over my pommel and drew my sword, "After them!" I did not think we would catch them. They had small, lithe horses and they had a start but I wanted to get as close to the river as I could. I had seen it in darkness. Now I needed to see it in daylight. This was a perfect opportunity.

Some of the younger troopers tried to overtake me. Sergeant Parkinson growled, "Get back in line you dozy bumpkins! We follow the officer!"

I knew that this would be a long ride to the river and I wanted to conserve our horses. I could not reload the Baker but I had two pistols in my belt. I regretted not bringing the holsters for the saddle. We had more pistols. At four paces you could not miss and in a hard battle they could be the difference between survival and death. I saw that the two wounded Frenchmen were struggling to stay in their saddles. First one slipped from the saddle and fell into the ditch and then the other. I shouted, "Lieutenant Minchin, have men secure those prisoners."

"Sir!"

They might eventually die but if we could learn about the enemy then it was worth four men who would secure them.

The road began to descend. We were getting closer to the river. I heard bugles and drums. The defenders at the bridge were preparing to give us a hot reception. I had no doubt that they would have the three-pounder loaded with grape. Three hundred yards from the gun's muzzle would be the closest we could approach. Some of the troopers at the rear of the French column were slowing. That would help us. I risked urging Donna on and we began to close with the ones at the rear. The troopers heard our hooves and they turned to see how close we were. They saw that we were less than forty yards away and well within carbine range. They spurred their horses. I could now see the bridge and the gun. I saw the crew preparing to fire. Even as I held up my hand and shouted, "Halt!" a nervous gunner applied the linstock. Although most of the Chasseurs had crossed the bridge, eight had not and the grapeshot scythed through horses and men. A piece scorched across Donna's flank. She veered away. I hauled back on the reins. We had been lucky.

"Fall back!"

I heard Captain Rogers shout, "Major, we have them! Let us charge!"

I saw Sergeant Parkinson roll his eyes.

I shouted, "Fall back forty yards and dismount! This is as close as we are going to go!" I patted Donna and said, in Portuguese, "Good girl. I will get you sorted, don't you worry." I nodded to Sergeant Parkinson. "You and Corporal Groves pick two good men and wait here." I handed him my Baker, "Think you can handle this?"

He grinned, "Yes sir."

"You have the range of the bridge. Get into position and then start to pick off the gunners. It will make them nervous. They may try to fire the piece at you."

"Don't worry, sir, there is cover aplenty here." He nodded, "Thank you, sir. I will look after this for you."

I smiled, "Never doubted it for an instant."

I dismounted and walked back to the picket line. The French began to fire their muskets. They were well short. When Parkinson began to fire the Baker, it would unnerve them. In a perfect world, they would try to shift us. The damage we could do might gain us the bridge. Unless they were complete fools they would not try to do so. The troopers, by and large, were doing as I had ordered. One or two looked to Captain Rogers. He was still on his horse and I thought he might trip over his bottom lip. I had no time for such things.

"Sergeant Sharp, take ten men and find the deserted house. We will use that as our headquarters. When you have found it send one man back here and then take the rest and try to annoy those infantrymen by the river."

"Yes, sir."

"Sergeant Fenwick!"

"Sir!" He appeared at my side, "Nicely done, sir. As smart a piece of work as I have seen in a long time. The two Froggies died sir. We have their horses."

"The horses will be useful. Sergeant Sharp is busy finding us a base. When his man comes then take half of the troop and get some food on the go."

"Sir." He turned and barked orders out.

"Lieutenant Minchin!"

"Sir!"

"I want ten men here with a good sergeant. They will take the first watch. I have a command post organised. Sergeant Fenwick will show you where it is."

"Right, sir." He looked happy. "Thank you, sir."

"What for?"

He shrugged, "I think you know, sir!"

That just left Captain Rogers. I waved him over. "Dismount, Captain. Come with me while I see to my horse."

He came albeit reluctantly. I led him far enough away so that his men could not hear and I put Donna between us and them. As I spoke, I first cleaned Donna's wound with vinegar and then smeared honey on it. The horse would lick the honey off but that was part of the healing process. The bleeding would be stopped and the vinegar would stop any infection.

I spoke quietly but with authority, "Captain, you will stop behaving like a petulant child. If you do not then I will put you under arrest and charge you with dereliction of duty. I will send you back to the general. You will be sent home and the money you spent on your commission will be wasted."

"My father is a judge!"

"And out here that means nothing! These men need you as a leader. Up to now, you have not impressed me. Some of your men have but not you. That changes now. Impress me!" He stared at me and his fists bunched. I laughed, "Oh please, try to hit me! That would make my day!" I saw fear in his eyes. I put my face close to his, "Captain Rogers I have been fighting since I was little older than sixteen. I have forgotten more than you will ever learn. All I am trying to do is to keep you alive. Forget the glory. Try to survive. This is your one and only warning. When I give an order then you say yes sir! Understood?"

"Sir, I came here to fight! I came here for glory!"

"Until you learn to be a soldier then you will do neither. This is like your first day at school. You will learn from the moment you rise until the moment you fall wearily into your bed!"

"Yes, sir!"

I should have known that he did not mean it. That was my mistake. His mistake was costlier.

Chapter 8

The setting up of a camp at the deserted farmhouse showed me the mettle of the troopers. The NCOs knew their business as did Lieutenant Minchin. They were organised and efficient. About half of the troopers showed that they had experience too, for they got on with jobs without being told. Some of the men, however, needed to be sorted out. I saw the frustration on Troop Sergeant Fenwick's face. He needed his officer to give him support and Captain Rogers was patently disinterested in how the troop was run. Some of the wasters just waited around the Captain admiring his weapons, uniform and generally, fawning around him to keep themselves out of work. The Troop Sergeant could do little while they did so. This was a distraction I could well do without. I heard the pop of carbines and the sharper crack of the Baker as Sergeant Sharp did as I had asked. I heard the sound of French muskets in reply. They were not firing in volley but individually. French infantry were notoriously poor shots. I had seen Napoleon despair of their inability to fire their muskets so much that he had once attacked using a column of men just ten files wide without even bothering to load their weapons. He had used them as a human battering ram. British infantrymen were better trained. Their voltigeurs and tirailleurs were better but our men would be safe enough until the French formed lines and sent volleys across the river. Sergeant Sharp would withdraw before the men were in any danger. Then I heard the sound of my Baker being used by Sergeant Parkinson.

As dusk fell the air was filled with the smell of food cooking. Some of the troopers showed initiative and the stew of salted meat was augmented with wild herbs and greens. I smiled when I saw Captain Rogers turn up his nose at the plate offered by his servant trooper. This food would be far better than the food we would be forced to eat once Sir Arthur's campaign truly got underway.

Sergeant Sharp returned. The men he had taken were in a good mood. I heard them telling their friends how many men they had hit. Alan smiled, "They did alright, sir, but not as well as they think they did. When Johnny Frenchman ducked they thought they had hit them. There will be a couple who will need to attend sick parade that is all. No casualties on our side."

"Thank you, Sergeant. Get some food and have Parkinson and Groves relieved."

Captain Rogers looked up, "It is not the way to fight a war, Sergeant."

Sergeant Sharp rolled his eyes but said, "Sorry, sir. I stand corrected." Turning back to me he said, "We hit five or six of them. Just enough to annoy them, sir, and keep their doctor busy."

After we had eaten, I had an officers' call. To the obvious annoyance of Captain Rogers, I invited the sergeants. Sergeant Parkinson had been relieved and he attended. He handed me back the Baker. He grinned, "Lovely little weapon, sir. I managed to hit three of them. They now have timber protecting the gun. You can still hit them but you can't see them."

I nodded, "You hit the gun crew?"

"Oh yes sir, Mrs Parkinson did not raise any soft lads. I hit the officer and the sergeant with two of my first shots. I couldn't tell if they were wounded or worse but they had to be carried off."

"Don't worry about that. They will not be at the gun anytime soon. You did well." The fact that I complimented him resulted in a glance at his own officer. Captain Rogers did not compliment!

When they were all seated, I noticed that Captain Rogers had his servant find the only chair from the deserted farmhouse. He was seated as though he was royalty. I was not offended. I preferred to stand anyway. "Tomorrow our real work begins. Lieutenant Minchin, I would like you to act as adjutant." He nodded. The captain appeared unbothered by my action. "Divide the troop into four. I will lead one section, Captain Rogers a second and you a third. The other quarter will remain here to guard the camp. They can also be the pickets for tonight. I want a good sergeant with the guards. Captain Rogers, you will probe to the west. There is a road of sorts which heads west. Follow it and get to the sea. When you reach the sea head to the river and work your way back. We need to know what the defences are like there. Lieutenant Minchin, you will head upstream. Find us another crossing beyond their last vedettes. The bridge is the obvious place for the general to cross but the more we can threaten their lines of communication the better. I will cover the area on the two sides of the bridge."

"Do we engage, sir?"

"With carbines, Lieutenant Minchin? Yes, we fire at them? Do we cross the river? No. We are here to scout and to contain. Lieutenant, I need a pair of messengers to take a report back to the general. One should be a corporal. The report needs to get through. If I am any judge of the general, he will be on his way north anyway!"

They all seemed happy about my orders. Even Captain Rogers looked less annoyed. I waved over Troop Sergeant Fenwick, "Sergeant?"

"Sir?"

"Try to keep out of bother tomorrow, eh?"

He looked aggrieved and began to bluster, "But sir I..." realisation dawned. He would be with Captain Rogers, "Right, sir. You can rely on me."

Sharp and I checked on our own horses before we retired. I saw that few of the troopers did. That could be costly in a long campaign. Minor irritations, unless dealt with promptly, could develop into major problems. This was not England. A trooper who lost his horse would be afoot. I rose before dawn. It was my way. I was pleased to see that the sentries were alert. I had wondered if the French might try to attack us while we were in camp. That they had not was due, I thought, to our initial aggression. They had probably stood to all night in anticipation of a night attack by us.

After checking that the sentries were awake, I made water and then washed. The fire needed attention and I built it up. Sergeant Sharp joined me and, between us, we filled the large dixie with water. Sergeant Parkinson joined us, "Sir, you shouldn't have to put the water on."

I smiled, "Why not, Sergeant? I will be drinking the tea we make."

"Yes, sir, but you are an officer."

"If you haven't noticed before, Sergeant, the lead balls which fly at us don't discriminate. This is not England and we are not in a barracks. Is my authority threatened by my putting on water?"

"Well no sir, but…," he shook his head, "you take some getting used to, sir. I will go and get the duty lads to get breakfast on the go."

"Thank you, Sergeant."

When he had gone Sharp said, "He asked the Lieutenant to be assigned to your section, sir. In fact, there were so many that he had to draw lots."

I shook my head, "Lieutenant Minchin is an officer. He should have made the decision himself. Still, I am flattered."

We had the first brew and had some hard tack and salt pork. The first rays of light dawned and reveille was called. I saw some of the older hands pour some tea on their pork and hard tack. It made for an interesting taste. Those with poorer teeth would find it easier to eat. I inspected Donna's wound. It no longer looked angry. If there had been any doubt, I would have ridden one of the spares. We saddled our horses and I loaded my guns. We had cleaned them the night before. By the time we had led our horses to the camp most of the troopers had breakfasted.

"Troop Sergeant Fenwick, sound 'boots and saddles.'"

"Sir!"

Even as the notes were dying away, I heard the bugle calls from across the river. It was 'to arms'! They had heard our call and were reacting. That was instructive. It meant they had not planned an attack.

I mounted and slung my Baker over my pommel. Lieutenant Minchin and his detachment were ready first and, saluting, he headed upstream. In many ways, he had the harder task for I knew not if there was even a trail heading east. Captain Rogers was still preparing himself when my detachment was ready, "Sergeant Rose, take charge of the camp!"

"Yes, sir and good hunting!"

We rode to the two troopers who were watching the crossroads, "Anything?"

Trooper Harris shook his head, "Not until you sounded the bugle, sir, and then it was like an ant's nest that had been disturbed. They are standing to. They filled bags with river sand during the night, sir, and built a sort of redoubt around the gun."

"Thank you for that. We will try to avoid giving them a target. Draw your weapons and single file. Sergeant Sharp, watch the rear."

I pulled Donna to the right and headed through the undergrowth. I picked my way north and east. We were sheltered by the trees but the infantry had a target as they saw occasional flashes of blue. I was not unduly concerned. They were wasting ball and powder. The range was over two hundred yards and there were so many branches that the odds on being struck were minimal. Having said that I knew that it would be disconcerting for the troopers. I said, over my shoulder, "There is more danger from river flies than these lead insects. Watch the trail and try not to fall off."

I had not yet travelled this trail and, in truth, I was not sure we would be able to travel very far but I needed to see if the army could attack from here. They only had one artillery piece and, as we had already seen, the troops we faced were not the best. The trail levelled out. I had a feeling it would end up where we had seen the French washing, just below our first camp. The trees thinned and I held up my hand. The troop halted. I nudged Donna forward. The river was just thirty paces from me. I saw a small island in the middle. In my experience that normally meant that one side was shallow and fordable. I saw the French. They were standing to. Unlike further upstream, they had not built any defences. However, if they dropped then they would have some protection from the undergrowth. I dismounted and, taking my Baker, moved closer to the river. I found a tree and I leaned against it. The river was almost at my feet.

I had, of course, been seen when I moved. Lead balls zipped into the trees. A French officer ordered them to cease fire and then someone shouted for tirailleurs. They would try to shift me with light infantry. I saw that they had a line of blue by the river but, further back, they also had log defences. They would be able to cover an assault across the river. Slow moving infantry would stand no chance. Beyond the river, I saw fields and open ground. Cavalry could use that. If Minchin could find a bridge or a ford upstream then Sir Arthur could exploit it. I was about to move when I saw the light infantry company arrive. It was under strength. There were just over fifty of them. They began to wade across to the island. I now knew which side was fordable. I shouted, "Sharp, be ready to give them a volley eh?"

"Sir!"

Above me, I heard the men dismount. The advantage we had was that the troopers could rest their carbines on the saddles of their horses. I aimed the Baker at the Captain who led the men. I fired as he was halfway to the island. He fell clutching his arm. Sharp shouted, "Fire!" The twenty carbines and the Baker fired together.

A French lieutenant belatedly shouted, "Fire!"

Our balls struck just as the French were taking aim. There was a volley of forty or so muskets but most hit the branches and trees. Smoke drifted across the river making it impossible to see the full effect of the volley. I hurriedly made my way back to my horse and I mounted. "That was instructional, Sharp, lead the troop back to the road. Let us see what the other side of the river is like."

I dropped to the rear. I saw the grins on trooper's faces as I passed them. Such tiny actions put heart into soldiers. They had fired their weapons in anger. They had hurt the enemy and we had come away unscathed. The first wound in the troop and even the first death would be easier to bear. We were still in single file as we crossed the road. With twenty men riding across the road we were in view for some minutes. The gun crew saw an opportunity for revenge. Perhaps Parkinson had managed to incapacitate the senior member of the crew and his replacement was young. Whatever the reason the gun was fired just as I neared the road. British gunners like to use roads to almost bounce their cannon balls. It was effective and, had they done so, then they might have hurt us. As it was the ball sailed over the heads of the two troopers who were on the road. We heard it crash through trees some two hundred paces behind us. The troopers cheered and jeered. I was across the road before they had reloaded. It was another victory. More importantly, the men had been under fire and had not run. I spurred Donna to overtake the troopers and retake the lead.

"Well done, men."

"Couldn't hit the side of a barn, sir!"

That was not true. French artillery was good. Whoever commanded the gun had made a mistake. We trotted down the trail and I soon reached Sergeant Sharp. He pointed ahead. "This is a bigger trail, sir. There are open fields ahead. I think this is the main route west."

I nodded, "Drop to the rear." I spurred Donna. The ground was flatter here. The trees had been cut and fields had crops growing. It was spring and so they were just green shoots. It meant that when we crossed them, we would be exposed. I held up my hand to halt the troopers when we reached the first piece of open ground. I took out my telescope. The French had better defences. I saw why. The river was much wider here, almost one hundred and forty paces wide but there were two islands. They were little more than mudbanks but cavalry could cross here. The other side of the river was cultivated too and I saw a farmhouse. A French flag had been attached to its roof. More worryingly there were also two more of the three pounders. Soult had kept his main batteries for the Douro but he had been happy to allow this detachment some firepower.

I waved my hand to lead the detachment west. I headed up the slope. The French were twenty or so yards back from the river and I rode across the fields. We were two hundred paces from the river. We were within range of the French guns but I intended to move quickly. I set Donna to canter. Single file meant that it was easier to move quickly. The field was flat and I risked looking to the right as the bugles sounded. The battalion was not understrength, in fact, it looked to be either a regiment or a brigade for I saw at least four companies form up. They were too far away for me to hear actual words but when I saw the two cannons belch, I knew that the command to fire had been given. It was our speed which saved us. Artillery, even well handled, needs a ranging shot. Their ranging shot was short and ploughed into soft, turned soil. Had it been hard pasture it might have bounced. By the time they had the range, we had passed. I saw that there were no more guns and I slowed. I took us closer to the river to inspect their defences.

The river widened a little more and there were fewer troops here. The French had been in the country for some time and Bonaparte had good engineers and map makers. He loved maps!

They would know the depth of the river and that led me to believe that it was not fordable. When we came to what appeared to be an undefended part of the river I reined in. It was now early afternoon. I led the detachment to the river. It was more than two hundred paces across. French muskets would not be able to hit us. However, just to be certain, I halted the men a hundred paces from the water, dismounted and led Donna to drink. The half a dozen French infantry who had been in the treeline emerged and catcalled me. They questioned my parentage. I smiled, calling me a bastard was not an insult, it was true. Donna drank and I watched the French. A couple of them popped off their guns and I heard the plops as the balls fell into the river. A French sergeant barked out orders and then waded in to smack the offenders with the flat of his sword. I took the Baker and loaded a ball. I did so carefully. It took until the smoke from the French muskets had dissipated for me to do so. The French had a company flag fluttering from a cut branch. I aimed at the branch. It was as wide as my forearm. I fired. The French ducked and when none were hit they rose. I heard the crack and watched the flag fall to the ground. The effect was almost magical. Instead of standing and facing us the half company dropped to the ground once more.

"Bring the detachment up, Sergeant Sharp. We might as well eat here. It is a pleasant morning."

My words were intended for French ears as well as Sharp. There would be English speakers amongst the French. I was trying to unsettle them. My men were in high spirits as they watered their horses and then, in pairs, went downstream to either make water or empty their bowels. It would infuriate the French. Then we ate and had water from our canteens. The river water would not be drinkable. With a couple of regiments using the river, not to mention their horses, it would be a short route to dysentery if we did so.

Sergeants Parkinson and Sharp joined me. "We will head south and try to find the road. Who knows, we may find Captain Rogers. I think we have seen enough now."

"Sir, how will the General get across the river?"

"This will not be a problem, Sergeant. We have three batteries of horse artillery. With six pounders and howitzers, we can easily take out the three guns we have seen. What I worry about, and I know the General will too, is the bridge. We cannot allow them to destroy it. That would slow up our advance."

Refreshed, we headed back towards the road we knew was south of us. We saw the horse dung left by Captain Rogers and his men. I wondered why we had not seen them along the river. His instructions had been quite clear. Ride to the coast by the road and then return along the river. Perhaps the sea was further away than I had thought. There was little point in pushing the horses and so we walked them back to the crossroads and our piquet. We were less than half a mile from them when I heard a bugle sound. It was the charge! Muskets popped and I heard the crack of the gun.

I spurred Donna as I shouted, "At the gallop!"

As we burst into the open, I saw, to my left, troopers at the bridge. I wheeled Donna and headed down the road. There were troopers in the road and dead animals. I saw Captain Rogers. He and his men were attacking the three pounder. The bugles in the distance told me that the Chasseurs were on their way. I had no idea why the fool had charged the gun but I had to try to extricate him from the situation. I drew my sabre. As I had expected, the French cavalry were coming.

"Bugler, sound the recall!"

The bugler made the call and I saw the troopers at the rear turn and head up the road. Muskets popped ineffectually at them.

"Sergeant Parkinson, have the men form a skirmish line."

"Sir!"

Then I saw the French Chasseurs hit Captain Rogers and the four men who remained with him. They had ignored the recall. Sabring gunners and hapless infantry must have seemed like an easy victory. It was not and his men were going to pay. The men who had obeyed the bugle parted to let me through. The Chasseurs had good swords. I know for I had used one. Even as I watched I saw Captain Rogers servant trooper, Henry, hold up his sword to block the blow from the French horseman. The blade bent and with a speed which must have mesmerised the poor trooper, the Chasseur slashed across Henry's face. It tore it open to the bone. The others with Captain Rogers suffered the same fate. I was less than twenty yards from the bridge. I yelled, "Captain Rogers, fall back!" I felt musket balls zip over my head.

The Captain seemed to realise that he was alone and he
spurred his horse. Caesar was a good horse. The Captain was also
lucky that he had bought a good sword to go with his captaincy.
He blocked the blow from the Chasseur and his blade held. As he
headed to me one of the gunners, although wounded, used his
short sword to hack into Captain Roger's leg and a Chasseur
slashed him across his back. He spread his arms and the sword
would have fallen if it had not been held by a lanyard. His horse
galloped hard. I drew a pistol with my left hand and as Caesar
clattered across the bridge, I fired at point blank range into the
face of the sergeant who led the Chasseurs. I whipped my sword
through the smoke and connected with the arm of another
Chasseur. He was a young officer and he was brave. He tried to
block my sword. He was too slow and I had quick hands. I could
not afford to be sentimental. I riposted his sword and struck him
in the throat. I had chanced my arm enough. I holstered my pistol
and wheeled Donna around. I sheathed my sword and bent over
my horse as I raced after Caesar and the Captain. I saw that Sharp
and Parkinson had a line of troopers behind their horses. They
were a hundred paces from the edge of the bridge. Caesar began
to slow. I saw that he had a wound. Rogers was slumped over the
saddle. I could see his backbone through his jacket. Blood poured
from the wound in his leg. The reins were loose. I grabbed them
for I could hear hooves behind me. The troopers parted before me
and we galloped through.

"Fire!"

The twenty carbines barked and I heard screams from both
horses and men. I reined in at the piquet. The survivors from
Captain Roger's detachment were there. As Caesar, wild-eyed
and distressed began to rear, Captain Rogers fell from the saddle.
I dismounted and two of Captain Roger's men ran to hold the
reins of Donna and Caesar.

I knelt next to Captain Rogers. He was still alive. He gave a
weak smile, "Damn, I thought I would be gazetted. I thought to
impress the old man. Next time eh, sir?" His eyes glazed over. He
was dead.

It was a waste and it was my fault. I should have realised that
he was a liability. In giving him the easier, safer task, I had made
a mistake. Captain Rogers wanted glory. His men had paid the

price for that foolish, vainglorious charge. I stood and looked down the road. The French had withdrawn. I looked at Captain Roger's bugler. He stood over me. He had a slashed face. "Sound recall and then get your face seen to."

He nodded and sounded the bugle. Captain Roger's Corporal said, "Is he dead, sir?"

"I am afraid so. Have his body and any other dead taken to the farmhouse."

"The other bodies are by the bridge, sir. The recall saved the rest of us."

I nodded, "Sergeant Sharp, Bugler, with me."

I mounted Donna and we rode to within a hundred paces of the bridge. Bugler, sound the bugle three times. Stop and then repeat."

"Sir."

The bugle sounded and I took off my hat. It was an unwritten convention that such an act meant we wanted to talk. I waited until the French bugle sounded three times and then headed towards the bridge. I stopped in the middle. A pair of French officers with a bugler and a sergeant approached on foot. I dismounted and handed Donna's reins to the bugler.

I saw that one of the officers was a Chasseur Major while the other was a colonel of infantry. The sergeant was from the grenadier company.

I spoke in French, "I am Major Matthews of the 11th Light Dragoons."

I saw the surprise on their faces at my perfect French. "And I am Colonel Leclerc of the 94th Line Infantry. What is it you wish?"

"We have both lost brave men, sir, I would suggest a truce until dark so that we may recover the bodies."

He nodded, "That is acceptable. The brave officer who led the charge, he is young?"

I shook my head, "No, sir, just inexperienced."

Realisation dawned, "Ah. And you, Major, where did you learn your French? You speak like a Frenchman."

I smiled enigmatically, "I have been fighting the French a long time and I am a quick learner. Until dark then?"

"Of course."

The Chasseur Major had not spoken but his glowering eyes told me that he was an angry man. "You and your men have killed my men, amongst them my nephew, Major, I will seek you on the field of battle."

I saw that the Colonel was unhappy with the Major but he said nothing. I smiled, "I look forward to it, Major." I mounted Donna and headed back to my men.

Chapter 9

We buried the men by the farmhouse. It was a sombre burial. The Captain had been a fool but he was a brave fool. It was the dead troopers I felt sorry for. They had followed a reckless officer. I wrote my report while the food was being prepared. The General liked his reports. That evening as we ate, Lieutenant Minchin asked what had happened. I told him. "This makes you acting Captain. With luck, it may be permanent. I shall speak with your Colonel and the General."

"It is not the way I would have wanted it, sir. I like not stepping in dead men's shoes."

"It is war, Lieutenant, and the Captain paid the price for not being ready for it."

"Captain Wilberforce will not be happy, sir. The two of them were friends. I think it was Captain Wilberforce who recommended that Captain Rogers should buy the commission when it became available." That did not worry me. I was not a member of the regiment and internal politics were irrelevant.

The smell of cooking horse meat drifted from the French camp. They had recovered the dead horses. They would waste nothing. We had benefitted too. We also had three more Chasseur mounts.

"What did you learn upstream, Geoffrey?" I used his first name as a sign that he had been promoted, albeit briefly.

"There are many places we can cross, sir, further upstream. We can flank them. They have the river guarded for a mile. Their last outpost just had a half company. We exchanged lead balls. There were no casualties."

"Then we wait for Sir Arthur."

The two messengers arrived back at noon the next day. "The army is on the road, sir. The General is with Colonel Hawker and the regiment which is leading the advanced guard."

I nodded, "Right, Troop Sergeant Fenwick, we had better vacate the farmhouse. I am guessing the General and his staff will want to use it. We will camp by the road. We might as well pick the plum position, eh? After all, we fought for it. Have some of the troopers clear the ground."

"Sir."

I smiled at the others, "It looks like we are rejoining the army."

While the camp was cleared and the house prepared, I waited with Sergeant Sharp at the crossroads. Captain Wilberforce and his troop heralded the arrival of the General. He saluted, "General Wellesley's compliments, sir, he is half a mile behind us."

I nodded, "We have a farmhouse prepared for him. Sergeant Parkinson, take Captain Wilberforce and his men to the farmhouse."

"Sir."

"Where is Captain Rogers, sir?"

"Killed in action yesterday."

I watched the Captain's face for they had been friends. If he was a sensible man, he would know that casualties of war are inevitable. Captain Wilberforce looked to be of an age with me. He simply nodded but I saw a cold look in his eyes, "That is the problem with chaps who have little experience. They need to be cossetted until they are comfortable. Captain Rogers should never have been given this task. I learned the hard way how to lead. This should have been my assignment!" He was criticising me and the Colonel. Captain Wilberforce was an ambitious officer.

"I think Captain Rogers learned too, but the lesson was too late in the learning."

The Captain led his men off. I heard the clatter of horses as Sir Arthur arrived. He had with him half a dozen aides as well as generals Hill and Sherbrooke. He wasted no time in pleasantries, "Right, Matthews, report!"

I mounted Donna and led them towards the bridge. I pointed out all of the salient features and told him what we had done. His reaction to the death of Captain Rogers was to widen his eyes, that was all.

"So, we are stopped by a battalion or two of infantry, two or three guns and a depleted regiment of horse?"

"Yes, sir."

"And we can cross the river upstream?"

"Yes, sir.

"Good, tomorrow we shift this obstacle and push on to the Douro. They haven't mined the bridge, have they?"

"No, sir, the troopers have been watching."

"There is somewhere I can use as a command post?"

"There is a farmhouse. Sergeant Parkinson, take the General to the farmhouse."

"I shall send for you later, Matthews. I will need you tomorrow."

My independent command was over. Colonel Hawker and the rest of the regiment arrived. I would need to tell the Colonel what had transpired. Acting Captain Minchin rode up and joined me along with Troop Sergeant Fenwick. Colonel Hawker dismounted and when he saw no sign of Rogers he frowned. "I take it we camp here, Matthews?"

"It is open, sir, and I guess the General will need more space at the farmhouse."

He turned, "Major Thirwell, organise the camp, eh? I will have a chat with the Major and Lieutenant Minchin. When we were alone, he said, "Something happened to Captain Rogers?"

I told him. He shook his head, "His father was a friend of mine. His father was a damned fine shot! He begged me to let Charles buy a commission. He seemed keen. I think Captain Wilberforce and Rogers knew each other. They were friends too. It seemed right to have him in the regiment but..." He shook his head. "He had the wrong idea about soldiering. I hoped that by letting him work with you, Major Matthews, the experience might have sharpened him up. You wrote a report?"

"Yes, sir."

"I shall read it later."

"Sir, excuse my impertinence, but Lieutenant Minchin's behaviour has been exemplary. I would recommend him for promotion."

The Colonel nodded, "Well goodness knows you deserve it, Minchin. Confirmation will have to wait until a report can be sent back to England but you are temporarily promoted to Captain. I am afraid there is no Lieutenant for you."

"That is not a problem, sir. The sergeants know their business."

"Right, and I had better see where I am sleeping, eh?"

After he had gone Geoffrey said, "Thank you for that, sir."

"Just speaking my mind, Lieutenant Minchin. You are a good officer. Never lose sight of where you began. It will keep you grounded."

I ate with Sharp and Captain Minchin. It was after dark when a young aide fetched me and Colonel Hawker. The farmhouse was packed with senior officers. Sir Arthur shouted, "Let the Major and the Colonel through! We have wasted enough time as it is."

I had learned that some of the regiments had not moved as quickly on the march as the General wished. He was not a patient man.

"Colonel, I want your regiment to go with Major Matthews tomorrow and head upstream. Cross the river and flank the French. I want you to roll them up. I will not risk men charging a narrow bridge. We have too few troops as it is. Our light companies will cross the river on both sides of the bridge and Lawson's Battery of Horse Artillery can support them. Their six guns should be able to deal with a couple of three pounders. When that is done, Matthews, then you and your sergeant can ride to the Douro. Find me a way across it!" The Colonel and I nodded. The General said, "Well, off with you. You will attack at dawn!"

We were dismissed. I said, "It was Captain Minchin who scouted the river, sir."

"Aye, Major but I can see that the General places much faith in you. A tricky task he has given you. You will be behind the enemy lines and in plain sight!"

I shrugged, "Actually, sir, following a retreating army might be a good place to hide. This might just work. Still, it would be wrong to count chickens. I would like to leave our spare horses with your supply train, sir."

"Of course. Well, I had better brief my officers."

For Sergeant Sharp and I, it was somewhat more complicated. We had to have with us all that we would need to get to the Douro and scout. I was lucky in that I had some names of men I could trust from Donna d'Alvarez. We would not be alone. I gambled that we might have a roof over our head and I had gold to buy food. Our cloaks would have to double as an emergency blanket and, if needs be, a tent. We cleaned our weapons. We reloaded our Bakers. I took out the whetstone and sharpened my sword. My daggers had not been used for a couple of days. When all was done and our bags ready next to our saddles, we retired for the night.

The night sentry woke me. "Sir, Troop Sergeant Fenwick said to wake you. It is three in the morning. Dawn in a couple of hours."

"Thanks, Harris."

I was annoyed with myself. I had overslept. Sharp had woken when Harris had entered our tent. We would leave the tent to be dismantled by the troopers who would be bringing the spare horses and ammunition. I hurriedly washed and then went to the field canteen. Now that the army was here there was hot food. I grabbed some sizzling ham. I soaked some of the slightly stale bread into the bacon fat and jammed the ham between it. It was delicious. Who knew when I would eat hot food again? Then I washed it down with some tea. Sharp and I, despite being late up, were the first to be ready. We had prepared the night before. We firmly attached our bags to our saddles ensuring that they were well balanced. We joined Captain Minchin and the troop. They would be leading along with Wilberforce's Troop.

No bugle was sounded. When Geoffrey had ascertained that all of his men were ready, he led off. The rest would follow. Our task was to lead the way to the ford and then silence any sentries we might encounter. Captain Minchin was heading for a landing to the east of the French positions but, in the last few days, who knew if the French had strengthened them? We rode in silence. The French were less than five hundred yards from us. They might hear the horses and the movement but by the time the news reached the bridge, we would already be over. The ford was in the open. I could see the ruts of wagons which had passed this way. This was an oversight on the part of the French. They should have guarded this section of the river too. Captain Minchin and Troop Sergeant Fenwick entered the water first. Sharp and I followed. The sound of the river would mask the sound of our hooves. Once on the other side, we listened. There was no sound of an alarm.

The previous night I had discussed with Captain Minchin what our plan should be. I led, walking Donna. We would use my French to get us close enough to attack. I noticed that there was

more farmland on this side of the river. It would allow the
Colonel to deploy the regiment into lines. Sharp walked ten yards
behind me and the rest of the troop followed in a column of fours.
The open nature of the land suited such a formation.

It was the smell of tobacco which alerted me. I handed my
reins to Sharp and drew a brace of pistols. I walked ahead. In the
dark, I might be taken for a French officer. I heard the two
sentries talking to each other. It was still night and there was no
moon. The two men had their heads together as they smoked their
pipes. They were coming to the end of a duty and were
anticipating breakfast. They were bemoaning the fact that they
were stuck in the sticks and their comrades were enjoying the
women and wine of Oporto. I saw a glimmer of light. There was a
false dawn behind me and I could just make out their faces. They
were facing south, across the river. I got to within ten paces
before one of them turned.

Before he could say anything, I snapped, "Smoking on duty is
a flogging offence. Where is your sergeant?"

My flawless French, cocked hat and confident manner made
them both snap to attention, their muskets held before them. "In
the camp, sir!"

I had kept on walking and I whipped up my pistols putting one
under each chin. "Drop your weapons and you live." They did so.
I whistled. Sharp arrived first with Donna closely followed by
Captain Minchin and Colonel Hawker. "'Pon my word,
Matthews, that was smartly done!"

I nodded, "Troop Sergeant, assign two men to watch these.
And now Colonel Hawker, it is over to you."

He nodded and said, "Form lines!"

I heard the French bugle from ahead. They had heard the
sound of jingling horse furniture as the troopers mounted. The
French bugle sounded boots and saddles. It was too little, too late.
Sharp and I joined the right-hand side of the front line. We were
next to Sergeant Parkinson. I had holstered my pistols and now I
drew my sabre. I was impressed by the way the regiment formed
their three lines. Colonel Hawker did not stand on ceremony.
Dawn was breaking. He had the bugles sound the trot and we
moved west. Positioned on the right we were in the more open
fields. The ones on the left would have to negotiate trees and

bushes. They would also have more men to fight. The French would be forming up for an attack across the river. They would not know we had flanked them. The French bugles and the shouts were more urgent now than they had been. When Colonel Hawker sounded the charge, I estimated that we were less than half a mile from the bridge and the road. Thus far we had seen no Frenchmen. Now we did. I heard the sound of the Horse Artillery as their guns struck the French gun. Muskets and rifles popped. The bridge was under attack.

The Chasseurs' camp must have been well away from the road. They had responded to the call and a squadron charged us at an angle. I shouted, "Wheel!" We needed to face them head-on. We would outnumber the troop three to one. They did not know that. We were in one line and galloping. They approached us piecemeal. We were closing rapidly with one another. I was not sure if the Light Dragoons had ever charged other horsemen. It was not a common occurrence. As Captain Rogers had found out, despite their smaller horses, the French were good cavalrymen. Sharp, Parkinson and I were on the right and facing an officer and sergeant along with three troopers. I drew a pistol and fired when we were ten paces away. I holstered it and watched a Chasseur grab his shoulder and then wheel away. It left a gap and I rode into it, swinging my sword as I did so. The officer swung his sabre at Sharp who blocked it. I backhanded my blade into the officer's side. He dropped his sword and I swung my blade to my left. The French sergeant had almost managed to break through Parkinson's defence. My sword struck his left arm. It bit through to the bone. It allowed Parkinson to hit the Frenchman with the hilt of his sword. The Chasseur fell to the ground.

Our troop was through but our orders were clear. We had to secure the bridge. First, we needed to negotiate the infantry who were hurrying back to try to form a second line. When we loomed up with the sun behind us, some dropped to the ground while most of them held up their hands. Behind us was D Troop. They could take the prisoners. The Horse Artillery had destroyed the guns on the northern bank of the bridge and I heard the muskets popping as the light infantry crossed. If they had not mined the bridge then Sir Arthur would have his first victory. Donna was tiring but she still had enough energy to lengthen the lead

Sergeant Sharp and I had over the others. The French were abandoning the bridge. I heard the bugle call for retreat.

I reined in Donna a little and sheathed my sword, "Sergeant Parkinson, we will leave you here. We are about to join the French army and retreat!"

"Good luck, sir."

We wheeled our horses and made the road. We followed some of the Chasseurs we had just defeated. I could see that they had been badly handled. They were not looking back. They had one idea in their head, get to the Douro before Marshal Soult destroyed the bridges and pulled all the ferries to the north shore. This was a race to Oporto. The losers would either die or be sent to a prison camp. Neither prospect was attractive. They did not even look at Sharp and me or, if they did, they saw what they expected to see. Our cloaks were brown and our arms covered in blue material. Sharp had discarded his hat and I wore the ubiquitous cocked hat.

One of the Chasseurs said, "What a mess!"

Another spat and said, "What do you expect, these were not *Vrai Bougre* who were on duty. They were the sweepings of Marseille."

"They were still killed by *Les Goddams*. They did their duty."

A Chasseur corporal said, "Aye you are right, my friend and we have horses. We might just make the Douro. The Marshal has many regiments on this side of the river. Perhaps we are stronger than *Les Goddams*!"

His friend said, "We might be stronger but we will be lucky to reach them. Not on this road. It is already getting choked. Their light cavalry might be reckless but they could destroy us easily on this road. I think we leave the road as soon as we can. We overtake the donkeys on foot, the *marche a terre*!"."

As they argued with each other I nodded to Sharp and veered Donna onto a more northeasterly course. If we slowed down then others might take more interest in us than these four Chasseurs. I saw, ahead, that the land was a mixture of farmland and heathland. It was undulating. It was land where we could vanish if we left the roads. When I saw a farmhouse ahead, I rode to the east of it and we disappeared from view for it hid us from the road. The Chasseurs would think we were going to loot. We could slow down now. In the distance, I heard an occasional musket popping. The skirmish for the bridge was over. We had forty miles to go. We would now travel a little slower. We had two horses to conserve. The road would be packed. Eventually, others would take the route we had chosen but we would have a head start by then. It had been when we were close to the river that we were in danger. I was not heading for Oporto. The French rearguard would be heading in that direction. We were heading upstream. If Sir Arthur found the bridges across the Douro intact then all well and good. I did not think that such a miracle would materialise! It was more likely that there would be a crossing upstream. We would have to find it.

One advantage we had was that all the French between us and the Douro were running away and the locals, the Portuguese, were on our side. Donna d'Alvarez had given me the names and addresses of a number of supporters who were patriots and wished to help the English rid their country of the Bonapartist menace. The paper on which they had been written was now destroyed but the information was burned in my head.

We passed few people. The disguise which had fooled the French also made the Portuguese wary of us. I knew there was at least one bridge over the Douro and that was at Oporto. Further upstream there might be others. I had to find them. We found a small village with a water trough. There were houses and farms dotted around but there was little else. It looked deserted although I knew that the villagers were watching us. We were soldiers and we wore blue.

I spoke loudly and in English. I hoped that someone might be curious. It worked. As we were preparing to leave an old greybeard emerged. I nodded and spoke in Portuguese. My Portuguese and Spanish were getting better but I sometimes mixed words up. Occasionally I slipped an Italian one in. Luckily the words were similar in many of the languages. "We are English soldiers. Could we buy food?"

Despite the mistakes, I had made he obviously understood me for he grinned and shouted for the others to come out. He rattled off some Portuguese; it was too fast and in a local dialect. I understood enough to hear the word, '*friends*'. We were given bread, cheese, ham and wine. More importantly, we were given information. Soult had regiments waiting south of the river. He was not relying on the defenders of the Vouga. Sir Arthur would have to fight to get to the Douro and that meant the bridges would be destroyed. There was one bridge close to Oporto and the nearest one to that was some days to the east and would involve mountain tracks which would not suit the artillery. I also learned that there were many ferries. Miguel, the head man of the village, suggested to me that the further upstream we went then the fewer French would be found. It sounded like a good plan.

We passed no one until it was almost dusk. We came across a small village. We were walking our horses and we surprised four old men who were sitting on a wall and smoking pipes. I apologised and explained who we were. As in the first village, our story won us smiles and a welcome. This time we discovered that we were just five miles from the river. The men refused to let us carry on for they wished to fete the soldiers who were coming to save their country.

"The French sent a cavalry patrol through yesterday. They took animals away and removed as much food as they could find." I looked down at the bowl of food before me. He laughed, "We are not so foolish as to keep our food where they can find it. We have learned how to thwart the French but the animals," he shrugged, "we cannot hide them."

We left the next morning with a different view of the Portuguese. They were fighting a war which was every bit as bitter as the war we fought. The difference was that they did not have guns and sword, they had to use their minds and their wit. As we approached the river road we descended along a twisting trail. When we neared the road I spied, upon its surface, horse dung. That had to be French cavalry. I cocked my Baker and removed my hat. I saw the river ahead. It was wide. The north side was definitely held by the French for I saw a French flag. Where they had mounted defences on the southern side I did not know. Oporto lay some miles to the west. We turned our horses and headed that way.

We heard the wailing long before we reached the village. It was a nameless village. It was not marked on the map I had copied in Aspley House. There were just a dozen houses. They touched the river and rose up the slope of the valley. The terraces to our left showed that they grew grapes in this part of the world. I had learned that, in Portugal, that meant they had sheep and goats keeping the ground clear of weeds but I saw none on the terraces. The wailing hid our approach until we were almost in the village. I saw the reason for the wailing. The villagers were gathered around two bodies. Uncocking my Baker, I raised my hands and said, "We are English."

A youngish man stepped forward. He had a gashed face. "I am José. You are welcome."

I dismounted, "What happened?" The two bodies were much older men. They looked to be in their fifties. I could see the ligature marks around their necks and the cut ropes told me how they had died. They had been hanged.

"French Dragoons. They rode from the east this morning. There were eighty of them. When they left they headed for Oporto." The soldier in me told me that it was a troop. The Portuguese knew the differences between Chasseurs and Dragoons. "They gathered our sheep and goats. My father and uncle protested and they were hanged." He touched his face. "For my trouble, I was struck. I remember the officer's face. He will die."

I nodded, "I am sorry for your loss. We are scouts for the allied army which is heading this way. Our general brings an army north. We are here to find a way across the river."

He shook his head, "All the bridges but one have been destroyed for many miles along the river. The French general has ordered all boats to be moored on the north side. I fear that your general will be too late. There is no way across the river."

Just then a younger version of José said, "That is not true, brother. The ferry of Juan the boatman is moored upstream."

"Are you certain, little brother?"

"I swear it is true. Do you not remember? He had an accident and the ferry was damaged. His crew brought him here."

"Aye, and his men took him to the nunnery but I thought they returned to their ferry."

"That was a week ago and they have not yet come back. I could show the officer. It is but half a mile upstream."

I dismounted, "I would be grateful if you were to do so." We tied up our horses and took our Bakers. If the boy was correct then this could be the answer to the general's prayers. As we walked, I noticed that the youth had a wickedly sharp knife in his belt. He could be no more than fourteen years of age but boys grew into men fast in this part of the world. He looked at my gun, "That is a fine-looking gun, sir. Have you killed many Frenchmen with it?"

"A few."

"I should like such a gun. I wish to kill many Frenchmen."

"You had better leave that to soldiers like us. The French do not treat guerrillas well."

"A man cannot allow his family to be hurt. What is the point of life otherwise? The family is all."

I noticed that the river had a bend in it. There was a sort of wooden quay. There, moored to the bank, was the ferry. I saw that it lay canted at an unnatural angle. We slipped aboard. It was obvious that the damage was minimal. It looked like it had struck a branch or a tree and there was a hole the size of my fist just below the waterline. It could be repaired! It looked like it would take half a company. "You were right." I took a couple of coins from my purse. "Here is for your trouble."

He shook his head, "It would be like blood money. Give me a weapon and I will be satisfied."

"I will try to get you one. Does the ferry normally come here?"

He pointed downstream, closer to Oporto, "No, sir. It operates closer to the town. The bridges are often crowded. There are people who wish to cross the river but do not need the city. There are many farms which grow wines on both sides of the river."

I turned to Sharp, "This is the news the General needs. Let us go back to the village. I have an idea."

As we had headed upstream, I had noticed a small fishing skiff tied to the bank. As we passed it, I said, "Cristiano, to whom does the boat belong?"

"Our family, sir. We use it to fish."

I nodded and began to speak in English, "Sharp, I want you to take the two horses and find Sir Arthur. Tell him about the ferry. There are no guns opposite. I think we could land a battalion in a short time."

"And what about you, sir?"

"I am going to cross the river. The General needs the Douro to be scouted and if there are no bridges then this is the only way!"

Chapter 10

Sergeant Sharp was not happy but he was a soldier and he obeyed my orders. I left my Baker with him and took a powder horn and a bag of twenty balls for my pistol. It was not a great number but I could always take French balls. They would do as they were, generally, of a smaller calibre than my pistols. He left after he had eaten. With two horses he could make the General in one long day. All he had to do was to avoid French patrols.

After he had gone, I spoke with José. They were curious as to what was happening for Sharp and I had spoken in English. "Will you stay with us, sir? You are more than welcome."

I shook my head, "No José. Tonight, I would like you to take me across the river and land me on the north bank. Could you do that?"

"Of course, but the north is filled with Frenchmen."

"Do not worry, my friend, I can pass amongst Frenchmen. Your enemies think you are a defeated people. When General Wellesley comes, they will learn differently."

I had an afternoon sleep. They called it a siesta. I knew that once I landed in French territory I would be in great danger and would need to be alert. I was woken by José's wife. I was fed well with plain wholesome fare. Like the other village, the animals might have been taken but they squirrelled away food in all sorts of secret places.

Cristiano came with José and me. I had my cloak wrapped about me and my cocked hat was folded into my jacket. I had nothing else with me save for my weapons. There was little point in leaving my sword behind. My boots and uniform marked me as a soldier. My cloak would just confuse any recognition and if there was a confrontation then I would have to fight my way out. The two Portuguese headed downstream; they knew the river well and the current would help us. They would have a harder journey back upstream. I wanted to be as close as I could to the city and I stared at the black shoreline with cliffs rising high above the water. José knew a good place to land. I had given him the address I had been given in Lisbon by Donna Maria d'Alvarez. She had said it was someone I could trust. He was a wine

merchant, António José da Silva, whose father had died during
the early clashes with the French. Donna d'Alvarez swore that he
was a man, although relatively young, whom I could trust. His
port house lay just a mile from the city. He had warehouses and I
hoped that I could use them to hide during the day.

The river was empty. The night and the water were both black.
The current took us towards the sea and José and his brother had
little to do except to find the one landing placed which was close
to the wine merchant's home. Returning back across the river
would be a different story. They would have to tack across the
river. They planned on fishing as they did so. It was unlikely that
the French would stop them but, if they did, then they had a story.

They would not be able to land me at the warehouse. It had a
quay and might be guarded. Instead, they would land me at a
small beach just a mile or so from it. I saw the trees begin to take
shape as we neared the north bank; they told me we were getting
close. We did not speak. They lowered the sail and allowed the
current and the rudder to bump us gently into the shore. Cristiano
slipped over the side and held us against the shore. I dropped into
the shallow water. I clasped arms with the brothers. Cristiano
clambered back aboard and, with the sail raised, they disappeared
into the night. I made my way up the slope to the road I knew lay
above me.

We were now into May and the nights were warm. I did not
need the cloak for warmth but it hid me. José had heard of the
wine warehouse and he had given me directions to find it. I
reached the road. I had no doubt that the French would have
imposed a curfew. That did not worry me. I would try to bluff my
way past any sentries with my French. I moved close to the
buildings to my left. They were mainly industrial and were empty.
I hoped that I would remain hidden. A dog barked to my right. I
kept moving as a Portuguese voice commanded it to be silent. In
some places, there were no buildings and I could see, to my left
the river. There I hurried to the next building. I entered the
warehouse district. I knew, from José, that many wine merchants
lived above their warehouses. I hoped that was true of António
José da Silva. It was dark but I could still read the signs above the
doors. Eventually, after walking three-quarters of a mile or so, I

found the premises of da Silva. As I had expected the doors were barred.

Before I knocked on the door, I would explore as much of the river and the bank as I could while it was still dark. Using the shadows and the doorways I headed towards the city. The main thoroughfare was wide but I spied many alleyways. We could slip men through them without a problem. I travelled, perhaps four hundred paces before I heard, ahead, the sound of French voices. I also smelled pipe tobacco. I moved more slowly and after two hundred paces I spied a battery of eight-pounders. They were obliquely aligned and were facing the bridge. They had just three sentries. I did not see any infantry. Turning, I retraced my steps to the warehouse. I walked back up the street until I found a passage between two warehouses, leading down to the river.

The cobbles leading down to the river were slippery and I had to move cautiously. I saw then that the warehouse had been built on a cliff. I guessed that they used the cool stones to create a better environment for the wine. My cousin had taught me much about viniculture. When I reached the river, I observed that the cliff overhung the river and provided shelter. To my joy, I saw that there were four large wine barges moored there. They were called Rabelo boats. They would be almost invisible to anyone looking upstream from the centre of the city. While I waited for dawn to break and people to begin to move around the streets above me, I explored the barges. Flat bottomed they were designed to carry huge barrels of wine from the vineyards upstream. They would be perfect for the transportation of troops. I estimated that almost a company could be boarded aboard each one. The four of them could transport almost four hundred men across the river.

By the time I had finished my exploration dawn was breaking and I heard a bell which, I assumed, marked the end of curfew. I headed back up the steep cobbled path to the warehouse. I waited across the road in the doorway of a building which looked like it might be a shop of some description. If I was found now it would be hard to justify my presence. Fate took a hand and no one questioned me. I saw four broad-shouldered men arrive from the east. One had a key and they glanced at me as he opened the door to António José da Silva's warehouse.

I stepped across the road, "Excuse me, I am seeking a Portuguese wine merchant, António José da Silva." I took out the letter of introduction given to me by Donna d'Alvarez. "I have a letter here."

One said, "You are English?"

My accent was not as good as I might have hoped. "Yes."

"Come inside quickly. The French send a patrol down here as soon as curfew is ended." Sure enough, I was no sooner whisked inside than I heard the sound of hooves clattering down the cobbles.

Don António José da Silva was a younger man than I had expected. I suppose that was because of Donna d'Alvarez. I later discovered that she had known his father better than the son. He read the letter and then embraced me, "You cannot know the joy your presence brings. Your army comes?"

"It does. Are the bridges still in place?"

He shook his head, "There is just one remaining. There were many men crossing it yesterday."

"In which direction?"

"They were heading south!"

"That means that the General is close."

"How can I be of service?"

"Those barges, they are yours?"

"Yes, they belong to my company but since the French came, they have not been used. We keep them hidden there because the French commandeered all the other vessels on the river! They cannot have them!"

"They would be useful in the transportation of troops."

He shook his head, "There is a battery of guns just one hundred yards from here. The French do not know they are there. They sank all the others yesterday. Only the high cliff hides them. As soon as we started to take them across then they would open fire. They are slow moving and would soon be reduced to firewood! Besides, the opposite bank is held by the French. Come, I will show you."

He took me to a balcony on the top floor. It afforded a fine view across the river. I saw blue uniforms moving. He was right. Just then I heard the unmistakable sound of British six-pounder cannons. In reply, I heard the heavier boom of nine and twelve pounder French cannons. The battle was beginning.

"Come, we will eat. We can do nothing while the battle rages."

"Could we take the barges across at night?"

"That is an idea worth talking about. It would be dangerous but possible. We will eat and talk."

He led me to a table which had been placed on the balcony so that we could view the battle. It did not sit well with me to rest while my comrades fought but my host was correct and there was little that we could do. It felt bizarre to be behind the enemy lines drinking coffee and eating freshly made pastries. We also had a fine view of the bridge. When I saw red-coated soldiers marching across it to the south, I started.

António laughed, "They had us confused too, Major. They are Swiss soldiers serving the Emperor. Mercenaries!"

By the time we had finished our breakfast the sound of muskets had grown and they were closer to the river. We saw ambulances and wounded men stream back across the bridge. At first, this was a trickle which grew to a flood and when the Swiss mercenaries returned along with blue coated battalions then I knew the French had lost the battle. It was mesmerizing. Neither of us could drag our eyes from the battle. Columns of smoke rose in the distance. We heard muskets and even the clash of sabres. A building burned and black smoke spread across the southern bank of the river. I had a better idea of what would be happening. Both armies would be using their light infantry and light dragoons to skirmish. Fighting in suburbs and towns was not the work of line infantry or dragoons.

The morning raced by. We saw no actual fighting but we did spy the results. Across the river, the blue battalions began to head towards the bridge which quickly became packed. If there had been a British battery with a line of sight to the bridge then the troops would have been massacred. They made it, albeit slowly, to the other side. Then I saw a sight which sent shivers down my spine, French engineers were beneath the bridge and they were placing charges. They were going to blow the bridge. This was where the British cavalry should have been used. If they could have gained a foothold on the bridge while men still flooded across it then there was a chance that they could take it and, with it, the city. There was still a mass of men tramping across the bridge. The engineers swarmed underneath the bridge with barrels of power and fuse.

I saw the last of the regimental artillery being dragged back to the northern bank and the sound of muskets replaced by that of carbines. The flood became a trickle and then I saw Chasseurs and Dragoons galloping across the bridge. I spied a French Engineer shouting. I knew what was coming. The last of the French had just left the bridge and a handful of red-coated soldiers were just on the southern end when an almighty explosion rent the air. The British soldiers knew nothing about it. They were thrown into the air with the bridge. Pieces cascaded down on both sides of the river bank and up and downstream of the bridge.

I looked at António José da Silva, "Well, it seems that we will have to find a way to take those barges across the river."

He nodded, "I can find men to sail them across the river but will your General be here and, if he is, where will we find him?"

"I have a good view here. If you can get me a telescope, I will spend the rest of the day looking for him but if we just land the barges on the opposite bank I can land and search for him."

"It is not as simple as that. They need to be out of sight of the French guns. A barge is not a warship. It is not robust."

"Do you have somewhere in mind?"

He pointed to the convent at Vila Nova. The largest south of the Douro, it lay to the south and west of us. I estimated it to be half a mile or so from us, "There would be a good place. Even the French will think twice about shelling a nunnery!"

The afternoon wore on. I saw more red coats as our regiments arrived. The Royal and Horse Artillery began to set up batteries facing us. When I saw the Union Flag raised above the convent I knew where Sir Arthur was. I shouted for António, "Sir Arthur, it seems, has read your mind. He is at the convent."

António beamed, "Then all is well. We can sail the barges there as soon as it is dark."

"And the curfew? I have a feeling that it will be enforced strongly tonight."

"You could be right. Perhaps we will wait until midnight. The tide will be higher then anyway. Will you be coming with us?"

I nodded, "My task was to find a way across the river and I have done so. Besides, my presence must place you and your people in danger."

"We are patriots and we are happy to place ourselves in such danger. When Sir Arthur lands he will find loyal men, who are willing to help him. We will help you drive the hated French from our land!"

The watching over, we dined and we dined well. António was a rich man and he had a good table. I was careful to drink as little as possible although I had to consume a reasonable amount as I did not wish to offend my host. While we ate, he told me all that he knew of the defences. The cliffs which appeared so formidable were also a weakness for they could not be defended well. It seemed that the bulk of the defences were towards the heart of the city. The strongest part of the defences were closer to the centre of the city. That meant we could land men close to the warehouse and gain a toe hold. The bell sounded the curfew. I heard the horses of the dragoons as they clattered down the cobbles.

The men who would sail the barges were already assembled in the warehouses. There were doors which opened directly on to the river. While we would only sail after midnight, we could prepare the barges. António would be sailing with us. I went on the barge with him. They had a simple sail arrangement. Our engineers would be able to sail them. Without any weight in them they would fly but, equally, might be prone to capsizing. I was glad that the men who sailed them knew what they were doing. António had a clock and we set sail at midnight. He bravely led. We had to scull away from the cliff but then the tide, current and slight breeze took us. We were totally silent. There was not even the snap of a sail or a sheet. I could not help but stare at the French bank of the Douro. There were sentries there. What would they make of the four shapes which ghosted across the river? As we moved across the dark river I suddenly wondered if we might have a hostile reception from the British. They might be nervous. I went to the bow and peered out. There was no quay beneath the convent. Instead, it was a rocky and sandy shore. António had assured me that they had landed in similar places. I saw two

English soldiers on the shore. Their faces turned and I heard the unmistakable sound of muskets being cocked.

I spoke loudly for I needed my words to be heard, "I am Sir Arthur's aide, Major Matthews of the 11th Light Dragoons. Hold your fire."

I heard a Geordie accent, "Tam, go and fetch the sergeant." I saw one of them scurry away. A red coat loomed up from the shadows. A bayonet was fixed to the end of a cocked musket, "Aye, sir, you may be who you say but keep your hands where I can see them and come slowly."

The barge ground ashore so gently that I was able to step down on to dry land. I heard footsteps and a sergeant appeared next to the private with the gun. "I am Major Matthews... I"

The sergeant nodded, "We were told to expect you. The General is waiting." He looked behind me.

"These are friends, make them welcome and keep them safe."

The Geordie said, "Aye, sir. Come on, gentlemen. I am sure we have a brew on."

Sir Arthur was camped in the grounds of the convent. Preparations were being made to assault the French and there was much movement in the camp. Part of it, no doubt, was heralded by the arrival of the barges. I had to wait but a short time as Sir Arthur was woken. He was not precious about his sleep. He had a dressing gown around him, "So, Matthews, you have worked your magic again. I have Sir John heading up to that ferry you and your fellow found and now I hear that you have brought me some ships! Is there no end to your talents?"

"Just to say, sir, that the people of Oporto are ready to rise and support you."

He took the tea his servant had brought him, "Pah! The last thing I need is a mob of civilians to muddy the waters." Cup in hand he strode off. "Come to the command tent. Let us see how we can exploit this God-given opportunity." His senior officers had been summoned. They knew the General and they raced towards the command tent in various stages of undress. I saw that Sir Rowland Hill had managed to don his uniform whilst some of the others were half dressed and, like the General, wearing dressing gowns. Lights were brought in. Dawn was not far away but the interior of the tent was black. There was a map on the table.

"Gentlemen, Major Matthews here has brought us intelligence and four wine barges. We begin our attack this morning. Sir John Murray is some miles upstream repairing the ferry Major Matthews found. The last news I had was that this would be repaired by noon. He has some light horse and artillery. We can cut off Soult from the east! I intend to attack this morning. Matthews, what do you know of the defences here?" He jabbed a finger just downstream from the warehouses.

"The main defences are towards the centre of the city. They are either side of the bridge. There is a battery here." I pointed to the bank half a mile from the warehouses. "If you land here," I pointed to the quay from which we had embarked, "then our men can land without fear of fire and the narrow streets would be perfect to build defences."

Sir John Sherbrooke asked, "How many men can you ferry at one time?"

"The river is calm and the barges are built to carry heavy weights. I would say sixty to eighty men in each boat."

Sir Arthur shook his head, "Too much risk of capsizing. The first wave will have just two hundred men. There will be fifty in each boat. Major Matthews will command. He knows the landing site best. General Anstruther, your men suffered the fewest casualties. Who would you recommend follow Major Matthews?"

He grinned, "Colonel Donkin and his mad Irishmen. He has the Prince of Wales' Irish and the Connaught Rangers. They have been itching to get into the fight. They need to be blooded. A bit of action might calm them down!"

Sir Arthur nodded, "Then your division will go in first. Matthews, secure a bridgehead and hold. You and Colonel Donkin will be in command until General Hill can land." He turned to the redoubtable General Hill, "Rowland, take your chaps and the Guards."

"Yes, sir."

"I want the Horse Artillery to support the attack. Have them placed to fire across the river. Knock out the French guns." He glowered around the table. "Any questions?"

Silence greeted him.

"We send the barges back as soon as they are assembled." He looked at me, "You had better leave the civilians here, Matthews."

"They won't like that, sir. How about we take crews over with us and I can leave them on the north side. Their families are there."

He stared at me, "Well, you know these chaps best. Good luck gentlemen and put some clothes on! It looks like a gathering of sepoys!"

General Anstruther followed me out of the tent. "I hope you don't take offence at this, Major Matthews, but I am not sure my Colonel Donkin will be happy about taking orders from a light dragoon!"

I nodded, "Don't worry, sir, I know my business. There are two divisions of troops waiting in the city, sir. A toehold is the best we can do and General Hill will be with the fourth wave. All I need to do is hold for an hour or so."

"Well, he holds you in high regard."

I was surprised. He had never intimated to me that he thought well of me. That was Sir Arthur's way.

We parted and I returned to the barges. Dawn had begun to break while we had been speaking in the tent. I strode over to the Portuguese. "We are going to attack as soon as the men are assembled."

They began to cheer when I told them. António rubbed his hands, "Now we fight back!"

"I think you should leave it to the men who wear red, António."

"If this was your land, Roberto, would you let others die for you? We are men of honour. We will do our part and besides, we can do what you cannot. We can slip through lines and appear in their rear, as though by magic. This is our city and we know it better than any. My father died fighting for Portugal. The least that I can do is to fight for it!"

They were adamant and would not be gainsaid. I prepared for battle. I had no Baker but I had my pistols and my sword. I put fresh powder in the priming pan and reloaded. Then I waited for the men I would lead into battle.

Chapter 11

Colonel Rufane Donkin was just five years older than me but, considering he led a brigade of Irishmen, was a remarkably calm and measured man. Perhaps that was why he had been appointed. "You are Major Matthews?"

"Yes, sir."

"I understand, from the General, that you are to lead my brigade?"

"Just until we establish our defences, sir. I speak Portuguese and I have been on the north side. It is just local knowledge which necessitates the arrangement."

He nodded, "Be careful with my chaps eh, Matthews? They are as mad as a bucketful of frogs but they are good chaps."

"Don't worry, sir." I realised that it was my Light Dragoon uniform which inspired his worry. "I am not a hunt to hounds sort of cavalryman. I was with Sir John on the retreat to Corunna. I know the mettle of the men you lead."

He looked relieved. "Good. I suggest we load the two light infantry companies first and then the grenadiers. I shall be with you, of course."

"Of course. But if I might suggest we send the rifles too?"

"Good idea. I will get them loaded. Sergeant Major!"

I clambered aboard António's barge. "There will be some engineers coming aboard. They will sail the barges back. If you would let them know the tricks to sailing these ships."

"They are simple! My grandmother could have sailed one!"

We had with us twenty-two Royal Engineers. Sir Arthur used them whenever he could not think of the perfect soldier to perform the duty he required. The Regimental Sergeant Major of the 88th also knew his business. These might be largely Irishmen, but he knew how to handle them. He loaded the ten riflemen who would be travelling with us. I did not know the Lieutenant but he seemed to know what he was doing. He ensured that the Bakers were loaded before we left land but not primed. The river crossing might damp the powder and make for misfire.

I nodded as he saluted me, "I served with riflemen at Corunna. I even have a Baker rifle."

Lieutenant Hay looked surprised, "A cavalry major who can use a Baker? I am sorry to sound so surprised, sir, but that is unusual!"

"Let us say, Lieutenant, that I am often placed in a position where being able to shoot enemies who are some distance away is a distinct advantage."

He smiled. Riflemen appreciated that advantage, "Will we be able to land unopposed, sir? What I mean is should we be ready to fire as we approach the shore?"

I pointed to the north-west. "There is a gun emplacement over there. I would have your men with weapons ready to prime but if we can land without firing a shot then this endeavour has a half decent chance of success. Our job is to gain us a bridgehead. The brigade holds until we can bring over half a division. The terrain should suit your chaps. There are narrow alleyways and buildings which look down on the enemy."

"You seem to know how to fight, sir."

I tapped my epaulettes, "As I was given these and did not buy them, one would hope so, eh?"

His eyes widened. Such promotions were rare. They were reliant upon a mixture of ability, luck and bravery.

We were loaded first. Colonel Donkin was the last to board. He left the Regimental Sergeant Major to load the other barges. We also had six engineers aboard our barge. I said, "Watch how the Portuguese sail. If you need to ask them a question then I will translate."

"Right, sir!"

"Push off, António."

The sail was unfurled and the breeze caught us. The tide had turned and we just had to fight the current. As we emerged into the river, I realised that we were leaving the safety of the convent. I tried to calculate how long it would take for the French to range their guns and begin to sink us. We had just a few hundred yards of the river to cross but the closer we came to the other shore the bigger the target we would make. They would spot us and a sentry would summon a sergeant who would look at us and then send for an officer. He would make a decision. The guns would be loaded and re-aligned. Each minute that I saw no activity made it less likely that we would be fired upon. When we sailed close to the cliff and the dead ground, I breathed a sigh of relief. We would have four boatloads of some of the finest soldiers in the British Army on the northern shore of the Douro. We had a chance.

I leapt ashore and, drawing my pistol and cocking it, ran up the steep cobbled slope to the street above. I heard orders being shouted behind me. It seemed impossible that the gun crew would not hear us and then I realised that there was a cliff between us and they were a good three-quarters of a mile away. The local markets were open and there was the normal street noise. Perhaps we had a better than average chance of survival. I heard the rifles and light infantry behind me, their boots pounding on the cobbles. We emerged on to the street. It was busy for the Portuguese did not know that an attack was taking place. They saw the red and green jackets and they cheered.

I held up my hands and shouted, in Portuguese, "Return to your homes I beg of you."

In response, some of the women ran up to us and began to kiss us. I know not what might have happened had not António shouted, "This is the day we retake our city! Return to your homes. My brothers, arm yourselves! Today we stand shoulder to shoulder with our British allies!"

It worked and the crowd dispersed. Colonel Donkin asked, "What did he say?"

"He told the men to arm themselves and join us."

The Colonel groaned, "That is all we needed. Orders, Major?"

"I suggest we let the rifles and one company of the light go as skirmishers with me. We get as close as we can to the gun emplacement. We need to build barricades and barriers. The ones who are following should collect as much material for barricades as they can. There will be plenty of barrels. Portuguese for barrel is almost the same as in English, *barril*. The Portuguese are on our side. They will let you have them. There are at least ten thousand Frenchmen in Oporto. Our men might be the best but they will struggle against those sorts of numbers."

"Quite. By my estimate, it took fifteen minutes to load the barge and reach here. It will take us an hour to bring one battalion over."

"It will be quicker than that, sir. The current will take the barges back quicker but I think you are right. We have an hour to build our defences."

He nodded, "I will organize the chaps as they are landed."

"Lieutenant Hay, with me. Have your men pair up and head along the street. Captain Turner, we need to get as close as we can to the French without alerting them to our presence."

"Yes, sir." The Connaught Ranger officer was English. Most of the officers would be.

The streets looked different in the daylight. I had to translate the black shadows I had seen in the night into the buildings I now saw. The Rifles and Light Company were doing what they did best. They were working as individuals and as pairs. They scampered through side alleys. I kept ahead with the Lieutenant and his Chosen Man. I smelled the pipe smoke and I held up my hand. Immediately the men I led dropped to one knee and aimed their weapons. Then I heard the tramp of feet. It was infantry! Gesturing for the others to remain where they were, I ran to the corner of the nearest building. I could see that the gun emplacement had been built on an open area or perhaps they had demolished a building. It had a good field of fire down the river. The road to the centre of the town turned to the right and I saw a company of French infantry. Their officer halted them.

The artillery officer shouted, "There are boats filled with soldiers in red!"

The infantry officer laughed, "Do not worry, they will be the Swiss. *Les Goddams* will be busy getting drunk on *Le Casse-Poitrine*. This will be another easy day. It is tomorrow they will bleed and the river will turn red. Carry on, Sergeant!"

The Sergeant shouted, "Piquets to your positions, Lasalle, get some water on to heat!"

Happy that they would not be investigating, I went back to my men. I waved over the Lieutenant and the Captain. The rest of the battalion had yet to arrive. I spoke quietly, "We make a barrier here. Lieutenant, get your men into the buildings and on to the top floors of the buildings. If they can get onto a roof then so much the better. There is a gun battery around the corner. Find somewhere you can fire down on them. Do not fire until you have to. We need to get as many men over as we can. Target officers and sergeants first." I knew that he would resent the extra command. The Rifles knew their business. However, I did not know the Lieutenant.

"Sir!"

He waved over his sergeant and led his fifty men into the buildings on both sides of the road.

Captain Turner asked, "Won't they tumble to our presence, sir?"

Shaking my head, I said, "They think the men in the boats are Swiss! I want every road blocking. Build barricades and have your men line them. Each moment brings us closer to battle."

"Right, sir!"

The barricades took shape. It was bizarre. The French were less than a hundred yards from us. All they had to do was to turn a corner and they would see us. An hour passed and they had still not reacted.

"Captain Hay, I want ten men to come with me. We will risk building a second barrier at the corner. Good men, eh?"

"Sir."

"Sergeant McMahon!"

The sergeant and nine men appeared. "Grab material to build a barrier and follow me. Keep close to the wall!"

We were just five paces from the wall when I heard a French bugle. The command to fire was given and the three guns belched forth. They had realised that they were under attack. It was the barges they had seen and not us. The French infantry officer shouted an order. Their eyes would be on the far shore and I took my chance. As the Bakers barked above us, I shouted, "Quick, lads. Build a barrier here!" I waved Captain Turner forward. "They will soon realise that they are under attack from above. Be ready." The smoke from the guns helped disguise us and I stepped into the open. As I had expected all the attention of the infantry and the gunners was across the river. When men fell in the gun emplacement and amongst the French infantry they thought the balls came from the four barges heading across the water. The Irishmen worked like demons. I had my two pistols aimed at the French while they laboured to build a second barrier across the corner.

The first shell from the British howitzer landed twenty yards to the west of the gun. The shell sent pieces of metal towards the infantry. At the same time, the officer of infantry pointed upwards and shouted. He had seen the Rifles. It was his last command as a lead ball hit him. The attention of the infantry was now on the roof. I looked and saw that there were twenty Connaught Rangers in position.

"Light Company, prepare muskets. Ready! Aim! Fire!" Their balls decimated the infantry and the howitzer had the range. One artillery piece was struck immediately. The Baker rifles thinned out the artillerymen and then a lucky howitzer shell hit the French powder. I was knocked from my feet by the blast and when I recovered, I saw that the guns were disabled and the French infantry was retreating.

One Connaught Ranger stood and shouted, "Away lads! Let's have the bastards!"

Sergeant McMahon's voice cut through the cheers, "Hold your positions or I will lay your backs open! They quailed. "And McIlroy, you are on pan bash for the next week!"

"Sorry, Sarge!"

Captain Turner helped to brush the dust from my jacket, "What now, sir?"

I turned and saw the grenadiers from the brigade arriving, "Have the light company occupy the French gun position. They will send men soon enough." I turned, "McIlroy, is it? Come with me!"

"Sir!"

I ran to the guns with the Irishman behind me. "You want to do something useful? Stand on the parapet and wave your shako!"

"Wave me shako, sir?"

"Can you think of a quicker way to let them know we have taken the position? The last thing we need, Private, is for our own artillery to start dropping shells on us!"

"Right, sir." He ran to the sandbags and clambered up them. He began to wave. I counted on the fact that there would be spotters and the sight of a British soldier in a red jacket waving his stovepipe shako would tell them that we had taken it.

Suddenly a musket ball struck the sandbags close to McIlroy's feet. As the Irishman jumped down, I turned and fired both pistols at the tirailleur who had appeared. I hit his arm and he dropped his weapon.

"Open fire!"

Captain Turner's voice sent a volley towards the French light infantry. I saw that half of the company were already with me and they levelled their muskets for a second volley. A different voice ordered a volley from the position at the corner of the road. The grenadiers had arrived. The Bakers continued to fire and take out officers as Sergeant McMahon shouted, "Sir, with respect, get your head down!"

He was right. I dropped behind the cannonball caisson from the eight pounder. "Thank you, sergeant!"

The light infantry duelled with the tirailleurs. I heard the tramp of feet as heavy infantry marched towards us. I had no idea how many men had landed but we had attained at least a toehold. It was a frenetic few minutes as the 88th, 89th and 60th all formed lines around our defences. The French were trying to do the same. I was busy trying to reload. The air was filled with smoke and both sides fired, almost indiscriminately at each other. Colonel Donkin took his life in his hands as he almost dived behind the damaged trail of the French Artillery piece. His bugler and the colour sergeant of the 88th followed him.

"Well done, boys." Raising himself to his full height he shouted, "Rifles and Light Companies continue firing. Brigade, form two lines." All around him musket balls zipped. There was so much smoke that little could be seen. They were not aiming at him. The French skirmishers were just firing blindly at chest height in the hope of hitting someone. The only one who was standing close to us was the Colonel but he seemed to bear a charmed life. His bugler and the colour sergeant stood with him. The colours of the 88th fluttered but few would be able to see them through the musket smoke. I stood and prepared my pistols. They would be of little use unless someone was close but I felt the Colonel and his men should not be the only ones who stood.

"Front rank, fire!"

"Second rank, fire!

The Colonel and the colour sergeant shouted out their commands twice more. There were fewer balls coming our way. "Cease fire!" The volleys had been kept company by the individual shots of the 60th and the light companies. Now the light companies ceased firing but the Bakers, in the lofty nest, continued to pick off the officers and sergeants who were beyond the smoke.

Glancing behind me I saw that the Guards were now being ferried over. The elite of our army would be in action within the hour. What had seemed like a long shot at dawn, now seemed a distinct possibility.

I heard moans from the smoke and then, in the distance, I heard the trumpet call which announced more battalions coming to attack us. We had broken the attack of the first men but the French would come again. In many ways, this was the perfect terrain for them. They were happy charging in a column which was eight men wide and up to a hundred men deep. That was the width of the road ahead.

Colonel Donkin shouted, "Reload!"

Just then I sensed, rather than saw the four French infantrymen who sought glory. They loomed up out of the smoke and ran at us with bayonets fixed and murder in their hearts. I fired my two pistols simultaneously, threw them to the ground and drew my sword. The Colour Sergeant used the standard to deflect one bayonet downwards. I slashed my sword across the face of the fourth man. The Colonel had an old-fashioned claymore and he drew it and hacked down so hard at the soldier whose bayonet had been deflected that he almost took off his head.

"I am obliged to you, Major, Colour Sergeant. Damned unsporting of them!"

The smoke had begun to clear and I heard the drums marking the beat as the next French column came from Oporto. This attack would not be piecemeal. The skirmishers would be like flies before the column. They would be trying to do what our light infantry were doing and picking off the officers. It was brave of the Colonel to be where he was. It was exposed but it allowed him to judge the moment to begin to fire better. The breeze had almost cleared the smoke and I saw the skirmishers. They operated like the Rifles. One man fired while the other ran. That might have been effective but for the men on the roof. Lieutenant Hay and his men had plenty of time to load their rifles properly and to keep up a withering rate of fire. The occasional ball got through but none hit flesh. I heard one ball ricochet off the artillery trail. The tirailleurs lost the battle of the light infantry and they moved to the side.

"Brigade, prepare to fire!"

I heard officers and sergeants, to my right, shout, "Steady! Wait for the command!"

"Present!" This time it would not be rolling volleys. The Colonel was unleashing a volley of three hundred muskets. It would act like an enormous shotgun. The British Army had perfected this art. The soldiers knew they just had to aim at the middle of the advancing men and fire. The blue mass which approached could bring, at best, sixteen muskets to bear. They relied on the momentum of the column to carry them forward. Often the men at the front might be dead, their bodies held in place by the ones behind them. The Colonel waited until they were sixty paces from us. The men would be able to reload before it came to bayonets.

"Fire!"

The cordite fog filled the space between the two forces. Men screamed.

"Reload!"

"Fire!"

I actually saw the musket balls tear through the French column just twenty paces from us. They also ripped the heart from the attack. I heard the bugle sound retreat. We had beaten them again but, even as this column moved back to the city, I heard a third column as they came up the road with drums beating and shouts of '*Vive L'Empereur*!'

The Colonel took out a hip flask and offered it to me. I shook my head. He took a swig, "Persistent beggars, what?"

"They are indeed, sir." I turned, "How are your men coping, Captain Turner?"

"Cuts, grazes and splinters, sir."

The smoke was dissipating once more but it still lingered making it hard to see what they were doing. This time the French tried something different. I heard the orders being shouted. "Sir, they are going to deploy into three lines and then attack."

Colonel Donkin looked at me in surprise, "You speak French then?"

It seemed an inconsequential thing to say, "Yes sir!"

"Reload!"

As the smoke disappeared, I saw that the French battalions had a frontage of sixty men. The street up which they marched made deployment difficult but they managed it. There were still one hundred and ten paces separating us. The French Colonel shouted, "*Avant*!"

They would march to within sixty paces of us and then fire. This would be a close-run thing. My pistols were already reloaded. Even as they deployed and prepared to fire, I heard the clipped voice of Brigadier Henry Campbell. He commanded the Guards Brigade, "Brigade, prepare! Brigade, Fire!" The Guards Brigade opened fire on the flank of the column.

Colonel Donkin shouted, "Fire!"

Attacked on two sides they broke almost immediately. Brigadier Campbell's voice echoed, "Advance!" The bugle sounded and we obeyed.

However, Colonel Donkin's brigade was Irish. They did not do the measured advance of the Guards. They gave wild cheers and hurtled after the French. I saw Colonel Donkin shake his head and then, sword in hand, he charged after his men.

Chapter 12

I followed. My part in this battle was done but I was a spy. I knew what to look for. The redcoats ahead of me would be intent upon killing Frenchmen and when that was done, they would seek alcohol. The French officer had been right. Drink was the bane of the British soldier. I had seen it during the retreat to Corunna. If there was an enemy to fight then they would fight. When the enemy was dead or fled then they fought themselves and drink. I knew that Sir Arthur would need to know what was happening here. As I ran, I saw more wine barges, filled with reinforcements, crossing the river. With Sir John Murray cutting off their escape then soon we would outnumber the French. Brigadier Campbell had been right. Now was not the time to take the bayonet from the Frenchman's back but where would Soult go? My money was on either Estremadura or Galicia. As I hurried after the screaming Irishmen, I dismissed Galicia. Soult was too clever a leader to risk being isolated. He would head north and east.

Ahead I heard muskets being fired. The redcoats were far ahead of me. There were screams and shouts. As we neared the centre it became a scene from Dante's Inferno. The Portuguese had taken to the streets. Men were wielding axes and pitchforks. They were firing musketoons. Any Frenchman who failed to join his fellows in flight was a doomed man. This was a rout. The French were leaving Oporto. I saw abandoned artillery pieces and discarded weapons. The defeat was so sudden that I wondered if Soult had already left the city. I stopped at what had been the French Headquarters. The French flag still flew. I found, in the entrance, scattered documents. I walked into a palace. It was the sort of place Soult would choose as his headquarters. I could smell food and I followed my nose. I saw a half-eaten sumptuous dinner. I picked up a lobster claw, cracked it and began to suck the meat from it. It gave me time to think. Soult had left in the middle of his dinner. What might he have missed? I would collect all the papers I could. I would search the headquarters and then report to Sir Arthur. He would be across the river as soon as he could. First Vouga River and now Oporto; if the General's luck held then Portugal would be free by the end of May and Spain, perhaps by the end of the year. I ate a chicken leg and washed it down with some wine.

Heading upstairs I began my search. I was soon rewarded by lists of regiments and numbers of men. There were maps. Soult had not meant to leave them. Our sudden and successful attack had given him no choice. It was flee or be captured. I soon had armfuls of papers which I carried back to the dining room. I collected the ones from the hallway. I had just begun to sort them when Sir Arthur walked in. I heard his dry laugh, "I might have known, Matthews, while others are racing around like headless chickens you are still gathering intelligence. Have you found much?"

"Yes, sir. Maps and reports about the strengths of units!"

"By God, we have them. If Sir John can stop the flight east then this victory will be complete." His staff followed him in, "Major Matthews has done the hard part! Take the papers from him and then begin to sort them."

"Yes, sir."

"Matthews, as soon as you are reunited with your Sergeant and your mount then report back to me. I have another little job for you!" He waved a hand and I was dismissed.

I picked up the rest of the chicken from the table and the jug of wine. Sergeant Sharp had been at the ferry. He would have crossed with our horses and the cavalry. He was a resourceful sergeant. He would head back along the river to find me. I walked east. I passed António's warehouse. I would not bother him. I found, just a hundred yards from the warehouse, a sofa which had been thrown from one of the houses. The stuffing had come out of it. I plonked myself in it and began to devour the chicken. It was late afternoon and my last meal had been with António before we had sailed across the river. It seemed a lifetime ago. I wiped my hands on the remains of the sofa and drank the wine directly from the jug. It was delicious.

"What are you doing here?"

I must have dozed off. I turned and saw António. I smiled. That was the effect of the wine. "The General has no need of me for a while. I am waiting here for my sergeant. He will be along soon."

António picked me up by the elbow, "We cannot have a hero sitting here on a broken chair. Carlos, come here." One of his men stepped forward. "Major, how will we know your man?"

"He will wear a uniform like mine and he will be leading a horse. He will have two of the rifles the 60th used."

"Good. Carlos wait here until you see such a man and then fetch him to the warehouse." He shook the jug and, seeing it was empty, handed it to Carlos. He took my arm and led me down the road. "This is not good enough. You are a hero. My people watched you. You saved the life of your general."

I shook my head, "He was just a colonel."

"Nonetheless you fought like a tiger. I am proud that Donna d'Alvarez sent you to me."

I do not know if it was the wine, the fighting or the long day but I felt ready to fall. "I am sorry about this, António, but I am tired."

He led me inside the warehouse. We climbed the stairs. "I have a guest room. I will have my man put you to bed. You can sleep and we will watch. It is the least we can do."

I was asleep before Stephano had removed my boots. When I woke it was dawn. I woke with a start and looked up at António who was seated in a chair smoking a cigar. "You should have woken me!"

He smiled, "There was little point. Your Sergeant Sharp arrived just thirty minutes ago. He is being fed. He and your horses are exhausted. I know not if your general wishes you to travel soon but that will be impossible until your horses are rested."

"Then you do not know the General. We have spare horses."

"Your Sergeant says that they are still with the baggage train?" He cocked his head to one side. I nodded. "They will not be here for at least a day and maybe two."

I rose, "Then we will have to buy some more." I made my way toward the stairs. "António, we have a great opportunity here to rid your land of the French invader. The enemy is in disarray. We must keep the sabre in their backs!"

He sighed, "Come, you must eat and I will get you two good horses. I am glad that I make wine and I am not a soldier."

Sharp was tucking into the bread and ham as though he had not eaten for a week. He grinned and made to rise when he saw me, "Sir!"

I waved him back to his seat, "We will talk when you have eaten."

Servants brought me my food and I ate well too. Sharp finished and wiped his mouth with a napkin. "Thank you, senor, that was most welcome."

António bowed, "You are welcome and now I will leave you, gentlemen. I have some horses to find."

He left us. Sharp leaned back and began, "Sir John crossed the river. We saw the army retreating but..."

"Sergeant!"

"Well sir, he made a mess of it. He didn't deploy properly. Colonel Hawker and he had words, sir. The upshot was that the French headed towards Amarante."

"Did Sir John follow them?"

"No sir, he held his ground and waited for more men to be ferried across. Colonel Hawker told me that there was little point in my hanging around and he told me to find you, sir. He is a good chap, that Colonel. He said he would watch out for our horses and war gear."

"Then we will report to Sir Arthur. I cannot see him being too pleased."

Sharp waved his arm around the room, "A nice billet, sir!"

"I am afraid, Sharp, that this is as close to comfort as we are going to get for a while."

It was as we walked to headquarters that the black clouds rolled in. We did not know it but we would have five days of torrential and unseasonal weather. As we wrapped ourselves in our cloaks, we could not have foreseen the effects of the rain. Aides and senior officers now filled the palace. Fortunately, I was recognised and taken to an anteroom to await Sir Arthur. I did not have to wait long.

Sir Rowland Hill himself fetched us in. "Damned foul weather eh, Major? Might as well be in England!"

"Indeed, sir, although as I recall this was the weather we had on the retreat to Corunna."

"You may be right but, as I recall, that was winter. This is supposed to be summer!"

The General had a map. He did not look up, "Matthews, here! He jabbed a finger north east of Oporto. "We have, apparently, allowed Soult to slip through our fingers. He will head for here, the Portuguese border. We will follow but the French can run faster than anyone I know. Marshal Ney is there. We will ensure that he leaves Portugal. General Beresford is pushing up towards Chaves from Lamego. What I need is information about Marshal Victor! He has a Corps which is the size of our army. If he were to join up with Soult then all our good work, hitherto, might be wasted. Find him for me, Major Matthews. He is between here and Madrid. Find him! I will be at either Coimbra or Abrantes."

I looked at the map. The distances were staggering. "Do I go as far as Madrid to look for him, sir?"

"Aye for if he has gone to Madrid then we have won!"

"And do you think, sir, that Soult will try to join with him?"

"No, Matthews. I think, now, that Soult will try to join Ney in Galicia. If we are quick enough then we might be able to trap him between us and General Beresford. Leave strategy to me, Major! Your job is to find the French!"

Duly chastised, I nodded, "Yes sir. This could take weeks rather than days."

"Fourteen days at the most, Matthews! That is all that I will allow you!" He waved over an aide, "Jeffers, provide Major Matthews with the funds he needs to buy horses and the like!" He turned to General Hill. I was dismissed.

I followed the Guards Captain and he went to a strong box. He smiled as he opened it, "You are honoured, sir. The General is short of funds. He seems happy to give you his gold. How much will you need?"

"Have you any French coins there?"

He took out a bag, "Yes, sir. This was found here when Marshal Soult fled."

"Then I will take that."

With a full purse, we left. The rain was torrential. If we had not been wearing our waterproof cloaks then we would have been soaked. When we re-entered the warehouse Sharp said, "I will oil these again, sir. It looks like we may be needing to keep dry."

"You do that, Sergeant Sharp, and I will see if António has our horses."

The winemaker was shaking his head as I went in. "This will do the grapes no good at all! And it will prevent you from leaving!"

"I am afraid not, my friend. We go no matter what the conditions. Did you manage to get me horses?"

"Yes, we have two. I will have my servants prepare provisions. Wherever you are going food will be in short supply. The French are like a plague of goats. When they pass over a land all is destroyed!"

"I know." As his servants prepared our supplies I said, "You know, António, I may be able to repay you in some small way for your hospitality. I am related to the Alpini family of Sicily. Their agent in London, Mr David Hudson, is a friend of mine. I could write a letter of introduction. I am sure he could act as your agent too. He has many contacts."

He beamed, "You do not need to repay me but I would be grateful for the letter. There are too many agents who would try to rob me, especially in London. If you vouch for the man then I know that I can trust him."

"I shall write the letter now while the servants prepare our supplies."

I was supplied with ink and paper. Sergeant Sharp arrived as I was finishing. "The cloaks are oiled again, sir. Mind you, if this rain keeps up then we will have to re-oil them again."

"It can't be helped Sharp."

It was early afternoon by the time we left Oporto and headed towards Amarante and then Vila Real. It was only forty miles and, in theory, should have been through friendly territory, but I knew that it would take us at least two days to negotiate the road. The rain continued to pour. Sharp led us the first ten miles for he knew it better than I. We caught up with the baggage train of Sir John Murray's column of horsemen but the 23rd had already moved north and we could not recover our other horses.

We reached Amarante after dark. There were British soldiers there. They were stragglers from regiments which had been pursuing Soult. They camped. I used my own coin to get us a couple of rooms in an inn. We left before dawn. The rain had continued all night but, as we rode, it stopped. Our cloaks had dried during the night and we had a much more pleasant journey without the persistent rain. The weather might have been more pleasant but the sights we saw were not. The retreating French Army had been harassed by guerrillas. They had reacted in their normal way. We saw bodies which had been hanged. The pursuing British had cut them down. We saw some being buried by British soldiers as we passed. We also spied the bloating bodies of abandoned French soldiers. They would, probably, remain unburied.

At Vila Real, we found General Beresford's column. He had more Portuguese troops than General Wellesley. I saw that they were being used to guard the baggage train which was lumbering up the road to meet up with General Wellesley. The town was crowded but, as they had defeated General Loison, they were in high spirits. The hold-ups on the road and the muddy conditions meant that we got no further than Vila Real on that second day. Once we passed through Vila Real, we headed south and east towards the border and the fortress of Cuidad Roderigo. This was a land which was without a military presence. The war had moved north. We saw the detritus of war: broken wagons and discarded uniforms. We saw the remains of dead horses but it was as if the land had been washed by war and was now at peace. The farmers farmed and people went about their business as the days lengthened and the rain, which had plagued us, gave way to sunny skies. I knew that it would be unbearably hot in a very short time. That was Spain. As soon as we were discovered to be English, we were welcomed. They had little to share and so we paid for our food and shelter.

Once we reached the border and the fortress which was Cuidad Roderigo then all changed. Here there was neither friendly nor neutral ground. The Spanish Army and the Spanish guerrillas were fighting a war against the French. Some parts were held by the Spanish and others by the French. I decided to avoid all fortresses, as a matter of course. I was not looking for strongholds. I was looking for the French army.

It was close to Plasencia that we found the first evidence of the French army. We had travelled for days without seeing a sign of war. It was almost our undoing. We had been on the road for more than ten days. We would not return to the General by the stipulated time! The two horses loaned to us by António were excellent horses and we alternated riding them and our other two horses. I still preferred Donna. We were using the road down the narrow valley which led to Plasencia when Donna neighed and her ears pricked. I had come to trust Donna. I knew not why she had stopped but I suspected danger. My hand went to the Baker as I reined her in. Sharp's hand went to his gun too. We had no need for words. Fighting together for so long had given us an unspoken understanding.

I looked ahead. The land to the side was both rough and untamed. This was the land of sheep and goats. Isolated farms dotted the valley sides. There were scrubby trees and bushes which littered both the side of the road and the hillside. There were small watercourses which trickled down the slopes. I spied one ahead and I followed, with my eye, its line down the slope. I saw that the road crossed it. There were trees nearby and through them I spied horses and green uniforms. There were French horsemen there. They were two hundred paces from us. If we had seen them then it stood to reason that they had seen us.

I said, "French horsemen ahead, Sharp."

"I thought I saw something, sir. Not too many places to hide around here are there?"

I glanced up the slope. There was a track of sorts. It led to a col. I knew there was a valley on the other side of it but I did not know if there was a road. The alternative was to go back. The French were below us. If they came towards us, we might have to try to escape. The decision was taken out of our hands. The six horsemen burst from cover and galloped up the road.

"Use the Bakers. Let us discourage them and thin them out, eh? Then we head up that trail to the col."

"Right sir. I'll take the one on the right."

As I aimed the rifle, I saw that they were Dragoons. One reason I liked Donna was that she was stable. She would stand stock still until I commanded otherwise. I saw that it was a Brigadier who led the detachment. We called them corporals. I waited until they were one hundred and fifty paces from us and I fired. I fired to the right, as I had been taught in the Chasseurs so as to minimise the chance of a backfire hurting my horse. Sharp fired a heartbeat later. I hit the Brigadier but he did not fall. Sharp unhorsed his man. The horsemen stopped and drew their muskets. Leaving my Baker on the pommel I turned and spurred Donna. The spare horses were tied to our saddles. Getting moving was always the hard part. The delay in the pursuit helped us and we were thirty yards up the trail before the Dragoons began to gain ground on us.

Two of the five who remained tried to ride up the slope. I heard the wounded Brigadier shout an order. It was too late for one man whose horse stumbled and threw him. It meant the wounded Brigadier led just three men. They had to ride to the spot from which we had fired and then follow us. As we rode, I was looking for the next place we could stop and fire. Half a mile up the trail I saw some rocks. The trail looked to turn around them. I could see that it continued up the slope.

"When we get to those rocks, we stop again! We fire one more time and hope that we can discourage them."

"Right, sir."

Glancing behind me I saw that they were now gaining on us. They did not have pack horses to worry about. The man who had fallen had remounted and was trailing behind. There were just four men we would have to deal with. We would try one shot each and then I would use my pistols and sword. We still had a lead of one hundred and thirty paces when we rounded the rocks. I quickly loaded the Baker. I just rammed the ball down. I spurred Donna to take her back to the trail. The four Dragoons were less than eighty paces from us. I lifted the Baker and aimed at the trooper who was ahead of the Brigadier. I saw the blood on the right shoulder of the French NCO. I could ignore him. The ball I fired was at relatively close range and hit the Frenchman in the chest. It threw him from the saddle. Sharp's ball hit another in the side. He retained his saddle. I let the Baker's sling slip to the pommel and drew my pistols. The Brigadier and the other trooper were now just forty paces away. I pulled the triggers of both pistols and they hit the last unwounded man. He fell from his saddle.

I shouted, "Brigadier, I can kill you in an instant! You have lost!"

He glared at me and then shouted, "Fall back!" The horses had obeyed the order before it was given. I watched the wounded men ride back to the one who had fallen. He had stopped and was aiming his musket at us. He fired but the ball fell woefully short. Sharp had reloaded. I watched them reach their wounded comrade at the road. They stopped and tended to their wounds. I knew that the Brigadier was watching us to discover what we were doing. They were a good half a mile away. There was a temptation to fire the Baker one more time but it would have been a waste.

I handed my Baker to Sharp to reload and, dropping Donna's reins, walked back to the two dead men. They were the 5th Dragoons. They had no papers on them. I had hoped for some intelligence.

"They are leaving, sir. It looks like they are heading to Plasencia."

I remounted Donna. "Then that rules Plasencia out for us." I looked across the valley. The range of hills was higher on that side of the valley but I knew that there was another main road there. I saw a trail leading up across it. "When they are out of sight, we head south-east towards Novaconjeo."

"What is there, sir?"

"Hopefully Spanish, but I don't know. The trouble with this land is that it is easy to block the roads. General Wellesley will have a hard job until we reach the plains."

They left and we headed, with the sun setting behind us, towards another road. If that was patrolled too then we might fail to do what Sir Arthur wanted.

We crossed the road and headed up the trail. This was a steeper slope and so we swapped horses. Donna had done her part. Travelling east by south meant we kept the sun behind us, warming our backs as we headed up towards the col and the pass to the next valley. I knew that we were pushing our luck but I wanted to be in the next valley before the Dragoons returned. They would return. We had used Baker rifles and that marked us as British. We dropped down the next valley and into darkness. The sun had not yet set but the mountain put us in shadow. There was enough light to see the trail and we followed it as it zig-zagged down the slope. We needed to stop before it became too dark but I wanted a decent campsite. The last thing I wanted was to perch precariously on a trail. We also needed grazing for our horses. We had some grain but I was conserving the little we had until we had to use it.

We had to dismount and walk. It was too dark now to see. When the ground flattened out and we were close enough to a tiny mountain stream, we stopped. Sergeant Sharp shook his head, "Not the most luxurious of digs, sir. But I guess that it will do nicely in the circumstances."

"The Dragoons will be after our blood, Alan. I am hoping that our diversion will put them off our trail. They might think we headed west, back to our lines. We will see."

"No fire then, sir?"

"No fire, Alan. Cold comfort tonight."

We saw to the horses first. We watered them and then tethered them close to grass. Before we left the next day, I would give each of them a handful of grain. Finally, we saw to ourselves. The ham which we had been given was delicious, but, after more than ten days on ham and stale bread, I yearned for something else. We had also finished the wineskin and were now reduced to water. The stream we had found was bubbling and so I risked filling our canteens from it. That done we used our cloaks as a groundsheet and wrapped ourselves in our blankets.

"We could always go back now, sir. We did find the French."

"True, but this could just be the garrison from Plasencia. We need to find their army, although you are right in one respect. It looks like we have driven the French from Portugal and that is not bad after just two small skirmishes. We have lost few men and Soult is finished. A good start."

"A long way to go, sir."

"As you so rightly say, Sharp, a long way to go."

It had been some time since I had been forced to camp in the open. Even when there had been no inn, we had found a barn in which to sleep. Straw was more comfortable than the hard ground. Perhaps the discomfort made my sleep lighter than it was normally. Or it may have been the whinny which Donna gave. Either way, I was awake when I heard the foot slip on the gravel. The pistol which lay next to me was in my hand in an instant. I gambled that these were not French. If they had been then they would have already fired their weapons. I spoke in Spanish.

"A little late to come calling, gentlemen!" The sabre was at my throat before I knew it. A Spaniard towered over me. My pistol was pressed into his groin. "If you stab me then my dying hand will pull the trigger. Not a pleasant way to die, my friend."

He laughed, "You are English." The sabre was removed, "You may remove your pistol, milord. We are friends of the English."

I stood and saw that there were six men. I said, "Guerrillas?"

He gave a mock bow, "I am Juan of La Calzada de Béjar. I keep these mountains free from the French."

I nodded, "But not the next valley."

He put a huge paw around my shoulders, "It was you doing the shooting! Miguel told me that he had seen two French Dragoons who had been shot! You are doubly welcome. Come, this is no place for such a hero. We will go to my village, La Calzada de Béjar. You shall sleep with a roof over your head." His voice became serious, "And we can discover what two English lords are doing here!"

Chapter 13

The village was a lot closer than I had expected it to be. I wondered why I had not smelled their wood smoke. There were only twenty houses. We later discovered that four of them just had a single person living in them. The French had taken hostages and shot them as reprisals for attacks. These were a tough people. They had simple homes and most had just one room in which they ate, cooked and slept. The one we entered was bigger and had two rooms. A table and chair were in the centre and I saw straw-filled mattresses around the side. When we had walked in to the village I had seen the communal oven. Our horses were unsaddled and tethered. I saw the men looking enviously at the beasts. They would be safe but the French would be fair game.

Juan was the head man. He had the largest house. We were taken there. He had a wife and six children. They stared as we entered. "Welcome to my home. While you are in La Calzada de Béjar you will be my guests. Maria, wine and cheese."

I knew that they would be offended if I offered them our ham and wine. I would leave them as gifts when we parted. "You are a gracious host."

His wife brought the wine and the home-made cheese. Both were rough and robust but they were also very tasty. Sharp smiled at Maria. His Spanish was a little like the cheese, rough but when he spoke it came from the heart and made Juan's wife beam, "Good cheese!" To emphasise it he rubbed his belly and said, 'Yum, yum!' The children giggled.

Juan's face showed me that he appreciated Alan's words, "So what are you doing here, milord?"

I knew there was little point in telling him that I was no lord. The Spanish seemed to think that every English officer was a lord. "We are seeking the French."

"It seems to me that you found them today."

"Not patrols, Juan, but their main army. My General wishes to defeat them."

"Good, but can he do it?"

"Sir Arthur was the General who defeated the French at Rolica and Vimeiro. Last month he defeated them at the Vouga River and drove them from Portugal after the battle of Oporto!"

Miguel, who had also come in the house with us, was obviously Juan's second in command. He nodded, "That explains those ambulances and wounded men we saw heading to Talavera!"

Juan nodded, "And that is where you will find your Frenchmen. There are two squadrons of Dragoons at Plasencia. The main army is at Talavera. It is between here and Madrid. The General there is called Jourdan."

I said, "Not Victor?"

"It was the one they called Victor but he has returned to the puppet they put on our throne."

"And General Cuesta, where is he?"

Juan spat into the fire, "There was a time when we had generals who had balls. The ones we have now are eunuchs. The French do not fear them. They fear us, the guerrillas but not the army. Cuesta is south of here. If he hears that your general has had a victory then he may come north just to claim credit."

I nodded and emptied my beaker. Maria took that as a sign I wanted more. She refilled my beaker. "Thank you for that information, Juan."

"So now you will return to your army?"

"I am afraid not. I will need to get close to Talavera. My general will need to know the make up of the army and the dispositions of the enemy. He will want to bring him to battle."

He frowned, "And how many men does your general have?"

"Between eighteen and twenty thousand men."

"Then he will be outnumbered. The French have three armies within twenty miles. They can field almost fifty thousand men! Even with General Cuesta's dubious thirty thousand men, you would be defeated." He shook his head, "Such a pity."

"When we attacked at Oporto, we launched the attack with less than two thousand men. The French had ten thousand and were dug in." I smiled, "We won and lost less than one hundred and forty men."

"Then your general is a magician. Perhaps Miguel and I will come with you tomorrow. We will show you the back ways to Talavera."

"You do not need to."

"But we want to. It is but sixty miles over the Sierra de Gredos."

As soon as he said that I knew we would have to let them ride our spare horses. As it turned out both could ride. We left our spare equipment and supplies in the village. When we headed south and east, I saw the mountain range we would have to cross. I knew then that we would have taken the road but for the chance encounter with Juan. He told us, as we rode, that it had been our skirmish with the Dragoons which had made them curious. They had not seen us but they had seen the dead Dragoons. It was the noise of our horses which had drawn their attention to us. They had thought we were survivors from the French attack and had thought to slit our throats!

The two Spaniards found the journey far easier than Sharp and I. We were not on roads; they were barely trails. Had Sharp and I been on our own then we would have been lost. I do not think that Sir Arthur would have discovered anything for we rode through a tangle of brush and almost invisible trails. When we stopped we camped on the eastern side of the mountain. Even though it was May it was cold and I was glad that I had my cloak. Juan was confident enough to light a fire. He laughed when I questioned him about lighting one, "Milord, the French will see the fire and assume it is a trap for us to collect more of their crown jewels. They will lock their doors and pray to God that the guerrillas do not come in the night."

When we awoke, I saw the town of Talavera in the distance. The town was protected on one side by the Tagus. The centre was higher than the plain before it. I could not see a town wall nor any fortifications. All looked good. Using my telescope, I also spied the French camp. It was huge with horse lines and an artillery park but did not look as though there were fifty thousand men there.

As we headed towards the town I said, "Juan, there are not fifty thousand men there."

"No, milord. There are other camps closer to Madrid and the garrison of Madrid as well. I can tell you that there are four armies within thirty miles of here."

I nodded, "We will not need to get too close to the French. If there is a piece of high ground I can count from there."

He looked relieved, "Good, then we just need to advance another ten miles or so and we can see their whole camp."

When we found the spot he had described, we dismounted and I took out my telescope. Sharp took down my words as I dictated the numbers of men, pieces of ordnance and horses we saw. There were two Corps as well as more cavalry than I had ever seen in my life. I estimated it at more than eight thousand horsemen. That was more than Napoleon had had in Egypt.

Perhaps we were complacent or more likely careless but the Chasseurs who galloped towards us were less than a mile away when we saw them. They must have seen us and approached using the dead ground between us. It was Miguel who spotted them, "Milord! The French!"

The three of us heeded Miguel's words. I jammed my telescope into its sheath and mounted Donna. I made certain that the other three were mounted and I spurred my horse. There are men who can ride and there are riders. Miguel and Juan could ride. The Chasseurs were riders as were Sharp and I. Inexorably the French Chasseurs closed with us. Our advantage was that we were heading uphill and we knew where we were going. The French would have the nagging doubt that we were leading them into an ambush. It was a depleted troop which followed us. I was able to glance around and I estimated that there were no more than twenty of them. They must have travelled four or five miles to reach us. I hoped our horses were in better condition than theirs. I was not certain.

Juan and Miguel were going much more slowly than we were. Sharp and I had to rein in to allow them to keep up with us. We had our Bakers loaded and, after two miles of the chase, I slowed, "Juan, Miguel, keep on riding. We will try to slow them."

"No, milord. There is no honour in that."

"We are better riders and we have the superior horses. We will catch you. I beg you to heed my words."

He nodded.

"Sharp, we turn and face them. Two shots from our Bakers should make them wary and slow them. The rest will help our horses and we can still catch Juan."

"Aye, sir."

We wheeled. The Chasseurs were four hundred paces from us. They did not see two cavalrymen. They saw two of Wellesley's messengers and they spurred their horses assuming that our horses were spent and that we had been abandoned by our guides. The two leading riders were the officer and the senior sergeant. They would be our targets. We dismounted and used our horses to steady our rifles. They were two hundred paces away. I said, "At one hundred and fifty paces we fire!"

"Yes, sir!"

I aimed at the officer's horse. If, as I expected, the ball rose then I would hit the officer. If not, then the horse would fall. The result would be the same. I fired at the same time as Alan. My gun fired true. I hit the horse in the skull and it died immediately. It tumbled over and threw the officer. Sharp hit the sergeant who fell and was dragged along the rough ground by his stirrup. We mounted and galloped. I did not turn around. When I heard carbines popping behind us then I knew they had stopped their pursuit. They could not ride and fire. I glanced around. They were four hundred paces from us and gathered around their sergeant and officer.

Juan and Miguel had stopped a mile ahead of us. We reined in. Juan nodded. "They are remarkable weapons. If you had an army with them then you would be unstoppable."

"They are slow to reload but they are accurate."

Two days' later we reached his home. I saw the relief on the faces of his wife and his children. He turned to me, "You are a brave man, milord. If you need me then just ask for me."

"And you, my friend, have helped in the fight against Napoleon."

We gave them half of the ham and half of the wine before we left. Juan sampled the wine and his eyes widened. "This is truly a great wine."

"Then the next time I come to see you I will bring you two jugs! And another of the hams."

"And you, my friend, are just that, a friend. If you know our people then I can give you no greater compliment,"

I was touched. Sergeant Sharp and I reached Abrantes on the last day of May. The guerrillas had proved to be more than helpful. They knew the times of the road patrols and our journey back was less hazardous. Summer was here and it was hot so we took longer to ride back than I would have hoped. We had no idea of the state of the campaign and all that we knew was that the Army would either be at Coimbra or Abrantes. The army encamped before Abrantes told us it was the latter.

As we rode through the camp, we saw that the victory had brought out the worst in some of Sir Arthur's men. We witnessed two floggings as we passed through the camps. As I well knew the British soldier was the best that there was when it came to facing the enemy and exchanging volleys of musket fire but put him in a camp close to a town and drink would change him. Sir Arthur would be keen to get my intelligence, if only so that he could move towards the French and battle.

I passed Lieutenant Hay and his Rifles. The riflemen were more disciplined than some of the other regiments. They could be relied upon to behave themselves. As we passed their camp, he and his Chosen Man stood.

"Major!"

"Lieutenant."

He nodded towards our Baker rifles, "I see that you are a good judge of weapons, sir,"

"They are very useful." I laughed, "Sergeant Sharp and I have often taken French horsemen unawares when they think we have a carbine. You and your men did well in Oporto."

"Aye sir but it was a sorry affair when we tramped north after the French. It was as bad as Corunna. The main difference was that we were doing the chasing."

His Chosen Man said, "Aye sir, but this time it was the French who abandoned their guns and equipment." He laughed, "We recaptured some of the guns we lost on the road to Corunna. Funny old world, eh sir?"

"It is indeed."

The Lieutenant stroked Donna's head, "And will we be moving soon, sir?"

"I know not for I am just the bearer of news. It is the General who makes the decisions. However, if I was a betting man then I would say we will be moving sooner rather than later and we will be marching into the sun." I smiled, "Of course I could be wrong."

"I doubt that very much, Major."

As we continued to the centre of the town, I saw that General Beresford and his army had joined ours. There looked to be twenty thousand men or more. What was missing was the Portuguese contingent. There were a few Caçadores in their distinctive brown uniforms but not as many as we had seen marching north with General Beresford.

Sir Arthur had made himself comfortable in a large house in the centre of the town. I dismounted and took the papers and notebooks I had compiled, "See if you can find a stable for the horses and a room for us."

Sergeant Sharp nodded, "It looks like we are the last to reach the party, sir, but I will see what I can do."

The Sergeant at the door did not recognise me but he knew my rank. I was admitted. I recognised many of the officers who milled around for they had been on the march to Oporto. There were others who were unknown to me. They were men who had followed General Beresford. I recognised one of Sir Arthur's aides, Lieutenant Newark who was a Guard's officer. I saw that he had seen me by his nod and then he disappeared. I knew better than to follow. Sir Arthur would be apprised of my presence and he would send for me when he was ready and not before.

"Major Matthews, you survived!"

I turned and saw Colonel Hawker. "And you too, sir. How are Captain Minchin and his troop getting along?"

"They are doing well. His time with you was well spent. He should have been promoted years ago but…"

The purchase of commissions was the reason but we could not mention that. Most of the men in the room owed their position to the system. They had sons who would benefit from it. I was just amazed that the British Army did so well in spite of it.

"So, Matthews, your dirty overalls tell me that you have been over the hills and far away. Action?"

"Not for me to say, sir, but I have found the French and that was what the General asked me to do. Any action will depend upon him."

"Aye well, if the French we meet are anything like Marshal Soult's men they will be good at running! Damned me but they can shift. We chased them right up towards Galicia. You would not believe the equipment they left behind them."

"Yes, sir. but the French are well supplied. Their guns and horses do not need to come by sea. They are supplied from France."

"You are a clever fellow, Matthews. I am surprised you are not a colonel."

I laughed, "Thank you, sir, but I am amazed that I am a Major."

Lieutenant Newark approached, "Major Matthews, the General will see you now. If you would follow me."

Colonel Hawker said, "When you are done come and join us at our camp. We didn't fancy the walk into town to get a drink and the prices are obscene. Bring your Sergeant. The Non-Commissioned Officers have their own mess too!"

"I might well take you up on that, sir."

The Lieutenant led me to a small staircase towards the rear of the grand house. From the condition of the handrail, this was used by servants. It was too narrow to have been used by the nobleman whose house this had been. The Guards officer knocked on a door at the top of the stairs and then opened it. It was a small bedroom. There was a table which was covered in papers and there was Sir Arthur and Colonel Selkirk.

Sir Arthur waved a hand, "Wait outside, Newark, see that we are not disturbed."

"Sir."

When he had gone Sir Arthur frowned, "You took longer than I said, Matthews!"

"The French were further away than I thought."

"Well, out with it! Do I have to ask twenty questions to get that which I need to know?"

I saw Colonel Selkirk smile.

"No, sir. Sorry, sir. The French army is at Talavera de la Reina sir. They have about twenty thousand men but there are three Corps close to Madrid and within marching distance of Talavera."

The General looked at Colonel Selkirk, "By God we have them!"

Colonel Selkirk took out a cigar and lit it from the lamp which burned in the dimly lit room, "Any idea who commands, Robbie?"

"Not for certain sir. It could be Marshal Jourdan or Marshal Victor, sir. A squadron of French Dragoons chased us off."

Neither officer was in the slightest bit concerned about the peril we might have been in. Sharp and I were a tool to be used. Our loss would merely be an inconvenience. "Any troops between here and there?"

"Cavalry patrols, General. They appear to have garrisoned the small towns with squadrons of Dragoons. The guerrillas harass them. It is a brutal war that they fight."

Once again, my comments were irrelevant and duly ignored.

"And did you see any sign of the Spanish Army or General Cuesta?"

"No, sir."

"You were right Selkirk. General Cuesta awaits us. The man has almost forty thousand men! He could take on the French at Talavera and then the back door to Madrid would be wide open."

The Colonel was never afraid of arguing with the General. I think Sir Arthur appreciated his honesty. "Don't forget that General Sebastiani is at Toledo with twenty-two thousand men and King Joseph has a further twelve thousand in Madrid."

"Then you have to get to Cuesta. I need the Spanish to move north. If we defeat the men at Talavera then we will outnumber the other two corps."

"Aye sir, but don't forget that General Wilson has reported Ney is heading from Galicia."

It was almost as though the General had not heard the Colonel but I knew he had. "Matthews, how did you reach Talavera?"

"I took the mountain roads, sir, and went around Plasencia."

"They can be used by artillery?"

"It might be difficult, sir, but it is the quickest route."

Again, he became silent and engrossed in the map. He suddenly jabbed his finger, "Here, Selkirk, we will meet with General Cuesta at Almarez on the Tagus."

The Colonel took a drag on his cigar. His words were carefully chosen, "And if the Spanish General will not come north, sir?"

Sir Arthur looked him in the eye, "Then we do not move from Portugal. If we are to recover Spain then the Spanish must show willing. God's blood, man, the Portuguese are here and they are willing to help the Spanish! The least they can do is to help themselves."

"I am sorry, sir, but you do not understand Spanish politics. They have no King and they fight amongst themselves. Each area is ruled by a junta. General Cuesta has the largest Spanish army but if he were to lose then another would be in power. The Spanish are worried about losing men. General Cuesta was wounded at the Medellin. He has been defeated once by the French and he will be wary."

"Then, Colonel Selkirk, you will need to be as persuasive as you can, eh?"

He nodded, "Yes sir."

"You two are dismissed. Selkirk, get to Cuesta and speak with him. Arrange a meeting. Matthews, you have done well. Take a couple of days to recover but I want you here each day. I may have need of you again."

As we went down the stairs the Colonel spoke with me, "The General understands his soldiers but not the politics of Spain!" The Colonel was right. My time with Juan had taught me that.

We stepped into the street. The Colonel leaned in and said, "The Black Widow is here in Iberia!"

"Spain? How do you know? Have you seen her?"

He shook his head, "I have seen her handiwork. A senior official in the Ministry of War for Portugal was seen with a beautiful, sultry woman. It sounded like the Black Widow. The official was found dead and the lady in question disappeared. She could be in Portugal, she could be in Spain but my money would be on Portugal. I arrived too late to help the poor fellow. Only you and I know the Widow. Everyone thinks it was a French assassin which of course it was but they are looking for a man and the dalliance with the Widow is ignored. I tell you because you would know her. If you see her then kill her. Shoot on sight!"

"This is a woman we are talking about!"

"And a deadly one at that." He shrugged, "You of all people should know that. I have warned you and now Angus and I had better head off and find this Spanish General. Take care, Robbie. You are a good fellow but you have an honourable streak which will be your downfall!"

He left me. I knew that Sergeant Sharp would come to find me and I needed a drink. Nearby there was a pleasant looking tavern with tables outside. The General had posted two men there to discourage the rank and file from drinking. I saw that officers were allowed to enjoy its fare and I sat. I ordered some wine and some bread. I had thought the Black Widow was just an unpleasant episode in my past but now she had reappeared. I knew that Colonel Selkirk was right and I had killed women before but could I kill this one?

Sergeant Sharp did not appear for an hour or so. I waved him over. The two sentries moved towards him. "He is with me, allow him through."

"But the General said…"

"And I am Major Matthews. I am one of the General's aides and I am ordering you to allow him through."

"Yes, sir!"

Sharp sat and I waved over the waiter. After I had ordered Alan said, "I can understand the General's order, sir. There was a bit of bother when the army arrived. Two soldiers from the 53rd were involved in a fracas. One was killed and the other badly wounded. Some shops were looted. There are provosts all around the town."

I nodded. The waiter brought another beaker and some more ham. When he had gone, I said, "And it is likely that we will be here some time. I can't see us leaving for a couple of weeks."

"That will give the horses a chance to recover. I have found where the 23rd are billeted, sir. We can get the other horses if you like." He sipped his wine. "That is, sir, if you think we will be needing them again."

"I think, Sergeant, that we will. We know the road to Talavera. I suspect the General will use us as his eyes."

The Sergeant had managed to get us a room above a shoe maker's shop. The man seemed happy to have an officer sleeping above his premises. After the attacks by the British Army, I could understand it. He had a yard and the horses were there. That was not a satisfactory arrangement and we led the four animals to the camp of the 23rd. Troop Sergeant Fenwick was on duty with the sentries and he seemed happy to be reunited with us.

"Good afternoon, sir. Come to pick up your horses?"

"The opposite, Sergeant. We have four more to join the others."

"No problem, sir, although this grazing won't last above another week."

"We passed a field just two miles east of the town. I will mention it to the Colonel."

"Thank you, sir."

"Give the Sergeant a hand, Sharp, and I will go and see the officers."

The officers had a mess tent but some, the younger ones, had spilt outside. Seeing a Major they snapped to attention.

"At ease!" I entered a smoke-filled tent. Cigars were much easier to obtain in Portugal and Spain compared with London. The officers had all taken advantage of the surplus.

Captain Minchin spied me and strode over. His pleasure at being reunited was obvious, "Major Matthews! This is a pleasant surprise. What can I get you to drink?"

Colonel Hawker's voice boomed, "The Major is our guest! Put his drinks on my mess bill, Sergeant!"

The orderly Sergeant nodded, "Yes sir." He turned to me, "And you sir, what will you have?"

"A glass of wine will suffice."

Captain Minchin said, "I am glad to see you, sir. I did not properly thank you."

"What for?"

"Why, my promotion of course sir. I would still be a Lieutenant but for you."

"You deserved the promotion. Colonel Hawker knew that." I looked around and saw that the usual cliques had formed. Captain Minchin and the young Lieutenant next to him appeared to be a little isolated. "And who is this young officer?"

The Lieutenant looked to be about eighteen years old. He was obviously nervous, "Lieutenant Frayn, sir. I have only been with the regiment for a couple of weeks."

Captain Minchin said, "Herbert here is my replacement. I suppose that means I have more chance of keeping my Captaincy."

"I think that is assured. There will be some hard fighting ahead. We were lucky at Vouga and Oporto. When we come up against a full Corps it will not be so easy." My drink arrived. "So, Lieutenant, where are you from?"

"Yorkshire, sir. My family has land near Malton. My father breeds horses. It was inevitable that I should join the cavalry. My father is a friend of Lieutenant Colonel Elley. We sold the Lieutenant Colonel his white hunter." The white horse and its flamboyant rider were a source of conversation amongst all of the cavalry regiments. "I am lucky that this is a regiment on active service. The alternative was a barracks in England or the West Indies."

"The graveyard of the English."

I nodded, "Quite so, Captain."

You say you arrived from England. When did you land in Lisbon?"

"That would have been the second of May. It took some time to find out where the regiment was. I was lucky. There was a lady on the ship and she took pity upon me. She rented a house and bought me a horse."

Captain Minchin laughed, "Now, had that been me, with my ugly features, then I would still be in Lisbon. This handsome young blood just flashes his smile, eh sir?"

The Lieutenant blushed and I laughed, "I think I would be like you, Captain. My scarred face would merely make them take pity upon me."

"Oh no, sir, it was nothing like that. She needed an escort. The lady was not young, sir!" I smiled. "But she was stunning, sir. Raven haired with eyes which stirred a man. I was disappointed when my orders came and ordered me to Coimbra."

Captain Minchin waved over an orderly who refilled his glass, "And was the lady disappointed?"

"Oh yes, sir. She became quite cross. She was recently widowed you see, sir, still I believe I served a purpose. She was invited to many balls and parties. After Oporto, the city seemed to celebrate."

Perhaps I had had too much drink but it had taken some moments for the Lieutenant's words to sink in. "This widow, did she have a skin which was tanned, as though she had lived in a hot climate?"

He looked amazed, "Yes sir, how did you know? Her husband had been a plantation owner in the West Indies, one of those islands where they speak French and English. She had sold the plantation when her husband died."

It was the Black Widow. Had Colonel Selkirk not told me I might not have made the connection but it was obvious. She had spun a similar story to the one she had used in London. "What was the lady's name?"

"Mrs Castle, sir. Why, do you know her?"

"I believe I do, Lieutenant, and you have been extremely lucky. The woman is a killer."

The young officer laughed, "You jest, sir! She is a lady!"

"Her servants were Indian?"

"Yes, sir."

"Then it is the same woman and I will not go into details but trust me, if you see her again then do not speak to her but seek me out!"

I saw the doubt on his face. Captain Minchin said, "Listen to the Major, Herbert! I believe him and so should you!" The Lieutenant nodded. Turning to me, Captain Minchin asked, "What is she doing in Portugal, sir?"

"What she does best, killing men!"

Sharp and I left after dark. We had been feted by the 23rd who felt that they owed us something. I just had a bad taste in my mouth. Had the Black Widow targeted the young Lieutenant too? She would, no doubt, have changed her name once more. She would take some finding and the ones who knew her were here at the sharp end of the campaign.

That evening I told Sharp what I had learned. Like me he was concerned but also offered reassurance, "London and Lisbon are places you would expect to find her, sir, but here? At the front?

She would stand out like a sore thumb. We will keep a watch for her. To do otherwise would be foolish but I can't see her coming here."

"You may be right, Sergeant. Did you get to talk to Parkinson and the others?"

Yes, sir."

There was hesitation in his voice. He was hiding something. "Sergeant! Spit it out!"

"It is Captain Minchin sir, some of the other officers resent his promotion. Most of them had to pay for their commissions. Colonel Hawker knows nothing about it, nor the Major. Captain Wilberforce is the one making trouble. He was Captain Roger's friend."

"Thank you, Sergeant." There was little I could do about it. It was not my regiment. Even if I told the Colonel his hands would be tied for Minchin was one officer. He needed harmony, especially going into battle. Captain Minchin was getting a lesson in life.

Chapter 14

More troops arrived each day. I met with the General once every couple of days. I reported to him but, until Colonel Selkirk returned then there was little for me to do. During one of our meetings, in a rare moment of unguarded comment, Sir Arthur confided in me that he was awaiting the arrival of General Crauford and his Light Division. Made up of the 43rd Foot, 52nd Foot and the 95th Rifles, they were, in my view, second only to the Guards as a fighting force. In many ways, they were superior, especially in the Peninsula. They had kept us safe when we had retreated to Corunna. I knew many of the men and officers from the 95th.

"I had hoped he would be here now, Matthews. The last I heard was that his transports had been delayed but he can only be days away!"

"Yes sir, but Lisbon is a long way from here."

"Quite. Even if Colonel Selkirk has not arrived, I want you and the 23rd to go to Plasencia and take it from the French Dragoons. It will be hard enough for the army to march over the mountains without the risk of an attack from Dragoons. Return in two days' time and bring Colonel Hawker with you." He smiled, "He likes you and that sort of thing cannot hurt."

The next morning, I went to the Colonel. I still did not know if I ought to tell him of the problem with Captain Minchin and his other officers. In the end, I did not. Sergeant Sharp told me that the sergeants and corporals of his troop were rallying round. They were as one with the officer. They trusted him and wanted him as their leader. They had seen the flaws in the character of Captain Rogers.

The Colonel looked at the map and then turned to me, "How far is it to this Plasencia then, Matthews?" Sir Arthur had no problem with maps and distances. Colonel Hawker obviously did.

"It is a hundred and fifty miles over rough roads and inhospitable terrain. Apart from Castel Branco, there is neither accommodation nor even a village worth mentioning along the route. We shall be camping. If it is any consolation then it will be

much harder travelling with the rest of the army. At least this way
we will have good grazing all the way!"

He nodded, "And what do we find when we reach this place?"

"French Dragoons; at least two squadrons of them."

"And all we have to do is to hold the town?"

"In essence, yes. We return to the General in two days' time.
He will have refined the plan by then but I would prepare your
men to move, Colonel. This will not be like the drive to the
Vouga River. Each step we take will be a step into the unknown.
The army may well be more than five days behind us."

He looked at me with a shrewd look on his face, "And you
know more than you are letting on."

I nodded, "But I cannot divulge what I know. The General
will tell you that which you need. I am sorry, Colonel Hawker, I
mean no disrespect."

"No Major, you have honour and I can respect that. I trust you
and I trust the General. All else is in my hands and the hands of
my officers."

The Colonel was nervous when we met the General. He was
putting his head above the parapet. He was risking an attack from
French Dragoons. They had a certain reputation. Personally, I felt
it was exaggerated but I was biased. I had been a Chasseur!

Colonel Selkirk was present. He stood in the background
smoking a cigar while the General spoke, "Gentlemen, I need you
to secure Plasencia. We will be travelling from there to Almarez,
where I shall meet the Spanish General who might help us to end
this oppression. The 23rd will act as our sentries. I want the
General and the other officers to be as safe as if we were in St.
James' Park. Do I make myself clear?"

"Yes, sir!"

"Then off you go and God speed. Major, any further
intelligence you can gather on the way would be most
appreciated. Those guerrillas you met, whilst not the sort of
people one would dine with, appear to be an asset I had not
identified hitherto. Use them."

"Sir!"

As we left the Colonel said, "It is obvious to me that you are a
far more important man than I am, Major. If you feel I am making
a mistake then I pray that you let me know."

"Do not worry, Colonel, you have a good regiment and they will deal with this easily."

We left the next morning. We moved more slowly than when Sharp and I had scouted. We had wagons with us and we had spare horses. I persuaded the Colonel to use different pairs of squadrons to scout. We had a pair in the morning and a different pair in the afternoon. If we used the elite squadrons there was a danger that the rest could become complacent. We did not need that. I rode with some of the other squadrons. I outranked all but the Colonel and Major Thirwell. I hated using my authority but bearing in mind what I had heard from Sharp, I felt I needed to get to know the officers of this regiment.

When I rode with Captain Wilberforce, I took the bull by the horns. It was necessary as, unlike the other officers, he tried to ignore me and would not speak with me, "Captain, how long have you been in this regiment?"

He gave me a cursory glance, "Not that it is any business of yours but five years."

I nodded and smiled, "Then the only action you have seen has been the battle of the Vouga River, the Oporto crossing and the pursuit of the French."

"Yes, sir. And I acquitted myself well in each action."

I shrugged. "That is for others to judge. There are officers in your regiment who have served since Egypt. There are officers and non commissioned officers who know what it is like to charge into battle and control the men who follow them."

"I charged at the Vouga River!"

I shook my head, "I led you then and I controlled your charge. Until you have led a charge then I would give more respect to those officers who have more experience. The only officer with less experience than you is Lieutenant Frayn and I would rather follow him into battle than you."

"You insult me, sir."

"I speak the truth and before you begin to get angry know that I have killed an officer in a duel. I am not a novice. I am here to offer sage advice. You take it or ignore it at your peril. I am not of your regiment. Your fate is of no consequence to me!" I made sure that I held his gaze until he lowered his eyes. I had won. I had done all that I could. All else was down to him.

We were half a day from Plasencia and I was riding with Captain Minchin when my sixth sense kicked in. There was danger ahead. The hills to our left were full of scrubby trees and rocks. The road ahead appeared empty but it was Donna who convinced me of the danger. Her ears pricked. I took my Baker and cocked it. Sergeant Sharp did the same but the rest of the troop were oblivious to the danger. I said, quietly, "Captain Minchin, Troop Sergeant Fenwick, there is danger ahead. Do not alarm the men but be ready to react when I command."

Both said, "Yes sir!"

They trusted me and that was half the battle won. I saw nothing ahead but I spied half a dozen places where we could be ambushed. I said to Sergeant Parkinson, "Sergeant, your horse appears to be labouring. Examine the foreleg, if you please."

He looked at me, "You what, sir?"

Troop Sergeant Fenwick growled, "Get off your horse and do as the Major says!"

"Yes, Sarge."

We were halted and it was easier to look ahead whilst we were not moving. I still did not know where the ambush lay but I saw that there was a watercourse and some scrubby bushes. Just at that moment, a half a dozen pigeons took flight from the bushes. There was a movement. I lifted my Baker and tracked them. I lowered the rifle and fired at the hint of a green tunic. I might have hit the Dragoon and then again, I might not but I spooked a rider and his horse. A dragoon burst from the shrubs a hundred and twenty paces from us. His horse had bolted. Sergeant Sharp did not miss. The wounded rider slumped over his saddle.

I shouted, "Charge!"

We had gained the initiative and we galloped after the Dragoons. There were twenty of them. I slipped the Baker onto the pommel and drew a pistol. I spurred Donna. She might not have been the biggest horse but she was a quick horse and she soon extended a lead on all of the horses except for Sharp's. The Dragoons were starting from standing and we soon began to gain. They were a mass of men before us and I risked wasting a ball. I was lucky and my pistol hit one in the back. As he fell, he knocked another rider to the side. When the rider tried to regain control of his horse Sharp shot him in the leg. There was confusion ahead and we gained on the Dragoons. It could not last. Inevitably they began to extend their lead. Their horses had been rested and ours had been riding all day but we had had the victory. I reined in when it was obvious that we would not catch them.

Lieutenant Frayn asked, "How did you know there would be an ambush, sir? I was studying the terrain and I saw nothing."

I patted my horse. "My horse warned me and once I knew there was danger then I looked for things which were unnatural. Dragoon green is not a natural colour. It jars when it is seen against leaves and grass."

The Colonel and his senior officers rode up. "We heard the firing, Major. Trouble?"

"An ambush." I pointed to the dragoon's musket in his hand. "They would have waited until we were level with them and given us a volley at less than twenty paces. They would have killed the officers and most of the sergeants." I pointed up the road. "I think the garrison will be evacuating about now. A depleted squadron of Dragoons is no match for a full regiment."

I was right. We entered the town where we could see the evidence of a rapid flight; there were discarded items littered around the headquarters and the flag had been cut down and not lowered. We were greeted as conquering heroes. Leaving the Colonel to secure our quarters, I led Captain Minchin's troop east. The horse dung on the road confirmed that the Dragoons had fled towards Talavera. By the time we returned to the town it was dark and the Colonel had secured the quarters recently vacated by the Dragoons. The Spanish had been harshly treated by the French and the tales they told hardened the hearts of the men of the 23rd.

The next day I took two captured Dragoon horses along with the swords and muskets of the Dragoons we had killed and rode with Sergeant Sharp into the hills. We headed for La Calzada de Béjar. I needed to speak with Juan. I knew we would be seen from far off and I rode bare-headed, despite the sun. Juan and Miguel rose like wraiths from rocks when we were half a mile from the village. "Had you been French, milord, then you would be dead!"

I had known they were there. I had learned, over the years, that a man smelled of how he lived and what he ate. It was a skill

152

which could save a life. I had detected with my nose. "Then I am pleased that we are friends. I bring you and Miguel these horses and weapons as a present."

Their eyes widened, "Truly, milord? This is a great gift. I swear that we will put them to good use. With horses like this, we can travel further and wreak our vengeance upon the hated French. Come, my wife would like to see you as would my children."

As we walked up to the village I said, "The General is coming with our whole army. There may be a battle here but that will depend upon your generals, Cuesta and Venegas." I dismounted.

Juan shook his head, "Then there will be no battle, milord, for those two hate each other!" Juan's wife fed us while Juan explained to me the politics of Spain. It seemed depressingly Byzantine! "There is hope, milord. Now that we have horses I can ride and meet with Chaleco."

"Chaleco?"

"Yes, milord. He is the leader of the guerrillas to the east of Talavera. He commands a thousand men. He may be able to help. You and your horsemen will stay in Plasencia?"

"Until the General arrives, yes."

"Then we will come to you there. I would like to see this general of yours. If he commands men such as you and your sergeant here then he must be a great man."

That evening I dined with the other officers in the mess. British cavalry regiments liked order and traditions. We were in the middle of Spain and living in semi-primitive conditions but that did not stop the Colonel from organising the regiment as though it was back in England. I told him of my meeting with the Spaniard.

Captain Wilberforce snorted, "A waste of a couple of good horses, if you ask me, Major. They will be eating them already!"

His cronies laughed. I shook my head, "Do not underestimate these brave men, Captain. If the French capture them then not only will they be killed but their families too. We are lucky, Bonaparte's boot has not yet set foot in England. I believe that he is busy adding Austria to his Empire. I have fought him and know that he is the equal of Sir Arthur. If he returns here with his Imperial Guard then we will need allies like the guerrillas."

"I do not doubt, Major, that you are a brave man and know your business but I know that this regiment will acquit itself with honour when we do fight a real battle."

Captain Wilberforce's cronies all banged the table in approval. Colonel Hawker shook his head. He spoke to me quietly so that no one else could hear, "I think there was a time when I might have endorsed the captain's views but the crossing of the Douro and the fatal charge of Captain Rogers has shown me that we still have some way to go. I believe that had Captain Wilberforce been leading the advance guard when we approached this town that he would have charged after the Dragoons."

"And he might have run headlong into the town and the rest of the squadron. Do not underestimate the French Dragoons, sir. They are good horsemen and while they might not have a reputation like the French heavy cavalry, they know how to fight. They are used as mounted infantry. Their officers are quite happy to dismount their men and let them use their carbines. They can even fight from the backs of horses. They are taught to fire from the right so that sparks from the carbine do not frighten the horse. Some even use muskets from the backs of horses."

Major Thirwell said, "You seem to know an awful lot about Dragoons, Major."

I nodded, "I make it a point to know as much as I can about the enemies I am likely to fight. I have been fighting for fourteen years. You learn to respect your enemies if you are to survive."

The Major looked surprised, "Yet you are what? Thirty years old?"

"Thirty-two."

"Remarkable! I was still riding to hounds when I was eighteen. I had not yet joined the army." He nodded to Captain Wilberforce, "Perhaps you should heed the Major's advice, Wilberforce."

The Captain said, "Yes, sir." But I knew he did not mean it. He would learn the hard way.

The General did not arrive until the end of the first week of July. By then the weather had become so hot that riding the daily patrols became a punishment. When he rode in, he had with him Colonel Selkirk and a Spanish officer. I was with the Colonel and Major Thirwell when he dismounted, "Well done, gentlemen. I take it that there has been no attempt by the French to push you from the town?"

"No, sir."

"Good! Good! Colonel, I want a troop of your men to accompany me tomorrow. I go to meet General Cuesta. Major Matthews, I will need you too!"

"Sir."

Colonel Hawker said, "In that case, sir, I will send Minchin's troop." He did not elaborate for the General but I knew he was using his common sense. Captain Minchin's troop might be the smallest in number but they had the most experience and had acquitted themselves well.

We had just twenty-six miles to ride to Almarez but the Spanish officer who led us was either a fool or deliberately misled us, for we did not arrive until late in the afternoon. The Spanish General had made his men stand to attention all afternoon waiting for Sir Arthur's arrival. It was not a good start.

General Cuesta was an old man. He had been injured at the battle of the Medellin and he travelled everywhere in a carriage now. He could not speak English and Sir Arthur could not speak Spanish. They could both speak French but the Spaniard refused to speak the language of the invader. We were lucky that there was a Spanish General who was of Irish origin. General Juan O'Donoju could speak both English and Spanish fluently. The three of them spoke while the rest of us watched. I could have translated but the General's English was infinitely better than my Spanish.

Colonel Selkirk sidled up to me, ostensibly to look at the Tagus below us but, in reality, to speak to me about the coming battle. "This does not bode well, Robbie. I had the devil's own job to persuade Cuesta to come at all. They were badly handled in the last battle. Between you and me I think he wants us to fight his battles for him."

"Sir, we cannot fight the French without their help."

"I know! Keep close to Sir Arthur, eh? He is our best weapon in our fight against the French."

"You won't be with us when we fight, sir?"

"No, Angus and I have…" he smiled, "other fish to fry." He was always enigmatic. We ate with the Spanish. There were tents for us. I noticed a distinct wariness on the part of the Spanish. Until just a year or so ago we had been enemies. It was hard for them to accept us as allies. I also heard mutterings and murmurings about the position of the Spanish General. His men would not accept orders from Sir Arthur and there was little likelihood of Sir Arthur serving under a Spanish General, especially as the general in question had been beaten so many times by the French already. I was not confident about the liaison.

There was no talk during the meal. That would be in the cold light of day. Once again, we waited while out betters spoke. The meeting went on for some time. There appeared to be some sort of agreement but the two generals did not look happy. When we parted from the Spanish I was, once more, in command of the escort. I made sure that Troop Sergeant Fenwick, Captain Minchin and Sergeant Sharp preceded the General and that Sergeant Parkinson and the Lieutenant were at the rear. I would take no chances with the General's life. I rode just behind the General and Colonel Selkirk. I was privy to their conversation.

"I fear that this collaboration will not end well, Colonel. The damned man wanted me to send half of my men north to face Mortier! In the end, I persuaded him to give me a thousand of his men. I will send Wilson with fifteen hundred of his men to watch the northern passes. We do not want to be flanked when we attack Talavera." He shook his head. "They do not want to fight. They want us to fight for them! It is their damned country!"

"It is not that, Sir Arthur. It is the fact that if General Cuesta loses then another of his rivals will become the most powerful General."

"Good God! Do they not realise that unless they join together then Boney will win?"

"Spain is a strange country, sir. What is our strategy then, sir?"

"We are going to ask General Venegas to bring his army to support General Cuesta. Our armies will meet at Oropesa and then march to Madrid."

The Colonel said, "I thought Major Matthews said that the French had a Corps at Talavera."

"They do but with Cuesta's men and those of Venegas, we will outnumber them. General Cuesta is of the opinion that our superior numbers will make Victor and Jourdan fall back to the capital."

"But you are not of that opinion, sir." Colonel Selkirk was astute.

"I am not. I have stuck my neck out. I am here with a tiny army and I am surrounded by many French Corps. Thanks to the nonsense of the Low Countries we do not have enough men to take on the French alone. We need the Portuguese and the Spanish. The Portuguese are reliable but the Spanish? I need Crauford and his men. I have half a mind to go back to Portugal and build defences."

"Sir, that would be a mistake."

"I know, Selkirk, but I think back six months to Sir John Moore's example. He did the right thing for Portugal and it ended badly for the British Army. Am I making the same mistake that he did? Am I doing the right thing for Spain and will it end in disaster?"

"Do not doubt yourself, Sir Arthur. You have bloodied the noses of every marshal and general the French have sent at you. I have no doubt that you will do the same here. If the Spanish prove less than reliable then it is a lesson learned!"

"But, Colonel Selkirk, it will be my red coats who pay the price. They may behave abominably when they are not fighting but there are no finer soldiers on this earth."

By the time we reached Plasencia, I had learned a great deal about Sir Arthur. Sir Arthur turned to me after he had dismounted. "The day after tomorrow, Matthews, you will be required to take a troop from the 23rd and scout out Oropesa." He nodded at Minchin's troop. "These fellows are not too bad. Take them! The French will, no doubt, have their own scouts out. Humbug them. You are good at that sort of thing!"

"Sir. Will you tell Colonel Hawker?"

"Of course. Leave at first light. Keep me informed of any developments."

Captain Minchin had been nearby and could not have failed to hear the order. I turned to him and he grinned, "My fellow officers may not think much of me but it is good to know that you and the General appear to have a higher opinion. I will get the men sorted, sir. I think they will be happy with the task!"

Sergeant Sharp had been at the rear. I told him what we would be doing. "Then I shall take two of our spares with us, sir. This land takes it out of animals."

"And buy whatever provisions you can. If we have two armies at Oropesa then there will be little to be had."

Chapter 15

The Colonel and Angus left us when we reached the camp. The General had orders to write. Sir Robert Wilson and his detachment were assigned to watch the north and the orders were given for the army to move further east. The behemoth that was our army would take three days to make its tortuous way over the poor Spanish mountain roads to the rendezvous. The next day I was with the General and his senior commanders offering advice about the terrain around Talavera when a sergeant of the Guards arrived, "Sir, there is a Spaniard outside. He says he has something for someone called milord. We have him held securely sir."

Sir Arthur said, "Sergeant. We are busy. Have the fellow given something to eat and send him on his way, I have no time to talk to Spaniards!"

"Sir, he has a French despatch bag and when we held him he asked for the Major." He looked at me. "I think he means you, sir."

Sir Arthur said, "Well, Matthews?"

"He could be one of the guerrillas, sir."

"Then bring him in, Sergeant. General Hill be so good as to cover the map eh?"

It was Juan. He ignored the General and held out the bag towards me, "I told you we would be of help. We captured a French General. He had this bag. I cannot read it but I believe you can, milord."

I opened the bag. I recognised Marshal Soult's signature, "General, these are despatches from Marshal Soult, Juan here says they were taken from a French General."

"A General?"

"Juan, where is the general now?"

"He is with Chaleco!"

"Are you sure he is a general?"

He shrugged, "he had a fancy uniform, like that one." He pointed to General Hill. "And he said his name was General Baptiste Franceschi."

The General did not understand all of Juan's words but he did the name. "Then, by God, I have them. Thank the fellow Matthews and give him some money. He deserves it!"

I shook my head, "He does not want money, Sir Arthur, he wants weapons to fight the French."

"Then see the Quartermaster and get him whatever he needs!" This was the most animated I had ever seen Sir Arthur.

He hurried inside to read the documents and left me with Juan. "Come, my friend, I will get weapons for you and your men."

"You are a good fellow, milord, when this battle comes, I shall watch out for you! None will rob your body!"

With that cheerful thought in my head, I took him to the Quartermaster. Juan selected four sabres and four carbines along with lead balls and powder. He was happy.

The next day the General told me that he now knew what Soult intended. He was gathering Corps to march south to meet us. Victor was to slow us down at the Albreche River. Sir Arthur knew how long it had taken us to reach this part of Spain. Soult and Ney were in Galicia and that gave us at least a month in which to strike towards Madrid. We would advance to Talavera. My scouting expedition, the next day, was even more vital now!

It would be our last dinner for some time and so the Colonel, after receiving the orders from Sir Arthur, insisted upon a more formal affair than we had previously enjoyed. It was somewhat spoiled by the attitude and snide comments from a section of the officers. It was a smaller group than hitherto. The fact that Sir Arthur had personally asked for the troop reflected well upon the regiment, but Captain Wilberforce and his clique seemed to resent not only Captain Minchin but also me. This insidiously divisive attitude was something unique to British regiments. In French regiments, there was no such snobbery. I chose to ignore it. However, Captain Wilberforce became so loudly obnoxious and his comments were aimed so directly at me that I could no longer restrain myself. I stood and, wiping my mouth, addressed the Colonel, "Colonel Hawker, you have a fine regiment, but I am afraid that I cannot suffer the loutish behaviour of Captain Wilberforce and some of the officers who seem to regard him as some sort of paragon. He is the very antithesis of a paragon. I bid you goodnight, sir."

Colonel Hawker stood, somewhat unsteadily, he had drunk a large amount of wine, "I apologise for Captain Wilberforce, Major Matthews."

That would have been the end of it had not Captain Wilberforce also stood and faced me, belligerently, "I do not apologise to an officer who is not even of this regiment. Should you seek satisfaction, sir, then I will happily oblige."

I went close to him. He was drunk to the point of staggering. The drink had loosened his tongue. "Three things, Captain: firstly, Sir Arthur has banned duelling. Secondly, I am an officer of superior rank and such a duel cannot take place." I lowered my voice, "and thirdly, perhaps most importantly, with any weapon I am your superior! If we did duel then you would be a dead man. The next time that you are sober and you see me I shall expect an apology."

He made the mistake of trying to take a swing at me. Such an offence would have resulted in dire consequences had he connected. I stepped back allowing the swing to miss me and he fell to the floor. He caught his chin on the back of a chair and was rendered unconscious.

"Colonel Hawker, I will leave you to deal with this officer unless," I glowered at the others, "any other officer wishes to risk my wrath?" They quailed, "I hope to God that you have more courage when you face the French, gentlemen, for they will make mincemeat of you!"

I was angry when I left the mess tent. I wasn't angry with the Captain, he was a buffoon. I was angry with myself for allowing him to get to me. I had defended Captain Minchin. I hated the unfairness of the system. It would not come to a duel. I had seen the fear in the Captain's eyes, even before he had collapsed. Sharp knew I was angry when I reached our billet. He smiled, "Sir, I managed to get some cocoa from one of the locals. That will make you feel better."

"How do you know I am not happy?"

"With respect, sir, you have a face like a slapped arse." His colourful language made me smile and began to diffuse my anger. "Whatever happened in the mess doesn't matter. The lads in Mr Minchin's troop know that. Just because a couple of officers haven't the sense they were born with there is no need to get upset. Tomorrow, sir, we will be east of here and all that we will need to worry about will be the French! And we know that we can deal with them!"

Sharp was down to earth and he had the ability to put everything in perspective. I sipped the cocoa. It had a kick!"

"Oh, I forgot to say, sir. The Sergeant Major gave me a couple of measures of rum. That is Navy cocoa! You will sleep well tonight!"

He was right and, as we headed east the next day, I felt like a new man. Politics and personal vendettas were forgotten. They were in the past!

As we headed east, I did not even bother to look at the tents of the 23rd. I had the best of the regiment with me. The troop had learned how to work as a unit. The best scouts rode ahead of us. They spaced themselves well and all of them had adopted my technique of riding with a cocked weapon across the saddle. The rest of the troop, although they chattered, were also scanning the sides of the road and the ground which might harbour ambushers. In theory, we were in friendly territory. With General Cuesta to the south of us and General Wilson to the north, we should have been the safest soldiers in the land, but it did not do to get into bad habits and make mistakes.

As we rode Captain Minchin spoke with me. "I feel I must apologise for Captain Wilberforce's words last night, sir. He was drunk."

"I know and that is why he is not on a charge at this moment. If an officer cannot handle his drink then he should manage his intake. What the Captain did was the same as those red coats who were flogged by their regiments. Should his rank protect him?"

"Probably not, sir."

"Put the Captain behind you. We have more important matters ahead of us. There will be a battle, Geoffrey, make no mistake about that. The General hopes that it is we who will have the superior numbers but I am not too certain about that. The Spanish are good soldiers. The guerrillas show us that but, hitherto, they have not managed to defeat the French. We are reliant on two Spanish generals doing what they have never done before, collaborating. Victor, Sebastiani, Mortier and Jourdan are all close to Madrid. If they combine then we would be outnumbered two to one."

"And you think, sir, that the 23rd will be called into action?"

"I do and Sir Arthur will use them however he can. What we do today is the best way to use light cavalry but I fear that the lack of cavalry in the army means he will use you to fight the enemy cavalry and for that the regiment is ill-equipped."

"Ill-equipped, sir? We have carbines and sabres."

"And your sabres are not the equal of the French," I lowered my voice. "Too many of your officers are like Captain Rogers, they think they are riding to hounds. They are reckless. If you are called upon to act as proper cavalry then be cautious. Keep your men together and watch the ground."

I had him confused, I could see that. "The ground, sir?"

"When you trained in England it was on open ground was it not?"

"Yes, sir. We had mock battles on Salisbury Plain."

"Look around you. Is this ground flat? Is it grassy? There are gullies and there are narrow streams and ditches. There are holes to trip horses. We ride bigger horses than the French and they are not as sure-footed." I patted Donna, "I am the exception. My horse is Portuguese. She is sure-footed."

We spoke for most of the day and I offered him advice garnered from all of my years as a cavalryman. I had less than a week to complete Captain Minchin's training. As Colonel Selkirk had intimated, I would be with the General when the battle began. Captain Minchin would be with the regiment!

When we eventually reached Oropesa we found a peaceful town. There were neither French nor Spanish in what was, in reality, a large village. It had taken us two days to reach the settlement. It would take the Army longer. Our animals had suffered. The July sun meant that we had to begin our ride before the sun had risen and, at noon, we were forced to rest from the sun's oppressive rays. We had been lucky. Our small numbers meant that we could find shelter in small woods and farm buildings. The twenty thousand men of Sir Arthur's army would not. They would bake in the heat. The woollen uniforms of the army were not suited to the hot sun of Spain. I took the decision to rest for a day before we explored the area between us and

Talavera. We were also fortunate in that the French gold I had been given was welcomed by those who lived in Oropesa. It bought us food and shelter. More importantly, it brought us intelligence. The French were to the east of Talavera. They were digging in along the Albreche River. They knew because some of those who lived in Talavera, anticipating a battle, had headed west. When I had scouted their army, with Juan, the French had been to the west of the town of Talavera. What had made them move? Then it came to me. They had had scouts out too. They had seen the movements of the British and Spanish armies. Marshal Victor was no fool. He was drawing us closer to Jourdan's Corps. If we attacked then he could call upon reinforcements. We had the best chance of destroying a French Corps but the allied armies needed to combine and do so quickly.

There were only ten of the troop's horses which were in a fit condition for a patrol. Leaving Captain Minchin and Troop Sergeant Fenwick to establish a camp for the 23rd, I led the other ten troopers and Sergeant Sharp, east. It was less than eighteen miles to Talavera. I decided to see how close I could get and confirm the news the Spanish had given to us. We were within sight of the town when we spied blue uniforms. We had just crested a rise and saw them ahead. It was a French light company. They were taking a noon break. There was a watercourse and the French were filling their canteens. Although there were just twelve of us, the French officer reacted quickly. The men who had been sheltering in the noon sun beneath tunics strung on muskets, quickly donned their tunics and shakoes and presented muskets. I had no intention of charging them. They were two hundred paces from us.

Sergeant Parkinson said, "What do we do, sir?"

"What I came here to do, Sergeant. We look for the French. This single company does not represent the French army." I took out my telescope. The French were forming three ranks. The front rank was already kneeling. Like me, their officer would be looking for the rest of our regiment to decide if he ought to form a square. I could not see any more French units. Talavera rose from the river and I could not see French flags. Glancing to my left I saw a hill which was a little higher than the road upon which we stood.

"Wheel left." Still holding my telescope, I led my patrol towards the hill. As I did so I heard the French bugle sound. The infantry took a defensive stance. The French officer was being cautious. Once we reached the grassy knoll, I raised my telescope. I was now above the line of trees which had masked the approach to the town. There was no tented town before Talavera. There were no French there. The light infantry was a patrol. It begged the question, where were the cavalry? They were the ones the French normally used to patrol. As I moved the telescope back to view the light infantry, I had my answer. A squadron of Chasseurs was galloping along the road. The bugle had been sounded to summon them. The twelve of us would be outnumbered.

"Right, chaps. Back to Oropesa! Lead them off, Sergeant Parkinson. Sergeant Sharp and I will show them our teeth!"

"Sir!"

After priming it, I lifted the Baker to my shoulder. I would risk a shot from Donna's back. The French Chasseurs were heading to cut off Sergeant Parkinson and the troop as they headed towards the road. The troop's horses were tired. Sharp and I had the two better horses. I aimed at the leading riders. It was a long shot; it was almost three hundred paces. I aimed at the two riders at the front. My rifle barked. Sharp's did the same and we were galloping after the troop when the two bullets struck. One hit a horse and the other winged a Chasseur. The French light infantry wasted one hundred musket balls as they fired a volley at us when we galloped towards the road. The Chasseurs reined in. The horse we had hit was the officer's. It took half a mile or more to catch up with the troop. Parkinson had kept them at a steady pace. Even so, they were still lathered.

Sharp glanced over his shoulder, "They are still following, sir. The sergeant has taken over."

"It can't be helped. Let us hope that Captain Minchin has sharp-eyed sentries. We may give these Chasseurs a hot reception back at Oropesa."

It was a good job that the French did not try to end the skirmish by galloping. If they had then they would have caught us. They were doing their job. They wished to discover if we had an army with us. By the time we neared Oropesa, even Donna was lathered. "Bugler, let Captain Minchin know that we are coming in and are being pursued."

"Sir!"

The bugle sounded and, was answered from ahead, I heard the response from a second bugle. There were other soldiers in Oropesa.

Sharp said, "Sir, they are gaining on us."

Then I saw that there were cavalrymen riding to our aid. It was a Spanish squadron. The Spanish had arrived. This time it was our allies who had the fresher horses.

"To the side and let them through!"

The Spanish cavalry rode through us down the centre of the road. Although the Chasseurs halted and tried to turn, the Spanish horses were fresher and they tore into the French Chasseurs. I reined in and turned to watch as the Spanish drove them from the field. It was then I saw that, even though the French were tired, they were better cavalrymen than the Spanish. It did not bode well for the battle. The Spanish lost more men than the French who managed to evade the Spanish Dragoons.

I rode out each day with different men and used one of my other horses to do so. The French still used their patrols but they were warier than they had been and I was able to ride beyond Talavera and view their army on the Albreche. I was summoned to the command tent where Sir Arthur was holding a meeting with his senior officers. "Well, Matthews?"

"There is one Corps facing you. It looks to be Marshal Victor. They are to the east of Talavera. They are dug in on the Albreche River. They have strong patrols to the west of the town." Since our first encounter, we had seen both Dragoons and Chasseurs within five miles of the village.

Sir Arthur looked happy about that. "Then when General Cuesta arrives, we can strike immediately and drive for Madrid. Good work, Matthews." I was dismissed and the council of war planned the battle. Captain Minchin and his troop rejoined their regiment but Sharp and I continued to stay in the house we had commandeered. The owner and his wife were happy for we paid them for our food, stabling and beds. When we left, he would be the richest man in the village.

Over the next few days, the two allied armies converged on our billet. Sir Arthur arrived on the nineteenth. General Cuesta a day later.

The Spanish camp was apart from ours. The Spanish General O'Donoju arrived just ahead of General Cuesta and he and Sir Arthur discussed the battle. It was as they were doing so that we heard firing. This was the second day that I had failed to ride on patrol. The Spanish had taken over that duty. A rider galloped in and reported that a Spanish patrol had run into a troop of Chasseurs. The Spanish Colonel with General O'Donoju reacted quickly and galloped off. I turned to Sharp, "Go and ready our horses. We may be needed."

The Spanish cavalry horses were fast and they galloped off. We could not see the skirmish. It was a mile or so from the village but we heard the neighs and the clash of steel. The two generals were distracted by the sounds of battle and their horses were brought.

"Matthews, be so good as to come with us, eh? We might as well see what is going on." Sharp appeared, as though by magic. I saw the wry smile on Sir Arthur's face. "As prepared as ever."

With the Spanish General and his aides, we rode east. We reached a good vantage point just as the Spanish cavalry struck the Chasseurs. It looked to me as though they had clashed and then reformed to charge each other. The Spanish were emboldened by the proximity of our army and the Chasseurs by their belief that they were the best cavalry in the world. It looked to me as though they would be driven from the field when I spied a regiment of French Dragoons approaching from the direction of Talavera. The Spanish still outnumbered the French but the Chasseurs were holding their own. The Dragoons swung the battle in the French's favour. Their muskets and carbines popped. I saw Spaniards fall from their horses. They reacted by charging into the French horsemen. Neither side could shift the other.

General Wellesley obviously tired of it, "Matthews, be a good fellow. Go and ask Brigadier Anson to bring his brigade and end this nonsense."

"Sir!"

Brigadier General Anson's brigade consisted of the 23rd and the 1st King's German Legion Light Dragoons. They were camped closest to the end of the village. I galloped to the camp and reined in next to the Brigadier's tent, "Sir Arthur's compliments, Brigadier; he would have your brigade ride to the assistance of the Spanish. There are some Dragoons and Chasseurs making a nuisance of themselves."

"Thank you, Major. Captain Hargreaves, boots and saddles if you please."

Thanks to the work they had done in Portugal the 23rd were an efficient regiment. The Germans were just as efficient and the two regiments, almost nine hundred men, were ready as fast as any Chasseur regiment. I rode with the Brigadier. I pointed to the left, "There are open fields there, Brigadier. We would be able to attack them from the flank."

"You have a good eye, Matthews!" He waved his sword and wheeled, "Three lines if you please!"

Behind us, the two regiments formed three lines. The horses were fresh and the open fields meant it could be done without fear of hidden gullies and ditches. Along with the Brigadier were his aides and bugler. The six of us would be at the fore when we charged. Glancing behind I saw Colonel Hawker to the left and the Colonel of the Germans to the right. I had made my suggestion about a flank attack for the alternative meant riding through our allies and I did not think that would have worked. The skirmish had now degenerated into a duel of carbines and muskets punctuated by individual combats between horsemen. We were four hundred yards from the French when we were spied. I heard French bugles.

Brigadier Anson had his bugler sound the charge. I drew my sabre, the Baker was still in the house in Oropesa, and I spurred Donna. We could barely keep up with Brigadier Anson's hunter. The French tried to disengage but it is hard to do so when half of your men are dismounted and firing their guns and your comrades are still duelling with their enemies. We ploughed into the French horsemen. I brought my sword down towards a Chasseur sergeant's head. He blocked it with his own sabre. I twisted and hacked at his middle. This time he barely managed to block it and my blade bit into the back of his hand. He kicked at Donna with his boot. Donna did not flinch and I hacked at his back. This time I ripped through his jacket and into flesh. My sword came away bloody. He wheeled away. I was about to go after him when I saw a Dragoon galloping towards Brigadier Anson's unprotected back. He was twenty paces from me and I would not reach him in time. I drew one of my pistols and fired. I did not kill the Dragoon but my lead ball hit his left arm and he dropped his reins. The bang of the pistol made the Brigadier turn. His sabre slashed across the Dragoon and the Frenchman fell from the saddle. The Brigadier saluted me with his sword and then wheeled his horse to pursue the French. I followed but the French had now managed to disengage. After a mile, he sounded the recall.

I reined in next to him. "Thank you, Matthews. I can see the value in having a pistol in your belt."

"You are welcome, sir. I learned long ago that a couple of pistols were an advantage in a battle."

Most of the Brigade had reined in and were returning to us but I saw the Brigadier frown as the bugle of the 23rd sounded the recall not once more but three times. The rest of the Brigade were already formed up when I saw Captain Wilberforce and Captain Jameson lead their men back.

Colonel Hawker rode up to us. Brigadier Anson pointed at the two captains, "Colonel, this is the first time I have led the Brigade and I am most unhappy that some of your officers required four recalls before they obeyed their orders. This will not happen again."

"No, sir."

"Major Matthews, if you would dine with me this evening then I would be honoured."

One did not refuse such an invitation. "Of course, sir. The pleasure will be mine."

Leaving the Colonel and me together the Brigadier rode off. Colonel Hawker was angry. "This is the last straw! The regiment performed just as I had hoped they would but Wilberforce!" He shook his head, "You are right about him. Now I must think of a way to curb him. The trouble is he has money and he has bought himself the favour of some of the other officers."

I had sympathy for the Colonel. He had a limited number of options open to him. "If I might suggest, Colonel?"

"Anything you can suggest would be welcome."

"The worst duty for any officer is to command the baggage train. One troop will be needed to do so. That would punish him and prevent any further incidents."

"Capital idea. I can see that you have far more experience at this sort of thing than I do."

I nodded, "I have been doing this for some time, sir." I did not say that much of that experience had been in French service!

Of course, when he received the punishment Captain Wilberforce knew who to blame. His irritation and obvious anger did not worry me. I was just happy that he would not be involved in any other action which might result in losses to the regiment. The only men we had lost in the skirmish were two troopers from his troop.

That evening I dressed for dinner. The Brigadier had his own staff. The two colonels were also invited. Colonel George von Braun was a good officer. He was a professional soldier. Most of the King's German Legion were. He and his officers could not understand Captain Wilberforce. Their opinion merely emphasised what Colonel Hawker now realised, Captain Wilberforce was a liability.

The Brigadier had had an ulterior motive for offering the invitation to eat. General Payne was the Cavalry commander and it was he who attended the meetings with Sir Arthur. As the general's aide, they knew I was privy to more information than they had. They were anxious to know the plans.

I had expected this. It was the same in every army. "I know little more than you, Brigadier. The General plans on striking towards Madrid. We have, now that our Spanish allies have joined us, over fifty thousand men. Marshal Victor has less than twenty thousand. A swift strike could give us the upper hand."

I could see that my answer had pleased everyone. Sir Arthur was known for his caution. An attack meant that the cavalry might be used offensively. Even professionals like Colonel von Braun preferred to be attacking than reacting to an enemy charge.

The next day I was summoned to a meeting with Sir Arthur. My presence was required as he would have General O'Donoju with him as well as General Cuesta. My Spanish was still not perfect but it was better than Sir Arthur's and he wanted me to listen to the way his words were translated by the Spanish

General. In many ways, it was good that I was there for I was able to confirm when I was asked later, what actually went on. Sir Arthur wanted the Spanish to attack the next day. He had devised a plan for both of our armies to advance on the weak Corps which lay on the far side of Talavera. It took some persuasion but I heard General Cuesta agree. After the Spanish left us, Sir Arthur summoned his own senior officers and plans were put in place.

We were all ready the next day when a messenger rode in. His news was disastrous. General Cuesta did not feel well and the Spanish would not be attacking! I had never seen Sir Arthur so angry. The messenger explained that it was just the delay of a single day. That one day proved crucial. That one day would cost many British soldiers their lives. More than three hundred horses would pay the price for the Spanish general's apparent illness. At the time we did not know that. The regiments were stood down and I went with Sir Arthur to the Spanish camp. This time it was not General O'Donoju who translated. It was me.

Glaring at the Irish Spanish General Sir Arthur said, "No frills, Matthews. Just translate my words exactly as I say them. I want General Cuesta to be in no doubt as to my intentions."

"Yes, sir!"

The General spoke in short sentences which I translated one by one. He wanted clarity and he had it. "We will attack tomorrow. This time there will be no postponement. If there is no attack tomorrow then I will take my army and return to Portugal!"

I saw the fear on the face of General Cuesta. He had almost forty thousand men and the French had less than twenty thousand but he could not defeat them on his own. The encounter between the cavalry had shown him that.

His attitude changed, "Tell Sir Arthur that we will attack tomorrow! He has my word on that!"

As we left, Sir Arthur shook his head, "All I want is the command of his troops but he will not allow it! He told me so at Albreche. I cannot defeat the French on my own! Damn Horse Guards and Parliament! They have tied my hands!" He turned and looked at me, "You didn't hear that, Matthews!"

I smiled, "Hear what, Sir Arthur?"

Chapter 16

The advance to the Albreche River began. It did not begin well. General Stewart who led the advance guard complained that the French rearguard was being allowed to escape because the Spanish were so slow. They managed to get across the Albreche River to the east of Talavera. By the end of the day, our army had all reached the river. General Wellesley sent a message to General Cuesta to advance a little more speedily. Sir Arthur found a pleasant house to use as his headquarters. Casa de Salinas was a large estate. It was surrounded by olive and cork groves but it allowed the General to view the land to the east. The French had managed to evade the cumbersome Spanish and were digging in. We could see their camps to the east. Sir Arthur had deployed our army behind him in a line from the Tagus to the Cerro de Medellin. The British were deployed along the Portina Stream. The Spanish had the area closer to the Tagus. This time Sharp and I were quartered with the General. General Mackenzie and his 1st Division were assigned as guards for the estate. I was pleased for it meant Colonel Donkin and his wild Irishmen were close at hand. He held a meeting with his senior staff and I attended. Sir Arthur was in a more ebullient mood than he had been. General Cuesta had assured him that he would begin his attack the next day and his men were already moving across the river. Once the French were engaged then we would launch our cavalry on the flanks of the French. It was a good plan.

That evening I dined alone with Sir Arthur. He was in an expansive mood. The intransigent Spanish appeared to be doing what he wanted them to do. "Your words appeared to have done the trick, Matthews. It might have been prudent to use you earlier."

"My Spanish is not as good as General O'Donoju's, sir."

"No, but at least it was accurate. I have a feeling that the Spanish General was trying to avoid hurting General Cuesta's feelings." I said nothing but I suspected that Sir Arthur was correct. He dabbed his mouth with his napkin. "I wager you would like to be back with your regiment, eh Matthews?"

"I miss them, sir. They are a good regiment"

"But if you stay on my staff then who knows what might manifest itself. You are a clever fellow. You could lead a brigade! Would you like that?"

I shook my head, "I am sorry, Sir Arthur, but I know what the soldiers in the regiments would think if I was dropped amongst them. If I was Colonel of the regiment that would be one thing but to be foisted on two regiments? No sir."

"That is a rare quality, Matthews. You are offered a brigade and you refuse. Don't get me wrong, I find it refreshing but I have not seen it before." He rose. "It will be an early start in the morning. If all goes well, we could be at Madrid in a week. By then General Crauford and his men will have reached us as well as the other regiments I requested. Perhaps things are looking up, eh, Matthews?"

"I hope so, sir."

I rose early and went, with my sergeant, to the stables. Sharp and I saw to our horses and then went to the kitchen to get some food. One only dined with the General when invited and I had not been invited. Sharp and I went to speak with the sentries who were in the olive groves. We followed the smell of frying ham. I had no idea where they had found it but the smell, despite the fact that Sharp and I had already eaten, was irresistible.

I saw Captain Turner and his men. They were the ones cooking the ham. The Irishmen cheered when they spied me. The Captain said, "They are pleased to see you, sir."

"I was drawn by the smell."

"Would you care to join us, sir?"

I shook my head, "We have just breakfasted, there." I turned and, pointing towards the house, saw Sir Arthur in one of the turret towers. He was looking east. I saw him take out his telescope. What had he seen?"

I turned and looked down through the olive grove. I thought the General might have been just looking at the advancing Spanish when I caught a glimpse of blue. I looked again and saw movement. I cupped my hands, "Stand to! It is the French!" Captain Turner looked at me as though I was mad. I pointed again, "The French are upon us."

Even as he shouted, "Bugler sound…" muskets barked.

I turned and ran. Sir Arthur had disappeared. I hurried to the stables with Sharp. "Saddle our horses."

I took Sir Arthur's saddle and had the General's horse saddled by the time Sharp had saddled his own horse. "Fetch our war gear and hurry back!"

I saddled Donna as Sir Arthur, his aide and a servant appeared. He nodded at me, "Obliged to you, Matthews. Damned if I haven't been humbugged again."

The firing intensified. I heard the shouts and cries as men were hit. Sir Arthur and I mounted our horses as the rest of his staff frantically saddled their own. I held the reins of Sharp's horse and my sergeant ran in to the stables. He unceremoniously threw me my Baker before fastening our bags to our saddles. Sir Arthur put his heels in his horse's flanks and galloped out of the stables. While Sharp mounted I primed my Baker. The two of us were just moments behind Sir Arthur. Even so, some French voltigeurs had broken through. I pulled up the Baker and fired. An officer fell, clutching his knee. Sharp joined me and we galloped after Sir Arthur. More red coats were hurrying to help the 88th which had borne the brunt of the attack. As we rode to the Portina we heard the crack of muskets.

I deduced, from the attack, that Marshal Victor had been reinforced. There was no way that he would have attacked twice his numbers otherwise. Cuesta's procrastination had cost us dear. Had he attacked when Sir Arthur had asked then the French would have been driven back to Madrid and we would have had a victory. The bugles which sounded ahead told me that the rest of the army knew of our dilemma. As we forded the Portina and climbed up the other bank I saw the Spanish troops streaming back too. Their attack had failed. It was we who were now on the defensive.

General Mackenzie's Division did their duty. They held up the enemy long enough for the majority of our troops to regain our lines. I found myself next to Sir Arthur on the Cerro de Medellin as he surveyed the allied army. The Cerro de Medellin was a plateau which had a good view of the valley below. Thanks to his meticulous planning they all knew where they should be but General Mackenzie and his division were still in disarray, having extracted themselves from the French attack. I dismounted and handed my reins to Sharp. He would take care of Donna for me as well as my war gear. I was still General Wellesley's aide and so I waited just behind him. It afforded me a fine view. It was now obvious that two or possibly three French Corps had joined together.

The Cerro de Cascajal opposite our position was a high piece of ground and I watched as a battery was set up on it. We had batteries already on our high ground and both sets of guns would ensure that any infantry which advanced across the plain would be subjected to a fierce bombardment. I saw Colonel Donkin and his men as they made their way up the Cerro de Medellin. They looked exhausted and they were depleted. They disappeared towards the reverse slope. I took out my telescope and scanned the battlefield. It looked to me as though the French were manoeuvring prior to an attack. General Wellesley did not appear concerned. It took most of the day for the French to advance to their chosen position and for our men to reach their allocated section of our thin line.

At about seven o'clock I observed a couple of regiments of French Dragoons. They rode from the olive groves close to the Spanish lines at the southern end of the Portina. I knew what they would do. They galloped up to the Spanish and, before the Spanish could even prepare their weapons, they each fired a volley from their pistols and then retired to the olive groves. I knew that there would be little damage to the Spanish but the poor light, the smoke from the pistols and the sudden appearance of the French Dragoons must have added to the anxiety felt by the Spanish. Suddenly, the whole front erupted as half of the Spanish Army fired. To my amazement, I saw Spanish battalions turn and flee. I counted at least three battalions do so.

Sir Arthur shouted for his horse, "Matthew, I need you to translate!"

"Sergeant Sharp!"

I was mounted before the General and we galloped down to the Spanish lines. It was now obvious that four battalions, two thousand men, had fled. There was little danger to the line for the cavalry who had attacked numbered less than a thousand and Dragoons are not fools. They had watched the flight of the Spanish from the safety of the olive groves. We arrived at the same time as General Cuesta. I saw him shout orders and two regiments of horsemen rode after the routed men.

General O'Donoju apologized to Sir Arthur, "The General is ashamed of the men who fled. They will be punished. He has ordered that when they are returned to the line one hundred will be shot by firing squad."

"That is unnecessary, General."

"It is a matter of honour, Sir Arthur. They have disgraced the General and Spain!"

We waited until the Spaniards were brought back, some of them with Spanish sabres encouraging them. Satisfied that the hole had been plugged we headed back to the Cerro de Medellin.

"Matthews, I fear that when the French attack in force then many others will flee. We are in a precarious position. I would have you remain mounted as shall I. I do not think that this will be a night where we get much sleep!"

His words were prophetic.

Darkness fell but many battalions were still finding their place in the line. There was confusion. The Guards were now where General Mackenzie should have been and his Division was spread out to the north. They had been shoved into a space in the line. The light was fading fast. The first French attack, when it came, was a complete surprise. It was ten o'clock and darkness had fallen when we heard musket fire from our left. Our men were being attacked. That was where the exhausted King's German Legion and Donkin's Brigade had thrown themselves down when they had arrived. In a perfect world, they would have set sentries and been watchful.

Sir Arthur said, "Matthews go and tell those Irishmen to behave themselves. I will not have random shooting."

"Sir!"

I did not think it was a random shooting. As Sharp and I galloped through the darkness I wondered at the mind of the French Marshal. This seemed like one of Marshal Victor's tricks. He was a clever man and a night attack, whilst risky, could bring him great rewards and, possibly, victory. We had almost reached the musket flashes when half a dozen Frenchmen appeared before us. I drew and fired my pistol in one motion. I drew my sabre and rode at them. Four Kings German Legion infantrymen rose from their bivouac and attacked the Frenchmen with their bayonets. I slashed down at the face of one of the Frenchmen. Two hurtled back towards their own lines.

It was an attack, "Sharp, ride back to the General and tell him that the French have broken through the front line." In an instant, I knew what had happened. The 1st Division had not realised they were the front line. They thought they were the second line. It would prove to be a fatal error.

"Sir!" He wheeled his horse and galloped off. I saw that he had his spare pistol in his hand!

I heard a German voice ordering his men to stop firing at shadows and wait until they saw a Frenchman. That was easier said than done, in the dark. It explained why there was so little firing. It was hard to see who you were fighting with and it would be sword and bayonet work.

Above the cacophony of clashing metal, musket pops and the cries of men being wounded, I heard a familiar voice in the dark, "Grenadier Company, form lines, damn you!" It was Colonel Donkin. I rode towards the sound of his voice. I saw him hatless, sword in hand trying to form his men into two lines. All around there were French, British and German soldiers desperately fighting hand to hand. In many ways, it was fortunate that it was the Second Brigade. They were Irishmen and this was their sort of fight. Then the Colonel disappeared into a confused maelstrom of arms and weapons. This was not the place for Donna.

I holstered my spent pistol and drew a second. Dismounting I tied Donna to a sergeant's pike which was embedded in the ground. The dead sergeant lay next to it. The occasional muzzle flare of a musket helped me to find my way to the fighting. I could hear the cries of men as they fought. French officers and sergeants encouraged their men to get at 'Les Goddams'. I could hear Colonel Donkin and I joined some more of his Connaught Rangers as they rallied to his call. I saw that some of them were hatless and more than a few bootless. They had been asleep when the attack had begun.

Even as I made the side of Colonel Donkin, I heard Sir Rowland Hill and a column of men coming from behind me, "Steady the 29th!" Reinforcements were on their way.

I made the side of Colonel Donkin. He shook his head. "I have just three companies of the 88th here and some Germans. God knows where the rest of the Division is."

From below us, I heard, "Vive l'Empereur!"

I shouted, in German, "They are going to attack with bayonets! Form two ranks." I then turned to the Colonel, "Bayonet attack!"

"Two ranks, 88th! Stand firm, Devil's Own! Who will separate us?" It was the motto of the regiment.

An Irish voice from the dark shouted, "No bugger, sir!"

The French column raced at us. From the side, I heard Sir Rowland Hill shout, "Prepare! Ready! Fire!"

As the blue-coated light infantry swarmed towards us out of the dark they were hit by the muskets of the 29th Foot. The muskets were fired at moving shadows. I levelled my pistol and, when the French were just ten paces from me, fired.

Colonel Donkin shouted, "Fire!" The front of the shadowy column of Frenchmen disappeared in smoke as muskets, pistols and carbines fired. It was inconceivable that any had survived but, remarkably, many did. A bayonet loomed out of the dark and it was rammed through the skull of the Irishman before me. As the Frenchman tried to pull out his weapon, I lunged with my sabre and my sword went into his open, screaming mouth. I tore it out sideways. He was dead before his hat hit the ground. The 88th were not the sort of regiment to take such losses lying down. They broke ranks and tore into the light infantry. French Light Infantry were like their British counterparts, they were small, agile men who were quick. When moving across open ground they were hard to hit. Here they were fighting the grenadier company of the 88th and the French were butchered. The Connaught Rangers did not fear a wound. They were almost like the Viking berserkers. It is hard to face a man like that.

Sir Rowland Hill was urging the 29th on and they initiated their own bayonet attack. Inexorably, the French were despatched or they fled. Long after the battle, we learned that originally three regiments had been sent for the night attack. Had they all reached us then they would have defeated the men who defended the line. Luckily for us, only one regiment made our line. The French 9th Light Infantry Regiment failed but not for lack of courage.

As the French fell back Sir Rowland shouted, "Take prisoners! Take prisoners!" An Irishman gave a wild and primaeval yell and Sir Rowland's voice said, calmly, "Colonel, control your men!"

"The 88th will reform! Sergeant Major!" General Hill plugged the gap with the men of the 29th and 48th regiments. Prisoners were collected up. Sir Rowland rode over to Colonel Donkin and I. He dismounted. Sir Rowland was a quietly spoken man not given to histrionics, "Colonel, what happened? Why were your men not stood to and defending the line?"

The Colonel's head drooped, "Sir, we thought we were in the second line. We believed there were Germans ahead of us."

"Dear, oh dear! Somewhat of an error, eh Donkin?"

I felt honour bound to defend the Colonel, "Sir, Colonel Donkin's men were with the vanguard this morning when the French first attacked. They had been marching all day."

"Ah, I see. Still, it was close."

Just then Sharp rode up with Sir Arthur and two of his aides. He surveyed the scene then he dismounted. Lieutenant Close of the 48th marched some prisoners towards us. I saw that one was a Colonel. Sir Arthur needed no translation for he could speak French fluently.

"Colonel, your men are brave but you are now a prisoner."

The Colonel saluted, "Yes, General, but had the rest of our men followed us then we would now be feasting on your breakfasts!"

Colonel Meunier was a brave man and he was right. "Take the Colonel away. Colonel Donkin, send word to General Mackenzie. This is his sector and I would have it defended properly. It is one thing for our Spanish allies to behave badly but I do not expect it of my regiments."

"Yes sir, sorry sir." He turned, "Sergeant Major, ask Captain Turner to send a runner to the General."

"Sorry, sir, Captain Turner is dead."

I had been offered breakfast by the Captain and his men. Now they were dead. Such was war.

"Then find another to do so."

"Yes, sir."

I recovered Donna and stayed with the two generals as they watched the red-coated infantry form lines and defensive positions. It was too dark to see my watch but I guessed that it was gone midnight. One of the sentries shouted, "Sir, I can see movement. The French are coming again!"

We nudged our horses towards the sentries. We could hear noise from the east. Almost as though Sir Arthur had ordered it the moon emerged and we saw, across the Portina, the French battalions as they moved below the Cerro de Cascajal. The noise became clear. The French were working on their battery atop the ridge.

Sir Arthur nodded, seemingly satisfied, "The moon is out. They will not risk it again this night. Sir Rowland be so good as to remain here until General Mackenzie stirs himself. Matthews, come with me."

We returned to view the rest of the army. Sir Arthur had been caught out. As we rode along the lines, listening to the occasional musket volley as men shot at shadows, he said, "Damned Spanish! I should have been on the Cerro de Medellin instead of worrying what the Spanish were doing. This should not have happened. I must confess, Matthews, I do not know if the Spanish will stand on the morrow. This ground is not one I would have chosen. Save for the Cerro de Medellin I have no reverse slope to shelter our men. When the French artillery gets to work tomorrow it will be hot work!"

It took some hours to ensure that both our flanks were secure and that sentries were on duty. It was our infantry who bore the brunt of such duties. The artillery and the cavalry were in the safer ground behind the front lines. They slept. Perhaps the volleys in the night woke them but they were in no danger. As dawn broke, we made our way back to the vantage point which was the Cerro de Medellin. We saw soldiers from both sides making their way to the Portina to fill canteens drunk dry. Fighting was thirsty work.

We rejoined General Hill who shook his head as he viewed blue and red-coated soldiers speaking with one another across the Portina, "Remarkable eh, Sir Arthur? There they are exchanging pleasantries at the stream and yet when the battle starts, they will try to kill each other."

"I have never yet fathomed it out, Sir Rowland." He waved a hand at the enemy positions. The open nature of the battlefield meant that concealment was almost impossible. The olive and cork groves by the Tagus were the only cover and their regular lines meant men could be easily seen. "They have fifty cannons over there, gentlemen, and we have but eighteen. What is even more crucial is that the French are using twelve and eight pounder cannons. Our six pounders are tiny by comparison. When the French begin to fire have our fellows lie down. It would not do to expose them."

One of his aides, Colonel Masterton, asked, "Sir Arthur, will they not attack across the whole line?"

Shaking his head, he said, "I think not, Masterton. Marshal Victor showed his hand last night. If they can drive us from this hill then the Spanish will fall like a house made of cards. The French saw them run when some Dragoons popped their pistols at them. He will want to humbug me and we must see that they do not. We rely upon the stout hearts of the red-coated infantrymen and the green jackets who will blunt their attack."

I knew that the Rifles were good but I doubted that the battalion we had with us could stop a French attack. As we waited for the attack, I loaded my weapons. I would be fighting, of that, I had no doubt.

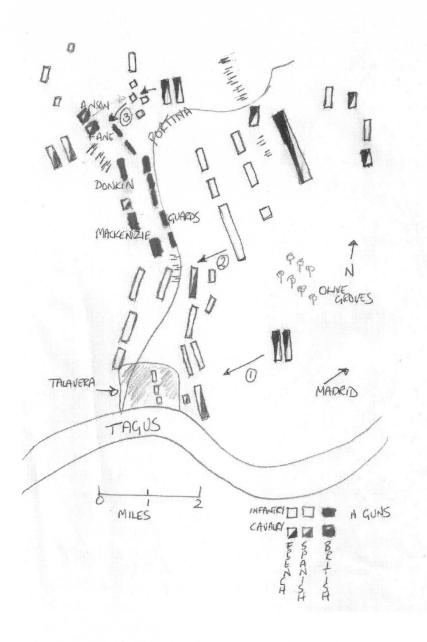

ANSON
FANE
DONKIN
MACKENZIE
GUARDS
PORTINA
TALAVERA
TAGUS

N
OLIVE GROVES
MADRID

0 1 2
MILES

INFANTRY
CAVALRY

FRENCH SPANISH BRITISH

↑ GUNS

Chapter 17

It was five in the morning when the single cannonball from the Cerro de Cascajal announced the start of the battle. When all fifty guns fired it soon became obvious that their target was the British artillery. The Royal Artillery fired in reply but as Sir Arthur had predicted it was an uneven duel. Balls from the French, which landed short, bounced their way through files of red-jacketed infantrymen. General Hill shouted, "The army will lie down!"

It did not stop men being killed but the balls could not take down whole files of men. The odd bodies which were pulverised by twelve and eight-pound cannon balls were just unlucky. The artillery batteries now began to be hit. As their fire withered so the French shifted their targets to the infantry below them. They ignored the Rifles. They were spread out like skirmishers. It would have been a waste of cannonballs.

The firing continued for forty-five minutes. Smoke wreathed the battlefield. It was hard to see the effect of the bombardment. Men groaned and stretcher bearers dealt with the wounded. We heard drums beating and a column of five thousand men began to advance across the battlefield. Voltigeurs, like insects, danced before the column. The Bakers of the Rifles barked and the French fell but the balls merely slowed down the inevitable. If we had had artillery left then the columns could have been struck by cannon balls and they would have been hurt. We had too few and the damage they caused was minimal. The blue behemoth advanced, unscathed. It moved steadily up the slope. When it reached the Rifles, the 5th Battalion scurried back to the main red line.

The Rifles, skirmishers and the occasional cannonball tore holes in the French column but there were so many men that it was hard to see the damage. Their officers and sergeants offered encouragement and cries of 'Vive l'Empereur' rang out. The drums continued their metronome-like beat.

Some of the newer regiments were intimidated. I heard a Sergeant Major shout, "Steady lads! These Froggies are full of wind and piss! Wait until they get close. A couple of volleys and then in with the bayonet. You will see them run then!"

The leading regiment was just one hundred paces from the ridge when Sir Rowland Hill ordered his six battalions to rise. They were safe now from French artillery which could not fire for fear of hitting their own men.

"Prepare! Ready! Fire!"

The first volley from eighteen hundred muskets was too much. The French were decimated. Volley after volley poured into them. They tried to return fire but the odd musket ball did no damage. I was close enough to see the flag they carried. It was the 24th Line Regiment. They broke and poured down the hill. Further along the hill, the 96th Line regiment was exposed and when the Germans launched a flank attack, they too broke.

Sir Arthur saw an opportunity, "Stewart, take your men and chase them back over the river!"

The three battalions were the 29th, the 48th and a mixed Highland battalion. With bayonets fixed they hurtled after the fleeing French. It was a rout. Wild Highlanders plunged their bayonets into the backs of Frenchmen who were already shell shocked from the musket fire. Of course, the Highlanders did not stop at the Portina. Sergeant Majors and senior officers managed to halt most of them but many jumped the stream and ran into the French battalions which had yet to attack. None had been lost in the pursuit. Two hundred and fifty of them were killed or captured when they crossed the Portina. The survivors returned to the ridge. The first phase of the battle was over.

Sir Arthur snapped at General Stewart, "Damn it, Stewart! I expected better of your men!"

"Sorry, Sir Arthur. They were carried away by the moment!"

Sir Rowland Hill suddenly shouted, "There is a chap coming to the stream Sir Arthur. It looks like he wants to talk."

Sir Arthur nodded to me, "Major Matthews, go and talk to the fellow!"

"Sir. Sharp, with me!"

We galloped through a charnel house. There were bodies which had lain there since the previous night. They were bloated in the heat. I knew what the French wanted, it would be a truce so that they could recover and bury their dead.

I reined in on our side of the stream. The French Major began in English. It was execrable. "I am Major Mortier…"

I waved my hand to silence him, "Let us speak in French. I speak it fluently."

Relieved, he nodded, "King Joseph asks for a two-hour truce so that we can recover our dead and wounded. He assumes that you will do the same."

"Two hours? Very well." I took out my watch as did the French Major, "Two hours then."

When I reached Sir Arthur, I told him the news. "Good, General Sherbrooke, see to it."

Sir Rowland Hill said, "Sir Arthur, the men are starving. The Spanish who fled yesterday ransacked our supplies."

"They will just have to forage for themselves." Sir Arthur had not thought his statement through. We were on a battlefield. Where would the men forage?

He took out his telescope and levelled it at the French lines. The plain was already filling with men, French ambulances and stretchers as bodies and wounded were removed. Whole regiments were going to the stream to fill their canteens. The water would have a salty taste; it was bloody. There were still bodies lying in it. I took out my own telescope and saw the same as the General. The French were having a council of war and, from the movements, the next attack would be on our weak left flank. The slope prevented the French from seeing the two batteries of German guns and the German brigade there but, even so, it was our weak area.

"Gentlemen, let us hold a council of war. We will ride to General Cuesta. Major!"

Once again, I was needed.

For once the Spanish were in a conciliatory mood. General Cuesta had seen how firmly we had stood and was impressed.

I translated as Sir Arthur rattled out his suggestions which were, in reality, de facto orders. He explained the threat and General Cuesta agreed to give us five thousand men to bolster our left flank. In addition, our weaker cavalry was to be supported by the Duke of Albuquerque's cavalry. We returned to the Cerro de Medellin in a much happier frame of mind. Now that they were supported Sir Arthur was able to move Anson and Fane's cavalry brigades to the western end too. The 23rd would be in action. Geoffrey Minchin and his men would be in their first real battle. I wondered how they would cope.

The two hours of truce and calm ended. I knew that little food had been found for our men. The French looked to have been treated better. I took my place with Sir Arthur. Donna had been rested. I looked at my watch. It was three o'clock. The French artillery fired. In the centre, where our lines met those of the Spanish, there was a battery at a place called Paja de Verergar. It was attacked by a whole French division. The French bombardment caused few casualties and the Spanish guns acquitted themselves well. The French stayed in column and when they were met by stiff musket fire then they fell back.

Sir Arthur said, "That is a feint. Their real attack will come further north." He pointed. There was a column of over fifteen thousand men. They had begun to move and they were aimed at the centre of the British line. The single column had almost as many men as the whole of the British under Sir Arthur's command.

I took out my telescope. "General, there are nine thousand men preparing at the northern end of their line. They are supported by twelve hundred horsemen."

"Are they by God? They mean to punch a hole in our line and then flank us. Major, ride to generals Anson and Fane. If the French close then they are to threaten their infantry. Make the French form square." His eyes held mine. "No foolish charges. They are just there to stop them and make them form square!"

"Yes, sir. Sharp!"

I galloped off away from the battalions who were already forming. The two brigades were not yet mounted. A rider did not mount prematurely in the Spanish heat. Brigadier Fane commanded the Dragoons and Dragoon Guards. As such he was senior. Some of the 23rd looked up in anticipation as I approached. I noted that Captain Wilberforce was there. I did not know why. Colonel Hawker had assured me that he would be watching the horses. I could only assume that he had been overruled by General Anson. In the scheme of things that was trivial.

"Brigadier General Fane, General Wellesley's compliments and he would like you to threaten the column which is advancing from the east. He does not wish you to charge them, merely to make them go into square."

"Good. Gentlemen, mount your horses."

"You should be aware, sir, that there are twelve hundred light horsemen supporting the nine thousand strong column."

"Thank you, Major Mathews. I appreciate the intelligence."

As I passed the Dragoon Guards, Lieutenant Colonel John Elley shouted cheerfully, "I wager you wish you were joining us, eh, Major?"

"Yes, sir!"

The Lieutenant Colonel was something of a legend. He was a Yorkshireman from Leeds who had joined the Dragoon Guards as a trooper. His advancement had been nothing short of remarkable. He now commanded a prestigious regiment of heavy cavalry. He owed nothing to the purchase of commission. He was a superb horseman and a great swordsman. Those who knew him said that he was fearless. I knew that he was reckless. He rode a huge white horse. When I had been in the Chasseurs, I had been warned off such animals as they tended to attract the attentions of enemy horsemen!

Confident that I had passed on the correct information, I rode back the short way to Sir Arthur. I saw that the column which was approaching our northern flank was not moving quickly. Sir Arthur was right. This was a diversion. The main attack was the larger column heading for the centre of the British line. They were marching in columns. With the artillery rearranged and the borrowed Spanish batteries in place, we began to pound holes in the French columns. They doggedly came on. I pointed out to Sir Arthur that the French Dragoons were massing behind the columns. When they broke through, we would have to endure a cavalry charge.

Then we heard firing from the south. The French feint attack was underway. When I heard the bugle sound the cavalry charge, I had to look. Every cavalryman was stirred by such a sound. General Cuesta had sent in his best cavalry, El Rey, the Royal Cavalry. They charged towards the French infantry scattering the skirmishers who fled back through the advancing column. It was an action every horseman dreamed of. The French broke ranks and fled. The cavalry did not stop but reached the French guns. They sabred the gunners and took the guns and caissons. The whole line cheered. It was a true victory. The British regiments to the side took advantage and, advancing, cut down even more of the fleeing Frenchmen.

The temperature was now so hot that I saw men fainting with the heat. This did not suit the British soldier but at least we just had to stand and endure shot and shell. The French were advancing in column. General Sherbrook was in command of the men awaiting the French columns. He rode along the line, apparently oblivious to the shells being fired by the French artillery and the musket balls from the skirmishers. "The Division will open fire at fifty paces. Fix your bayonets and when you have fired three volleys await my order to charge! None crosses the Portina! Is that clear?"

"Yes, sir!"

The roar must have sounded like a battle cry to the French. The General returned to his position behind the line so that he could judge the moment. He had five thousand muskets at his command and even though they were outnumbered three to one by the advancing columns, I was confident about the outcome.

All the while I was glancing to the north. I saw that General Fane had his men prepared for their focussed charge. The King's German Legion Hussars and the 23rd would be in the front rank. I saw their standards. Like General Sherbrooke, Brigadier Fane would have to judge his moment well. I was surprised to see Lieutenant Colonel Elley on his white horse. He was with the Hussars. I wondered at that. I estimated it would be half an hour before they were ready to attack. I returned my attention to the encounter before me. It was now obvious that the French Marshal was using Sir Arthur as a target. It was as though he and his staff were the subject of the whole attack. The drums filled the air as the French marched. The drummer boys at the fore would all be slaughtered. The Rifles had duelled with the voltigeurs and both skirmisher screens had now withdrawn."

"Prepare."

Muskets were primed and brought up.

"Ready."

The muskets were aimed.

"Fire!"

Five thousand muskets barked and the world before us became a thick pall of smoke. The cracks sounded like thunder and then there were the screams of the wounded and the dying.

"Fire!"

A second volley followed. This time it was slightly more ragged.

"Fire!"

The third volley was even more ragged.

"Charge!"

We could see nothing but we knew that the enemy were just fifty paces away. The double line launched themselves at the shattered and shell-shocked Frenchmen. None could withstand such an onslaught. As the Guards and the grenadier companies led the attack the French saw the largest men in the British army charging towards them. They heard the screams, curses and obscenities of men who had endured French artillery fire and now wanted vengeance. I could see little but I could imagine the bayonets tearing into men whose ears were still deafened by the volleys. The wind began to shift the smoke and it was a barbaric scene which greeted me. The field was filled with the red and the blue. They were tearing at each other with sharp-edged weapons, or simply clubbing at each other with their muskets. The fresher English troops prevailed and the French fled.

As the smoke thinned even more, I saw that Fane's and Anson's brigades had begun their ride. Sir Arthur shouted, above the cacophony of battle, "Matthews, report on the charge for me. Let me know how it goes."

"Yes, sir. Sergeant Sharp!"

I needed no encouragement. The battle in the centre was over. As I rode north, I saw the red wave flowing down towards the Portina. These were the Guards. These were not the wild Scotsmen who had overreached themselves so dramatically just a few hours ago. This time history would not repeat itself.

The two regiments which led the charge towards the northern French column were keeping perfectly straight lines. I heard the bugles sound the increase in pace. Drums rattled and the French went into square. As soon as they did so the artillery on Cerro de

Medellin saw their opportunity and wreaked their revenge on the French. They had suffered just half a day ago and now they had their revenge and scythed huge lines through the immobile squares. They kept firing as long as they could. It was as I turned to glance at the attack across the Portina that two things happened at once. The horsemen of the 23rd disappeared into a ravine just fifty yards from the French squares and the Guards, along with the other regiments, disobeyed their orders and flooded across the Portina. It was the French's turn to pour volley after volley into them.

Turning my attention back to my comrades in the 23rd I witnessed a piece of superb horsemanship. Colonel Elley had a thoroughbred and he cleared the ravine. Miraculously other troopers clambered out of the ravine. However, instead of obeying orders and returning to their own lines, they charged on. I recognised Captain Wilberforce and his troop. Like Captain Rogers, he would have his moment of glory. The King's German Legion Hussars did halt. They pulled carbines and pistols and began to duel with the French. It was one-sided, the French had many more muskets. In square, they could bring three ranks of every square to bear. The Hussars fell back. The two cavalry brigadiers did the right thing. They reformed their remaining regiments into lines. The squares might be able to massacre the 23rd but they could not advance against cavalry.

Colonel Elley took off after the troopers who had now lost all sense of reason. It was a brave gesture from a true cavalryman. I had no need to ride any closer but something drew me towards the men I had led. None of the 23rd had made it back to their own lines, yet. The French cavalry was preparing to charge Colonel Elley and the men he led. The officers who remained with the 23rd were trying to help their wounded comrades from the ravine. I was now just two hundred yards from the ravine. I was out of range of the muskets but not of the cries of wounded men and the pleas for help.

"Sharp, ride back to the General and tell him what has happened."

"What will you do, sir?"

"Try to help as many of those poor souls as I can, Sharp."

"Then I will help you, sir. Sir Arthur has a good telescope. He can see for himself what is going on!"

His face told me that he was determined. Picking up my Baker, I said, "Right then. Let's get to it."

We rode to the ravine. The sight which greeted me haunts my dreams to this day. Dead and dying horses lay tumbled in the bottom. One or two falling there might have survived but horses had fallen on other horses. Troopers lay crushed or dying. I watched as Captain Minchin and Sergeant Parkinson jumped the ravine to go to the aid of Troop Sergeant Fenwick whose leg lay pinioned under his horse. The nearest French square, the 27th Light Infantry, was a huge square and lay just forty paces from them. The two brave men ignored the musket balls flying all around them as they ran to the Troop Sergeant.

I saw a Lieutenant directing the fire of the square. He was less than two hundred yards from me. I dismounted and used Donna to steady my gun. I fired and he fell back. Sharp joined me and he hit the sergeant. Angered the company began firing at us. They were wasting lead for we were too far away but it stopped them firing at Captain Minchin. I reloaded properly and aimed at the next officer who strode towards the square. My ball spun him around. As I reloaded a third time, I saw that Sergeant Parkinson and Captain Minchin were half carrying the Troop Sergeant. They were using their horses for cover. Sharp and I were firing as fast as we could. We had disrupted the musket fire and more of the troopers were dragging themselves from the ravine. Miraculously some of the horses had survived. The German Hussars hurried back to their own lines but the troopers from the 23rd joined Sharp and I to harass the squares.

I began to think that the three men might make it when the square of the 27th Light Infantry began to fire at the two horses and the three men. The horses were hit by a volley. The two dying horses protected the bodies of the three men but not their legs. All three were hit in the legs. The horses fell as did the men. Still, they did not give in and they crawled towards the ravine. The carcasses of the two horses afforded them some protection but they were still twenty yards shy of safety.

"Trooper Harris, hold our horses! Sharp, come with me." I ran to the ravine and threw myself in. I landed on the soft and bloody corpses and carcasses of men and horse. It softened my fall. I clambered up to the other side. I aimed my Baker at the officer commanding the 27th Light Infantry. When he fell his men began to fire at the ravine. It was a mistake for most of the lead balls fell short.

Slinging the Baker over my back I clambered out of the cavalry grave. I half crawled to the three men. The Troop Sergeant was in a bad way. I grabbed Captain Minchin and began to pull him to safety. "Sir, Fenwick!"

"I will come back for him. One at a time, eh?" Sergeant Sharp had made the ravine and he began to clamber out, "Keep firing at them!" I almost pushed the Captain into the ravine and then went back for Sergeant Parkinson. The ravine which had caused such carnage was now a haven for the French could not hit those sheltering in the bottom of it.

He grinned at me as I dragged him, "Sir, can I be cheeky and borrow the Baker again? Those buggers killed Betsy. I would like to pay them back!"

As I dropped him in the ravine, I slipped the gun from my shoulder. "You are welcome! Use it well!"

The Troop Sergeant was the hardest to shift. He was the biggest of the three and he was unconscious. I am not sure I would have made it had not Lieutenant Colonel Elley and the six survivors from the encounter with the lancers and the Chasseurs galloped by and drawn the fire of the two nearest squares. By the time the sergeant and I were in the ditch, I was exhausted. I drew my pistol and popped a shot at the square.

Then I heard a bugle. The rest of the Brigade was coming to our aid. Now that the land around the squares was free from any living cavalrymen the artillery started to fire again. I watched as the two squares were pulverised. When I heard the horses behind me, I knew the squares would not remain before us for long. A bugle sounded and the squares moved, somewhat crab-like, away from the guns. The surviving troopers from the 23rd helped to take the wounded men from the ravine. Unlike the French, we had no ambulances. The three men were slung on to the backs of horses and taken to the doctor at their camp.

I found Harris who held our horses. Brigadier Anson nodded, "Damned brave, Matthews. Not our fault, you know? Tell the

General that. How were we to know there was a damned ditch there?"

"How is Colonel Hawker? I didn't see him."

"He was knocked from his saddle by an artillery shell. Damned unlucky. He and the Major fell. Wilberforce took over. Damned brave of him too, but reckless."

As we headed back to the Cerro de Medellin, I reflected that his recklessness must have cost the regiment more than two hundred troopers. I had not seen him following Lieutenant Colonel Elley and I assumed he had perished.

By the time I reached Sir Arthur, the last survivors of the attack across the Portina had returned. They were shamefaced. "Well done, Matthews. What a waste eh? We have few enough regiments of cavalry as it is!" He peered across to the French, "And now what will they do?"

I knew what he was thinking. Our combined allied army outnumbered the French but they had more than enough to attack again. He knew, from the captured reports, that Soult and Ney were on their way south. The document had made it clear they would not arrive until August. Would the French attack before the five Corps could combine?

We had our answer when we saw the northern column begin to trudge east. As they dismantled the battery on the Cerro de Cascajal then we knew the battle was over.

We stood to until dawn. By then it was clear that the French were pulling back to the Albreche river. I was sent to collect the musters after the roll call. It made for sad reading. General Mackenzie had paid the price for his mistakes and he was dead. Thirty-four officers, six hundred and forty-three non-commissioned officers and enlisted men had perished. More than four thousand officers and men were wounded and there were six hundred and fifty officers and men missing. We had lost a quarter of our force. Had we won the battle? The French had lost more and they had withdrawn. We had fought superior odds. History said we had but, on that July morning it felt like a draw, at best.

Chapter 18

The day after the battle General Cuesta rode into our camp. Once again, I was invited to the meeting. The Spanish General was in the best mood I had yet witnessed. That, in itself, was not a surprise. He had lost less than five hundred men for the French had concentrated their attack on us. He brought news that his fellow Spanish General, Venegas, was approaching Toledo. He urged Sir Arthur to attack Victor and march on Madrid.

General Wellesley was not going to do that. He agreed, in the short term, for General Wilson to threaten Madrid. By doing so it would help the other Spanish Army. I explained to General Cuesta that, unlike his well-supplied army, ours was starving and the men could not fight without food. I also pointed out the large numbers of men in the hospitals. I chose my words carefully. Sir Arthur's words had been, at best, terse. The argument gave Cuesta the opportunity to agree to wait a few days.

When General Crauford's Light Division arrived a day later then we all became more optimistic. They had marched over fifty miles in twenty-seven hours. It was a remarkable feat. Of course, after such a marathon march, they were in no condition to move. It would take a day or so for them to recover.

Sharp and I took the opportunity to visit our wounded friends. We went to the camp of the 23rd first. Captain Minchin and Sergeant Parkinson were lucky. The musket balls had almost been spent when they had hit them. Sergeant Parkinson's fibula had been broken but the surgeon had set it. He would make a full recovery. Captain Minchin, who was now the senior captain in the regiment, had had two musket balls removed from his right leg and he was walking when we saw them. Both men were in the sick bay at the camp of the 23rd as the hospital needed the beds for the more seriously wounded. The regimental doctor and his orderlies saw to them.

Captain Minchin spoke for all of them, "Parkinson, Fenwick and I would like to thank you, Major Matthews. I have no doubt that we would have perished but for you and Sergeant Sharp's brave action."

"You are brave men. I am sure that you would have managed somehow."

Captain Minchin shook his head, "No sir. You and I know better. Do you know what is going to happen now?"

I could not tell the captain all for rumour and gossip would exaggerate my words. I was able to give him some news, however. "Your regiment has suffered so many losses that it is heading back to Portugal. It will escort the wounded who can be moved."

"And Troop Sergeant Fenwick? He is still in the hospital."

"He and the others will have to wait until they can be moved. Sharp and I will visit him this afternoon, after the siesta." I did not mention that, if we had to move out of Talavera suddenly then the wounded would be left to the French.

"Then we shall see you in Lisbon, eh sir?"

Sergeant Parkinson nodded, "Aye, and Lieutenant Frayn will be glad to have the Captain back."

"He survived too?"

"Oh yes sir, a game 'un is Lieutenant Frayn!"

Captain Minchin pointed to Sergeant Parkinson, "And this is the new Troop Sergeant."

Sergeant Sharp grinned and patted his fellow sergeant's back, "Well done! Well done!"

"Aye well, I have some big boots to fill."

The words of Acting Troop Sergeant Parkinson seemed hollow when we reached the hospital. Troop Sergeant Fenwick had lost his left leg below the knee and, from the look of it, his left eye. His left arm was also bandaged but I saw fingers; he had not lost the limb. He still smiled when he saw us. "Sir, this is an honour. I am pleased you came, sir. It gives me the opportunity to thank you for saving my life."

I nodded, "I confess that I thought you would succumb to your wounds."

"Old Joe Fenwick is tough, sir! I will survive." His good eye lowered and his voice became thinner, "Of course, I have no idea how I will earn a crust back in England." He sighed, "Probably join the other beggars in St Giles' Rookery."

The mention of The Rookery suddenly gave me an idea, "Sharp, go and find me a pen and some paper."

"Sir!"

"Troop Sergeant, you are good with horses, are you not?"

His face broke into a proud smile, "Aye, sir. I have been around them all my life. I know how to look after them alright even in a hell hole like Spain."

"I have a small estate north of London, Bilson's farm. At the moment it is in the process of being built. When time allows, I intend to return there and raise horses. I have another ex-soldier, Rafe Jenkins, as a caretaker. You could go there to recover and when you can walk again, you could look after the horses I intend to buy. You will be able to walk, won't you?"

He said, "Aye, sir. It might be a peg leg but a man would be a fool to turn down an offer like that." Sharp reappeared and handed me the paper, ink and pen. "This is not out of sympathy is it, sir? That would not suit at all!"

"No, Troop Sergeant Fenwick, I do need someone who knows horses. You would be doing me the favour. I need men around me whom I can trust. If nothing else you have proved that many times over on this Iberian adventure."

"Then sir, I will accept your very generous offer."

I wrote the letter and addressed it to Rafe Jenkins. I added a note to Mr Hudson to add Fenwick to the men he would pay. I folded the paper and addressed it. I had a sudden thought, "You can read, Troop Sergeant?"

He grinned broadly, "My dad couldn't so my mum taught me my letters. I have kept it up. Aye, sir, I can read!"

I felt much better when I handed him the letter. If he could get back to Lisbon and thence London, he had a chance of a life. Otherwise…

Reports came in from generals Wilson and Venegas informing Sir Arthur that they were both closing with the French and all seemed to be going well. Most of the wounded, including Troop Sergeant Fenwick, were evacuated. As we were uncertain about the northern road we had taken they were sent by a more southerly route and the fortress of Badajoz. There would be more than fifteen hundred who would remain in the hospital.

On the 1st of August, Sir Arthur sent for me. "Matthews, I need your eyes, ears, mind and your contacts with these guerrilla chaps."

"Sir!"

"Now that General Wilson has headed east, we are blind about the road to the north. Head to Plasencia. Find that fellow who brought you the despatches, what was his name?"

"Juan, sir."

"Yes, well, find him and see what he knows. I am not going to head east until I know that the road to the west is safe. Do not tarry. Time is of the essence."

"Yes, sir!"

Although our horses had recovered since the battle, the distance we would have to cover necessitated us each taking a spare. We set out immediately knowing we would have to halt for three hours in the heat of the day. If anything, the weather was becoming hotter! It took two days to reach the town. We rode mainly while it was dark for it was cooler. We rode into Plasencia at ten in the morning. They had a market and the town seemed to be agitated. Our British uniforms were recognised and information was easily gathered. Marshal Ney and Marshal Soult, it seemed, were heading for Plasencia. The townsfolk not only offered me that information they asked when General Wellesley would return to save them from the French devils. I could not give them hope and I told them that it would take time for our army to come to their aid.

I turned to Sharp. "You must return to the General and give him this dire news. It changes everything. He will need to evacuate Talavera and take the Badajoz road. If these people know that the French are on their way then the enemy will be here sooner, rather than later."

"What about you, sir?"

"I have to find Juan and to verify this news. It could be just a large patrol or the vanguard. I will use the back roads."

Although reluctant, the Sergeant was a soldier and he obeyed me. We bought food at the market and then, a little earlier than we might have liked, we separated. I took the trail over the mountains and Sharp headed back down the road to Talavera.

I would be sleeping rough. It would take me a whole day to reach Juan's village and I did not want to arrive in the dark. I headed up the trail which I vaguely remembered from all those months ago when I had scouted out Talavera. The land looked even more lonely now. The hot summer sun seemed to bake the landscape. The heat began almost as soon as the sun rose and it grew to be an oppressive blanket when men could not move and horses could die through heat.

I camped in what the Spanish called an arroyo. It was a gully which would be deep enough to give me some cover. I chose it because there was water bubbling along the bottom. I reached it in the dark and I was drawn by the sound. Donna and my other horse, Goldie, hurried towards the stream. They could smell the water and they were thirsty; like me, they had been on short rations. I unsaddled them as they greedily gorged on the refreshing water. I saw that there was a little grazing. Sheep had been in the valley but they had not destroyed the pasture. Leaving them to graze I put the saddles on the ground and then I ate. I chose not to light a fire. It might have drawn Juan and his guerrillas to me but, equally, it could have attracted French patrols. I knew that Soult and Ney would have men ahead of them scouting out the land.

It was as I lay down to sleep that I caught the whiff of woodsmoke in the air. That heartened me. I was close to houses and I wondered if I was close to Juan's home. It was too late to investigate them but as the trail was just below a col, I hoped that when I rode, in the early hours, that I would see houses and, hopefully, find guerrillas.

I awoke in the dark and I saddled my horses and then walked them up the long slope leading to the col. It was at least two miles away. The nights in Spain were never as cold as one might expect and I found myself becoming hotter as I neared the top. I stopped to unfasten my jacket. I even contemplated taking it off but thought better of it. I glanced behind me and saw the thin line that was the sun beginning its rise. Here the sun rose faster than in England. I could make out the col ahead. The trail passed between two jagged rocks. The trail looked a little flatter and so I mounted Donna. I had given them both adequate rest and I was becoming uncomfortably hot. As I mounted, Goldie snorted. I laughed, "I will ride you later, I promise." She gave a whinny in reply and I moved on. As I reached the top, I looked expectantly to the valley below. I saw no houses. What I did see, just forty paces from the top of the col, were the barrels of six Chasseur carbines and they were pointed at me. I had stumbled into the camp of a French patrol. The Sergeant said, "We have a juicy treat to take back to the regiment. Brigadier, secure his weapons. If he moves his hand towards his gun then shoot him."

He did not know I spoke French and I did not enlighten him. I raised my hands cursing myself as I did so. I was slipping. The woodsmoke I had smelled the previous night should have warned me to be wary. I had allowed my animals to make noises. Worse, I had spoken.

While the troopers kept their guns on me the Brigadier grabbed my sword, my pistols and then my Baker. He examined it. The first rays of the new dawn peered over the skyline. He shouted, "Hey, Sergeant, this is one of those rifles used by the Goddams!"

"Let me see his face." He strode over and, taking the Baker from the Brigadier looked closely at me and then my horse. Cavalrymen know horses. He began to laugh, "Boys, we have dropped lucky here. Do you know who this is?" Without waiting for a reply, he said, "This is the English Major who killed Major Laisse's nephew in Portugal. There is a reward for him. We will treat him with kid gloves but watch him. He is tricky and he speaks French like a Parisian!" I had been recognised and escape was now a remote possibility.

My hands were tied before me. They were well tied but it was a figure of eight the Brigadier used and I was able to hold the reins. This was a disaster. To fall into French hands was bad enough but to fall into the hands of a Frenchman who was also an enemy meant that my chances of escape were minimal. The Chasseurs were in no hurry to move. I guessed they did not want to risk riding in poor light. I was unfortunate to have ridden into their camp. The Brigadier rode next to me and a trooper led Goldie. These were veterans and knew their business. Each time we came close to a stand of scrubby trees or bushes the Sergeant sent a trooper ahead to investigate. He only began to relax when he saw the road ahead. It was a mile away and there was nowhere for us to be ambushed. In fact, the ground had been completely cleared of bushes and trees. It was so flat that it looked to have been swept. The only cover was four hundred yards up the slope where there was a large rock.

Suddenly, even as I watched the rock, I saw a figure rise and raise a musket high above his head. It was a guerrilla. The Sergeant and the other troopers all stared in that direction.

The Sergeant said, "What is he doing? Signalling?"

I sensed, rather than saw Juan and the rest of his guerrillas rise from the holes they had dug in the ground and attack the horsemen. I watched the Brigadier as he began to pull his pistol out, I did the only thing I could do, I launched myself from the saddle. Putting my arms around his neck we both fell to the ground. The Chasseur's horse galloped off. As we fell, I landed heavily below him but I had the ropes around his neck. I wrapped my feet around his legs and pulled hard. He wriggled but I held him tightly around the neck. This was a fight to the death. Unless I could kill him then he would kill me. The guerrillas had taken the Chasseurs by complete surprise. I heard screams and shouts. I heard the clash of steel. I could see nothing for the Brigadier's head was in my face. I pulled the rope hard against his throat. He began to choke. I heard his breath rasping. What I did not hear was a pistol. The Spanish did not want to alert any nearby patrols. I kept pulling. The Brigadier's struggles lessened. I gave one final pull and felt his neck snap. Rolling him from me, I removed my arms and stood, somewhat unsteadily.

Juan was wiping his sword on a Chasseur's tunic. He grinned at me, "Milord! It is you. We saw just the Chasseurs. We spied them last night when they camped and planned this ambush. It worked, eh? We now have horses, more swords and more carbines."

I saw that they had kept three alive. "And what will happen to them, Juan?"

He shook his head and walked over to sever my bonds, "Better that you do not ask, eh milord. And you? Why are you here?"

"I was scouting for Sir Arthur. Are there any French troops nearby? An army perhaps."

He held up three fingers, "There are three armies. They are all heading for Plasencia. One of their armies is there already. They arrived yesterday afternoon and sent out patrols. We followed this one."

I collected my weapons and mounted Donna. She had not wandered far, "Thank you for the rescue."

"Now where will you go?

"I must get back to Talavera and tell my general the news."

"That would be suicide. The roads are filled with French."

"Nonetheless I must go."

He nodded, "Miguel, take most of the men home. Keep the prisoners until I return. Sergio, come with me. We will escort this Englishman to Talavera."

He leapt on to the dead sergeant's horse. It was the best of the Chasseur's mounts and he led us due east. We rode the whole day. The only concession to the heat was that we walked our horses at noon. Juan seemed to find the shady defiles and tiny patches of woodland to give us some relief. We rarely went near to a road. As darkness approached, I wondered if we would sleep or keep marching on through the night. When the guerrilla turned to head south and east along the road, I had my answer.

He answered my unspoken question, "We will sleep, milord, but let us use the cool of the evening to cover as much ground as we can. There will be no Frenchmen out this night. They fear having their throats cut."

Again, as a concession to our horses which were weary beyond words, we walked and it was that which saved us. We heard, galloping along the road behind us, a rider. We heard him from a long way away. Juan said, "He must be French." He cocked his pistol.

I restrained him, "But he may be English. Before you open fire let me speak to him in French. If he is English and a despatch rider, he will answer me in bad French and I will know." I took out my own pistol. "If he is French then I will help you to take him."

"Very well, milord. Sergio, come with me." They headed to the drainage ditch on the other side of the road.

The hooves galloped closer. There was no moon. It was a pitch-black night. I saw the shadow that was heading down the road but, because we were still, I did not think that he would even know that my horses and I were there. It was obvious that he was alone. When he had passed the place where Juan and Sergio waited, I moved my horses across the road and said, as he jerked his horse to a halt, "Can you help me, my friend. I am a little lost?"

His voice was angry, "Out of my way, fool! I am carrying despatches from Marshal Soult!"

That was all I needed to know, holding my pistol out I said, "Then I am afraid he will never receive them. You are my prisoner." I shouted, in Spanish, "Juan, he is French!"

In answer, he drew his own pistol. Even as I raised the pistol to fire at him, and, no doubt, alert the nearest French patrol, a figure leapt upon the back of the Frenchman's horse and dragged his knife across his throat. Sergio threw the body into the ditch. He said, "And this is a much better horse."

Juan ran to the body and retrieved the man's purse, sword and pistol. I grabbed the leather despatch case. Juan was pleased, "Soon we will have a horse for every one of my men. We had better mount now and head across country. We will make camp soon."

When we made camp, we had cold rations but they were washed down with good wine taken from the Chasseurs and despatch rider. He had been a colonel. I desperately wanted to read the despatches but I dare not risk a fire. We left the camp in the middle of the night and headed for Talavera. I did not have time to read the despatches for we needed all of our eyes to keep a good watch. We descended from some rough ground and saw the road below us. I recognised the 16th Light Dragoons who were on patrol. One of their squadrons was riding along the road. Juan said, "Your men?" I nodded. "Then we will leave you here. Good luck, milord. We have helped each other, I think, and that is how it should be." He clasped my arm in a warrior's grip, then turning his horse, he and Sergio headed back up to the hills.

I turned as hooves galloped up to me. It was a sergeant and a trooper. The sergeant recognised me, "Major Matthews! Should we get after those fellows?"

"They are friends. I have despatches for the General. It is vital that I get to him!"

It was after noon when we reached Talavera. The town was asleep but not Sir Arthur. When I entered, he looked pleased to see me, "Your fellow, Sharp, was most anxious about you,

Matthews! I damned near had to clap him in irons to keep him here. Well?"

I handed him the despatches, "I took these from a Colonel last night. They are from Soult!"

He grabbed the bag, tore it open and began to read. It did not take him long, "By God, Matthews, but you are a magician." He flourished a piece of paper. "Five French Corps are converging upon us with a sixth in reserve. There are more than one hundred thousand men heading for Talavera. They mean to cut me off from Spain and destroy me. Baird!"

An aide rushed in, "Sir Arthur?"

"Send a rider to General Wilson. Tell him to get to Portugal anyway he can. All previous orders are cancelled."

Sir Rowland Hill, clearly wounded, came in, "What is amiss, Sir Arthur?"

"We are surrounded and about to be destroyed. We leave tomorrow. Matthews here can fill you in. I must ride to General Cuesta. This time I do not need you. General O'Donoju will have no choice but to translate my words exactly as I say them. We are heading back to Portugal. This fiasco has ended."

Sir Rowland shook his head as Sir Arthur left. He took in my dusty clothes, "More adventures, eh Matthews? Tell me all."

When I had finished, he said, "Well I can see what has caused the General so much concern. There are still over one thousand five hundred men in the hospital. They will have to be abandoned. You had better get some rest. I think when Sir Arthur returns, he will give us all a myriad of tasks."

I went directly to my quarters. Sharp met me outside, he had been watching for me, "Sir, you had me worried."

"I will tell you all as we pack. We leave tomorrow and that means, I think, before dawn. Tell me, have you had a chance to visit Fenwick again?"

"He left yesterday, sir. He is a tough one and the surgeon let him go."

"Good. The rest are being left here. The French will be here in days, if not hours."

"Poor sods, sir."

He was right but there was little we could do for them. The French had good surgeons and, in my experience, they respected the English. We began to pack our bags. It was a long way back to Portugal and at least two French Corps would be in striking distance of us."

Chapter 19

The road back to Portugal was long and it was torturous. We had, thanks to the French occupation of Plasencia, over three hundred miles to travel through the August heat. We were lucky that General Crauford's men had recovered and were able to act as a rearguard. The first sixty miles, which took two days to travel, were the most nerve-wracking for they were within striking range of the French columns.

I had heard that the meeting between the two allied generals was acrimonious. Sir Arthur was accused of abandoning the Spanish. The Spanish marched with us as far as Arzobispo. There was a bridge there and General Cuesta hoped to defeat Soult's Corps at the river junction. He outnumbered the French but I was not hopeful. The single action by the El Rey regiment was an oasis in a desert of incompetence. However, once we had passed the bridge, we knew that pursuit by the French would be unlikely to catch us. Even if the Spanish lost the bridge and town, it would take Soult some time to negotiate it.

We were three days beyond Arzobispo when the news of the twin disasters reached us. General Venegas and his army of La Mancha was destroyed at Almonacid in the east of Spain. Three days later General Cuesta lost the battle of Arzobispo. His army was not destroyed and, although he lost over a thousand men, he was able to retire in good order.

My exploits at Talavera meant that Sir Arthur's generals were happy to talk to me. I had been responsible for the two sets of despatches which had saved our army from a battle we could not have won. They thought me something of a lucky charm. Sir Rowland Hill, who had seen me close up on the battlefield was especially chatty as we headed towards the border fortress of Badajoz.

He pointed ahead to the solitary figure of Sir Arthur, "Damned lonely leading an army, Matthews! The weight of the world is on his shoulders. I must confess that I, for one, will be glad when we reach Badajoz. It means that Portugal will not be far away. I thought the mountains and passes of Portugal were hellish enough but," he waved an airy hand, as though to fan the sun, "this heat desiccates a man. You know we have lost five men already and that is when we are not under attack? This is not like Corunna, the men are not deserting, they are dying from the sun."

"And yet the French cope, Sir Rowland."

He cocked an eye at me, "You are a clever chap. I suppose France is a little more like Spain."

His aide, Major Carruthers said, "The question is, Sir Rowland, does Boney want Portugal too?"

"He might. What do you think, Matthews? Sir Arthur seems to think you know the French mind better than most. Certainly, Colonel Selkirk does."

This always made me uncomfortable. I was not lying to my new comrades but I could not tell them that I had been as close to Napoleon as I was to Sir Arthur. I decided on obfuscation. "Napoleon will not be happy that Sir Arthur has bested his marshals. Now that General Venegas has lost his army then Spain is at his mercy but he went into Portugal in the first place to punish the Portuguese for supporting Britain. However, he is in Austria."

Sir Rowland nodded, "Aye, he has trounced the Austrians at Wagram. There are just two countries now which do not bow their heads to him: Britain and Portugal."

Major Carruthers frowned, "Then he has a huge empire already. Why bother with Portugal? It is just full of rocks and mountains as far as I can see!"

I knew more than a little about the Emperor, "His title, Major, is Emperor. He has yet to lose a major battle as Emperor. He chased Sir John and the British out of Portugal. He sees Portugal as being lost. He will want it returned, as he sees it, to the Imperial fold."

"Then he will return?"

"Perhaps, Sir Rowland, but the one thing in Sir Arthur's favour is that the marshal who now commands in Spain, Soult, was defeated at Oporto by Sir Arthur. Victor and Jourdan were beaten at Talavera; they retreated and we held the field. Their confidence will be low. I think Sir Arthur has time to have more men sent from England and build defences. When the French come they will want a huge army to ensure that they defeat him this time."

Sir Rowland snorted, "The debacle at Walcheren means that there will be fewer men available to us."

"We have the Portuguese, Sir Rowland. I think they are a better soldier than the Spanish or, more likely, they are better led."

The general looked at me, "What do you mean, sir?"

"The Portuguese are brigaded with us, sir. General Beresford commands their army. They fight like we do. The Spanish are good soldiers. I met many guerrillas and they are brave and resourceful. However, they are poorly led. If they had been well led would two thousand of them have fled in the face of a regiment of Dragoons?"

"Interesting, Matthews. I can see why Sir Arthur holds you in such high esteem. If you were the general of this army, what would you do?"

"The French will come again. Napoleon will appoint someone who has yet to be defeated by Sir Arthur. He has many young generals who are eager to catch the Emperor's eye. Until we are reinforced then we have to defend. I would defend the area around Lisbon. General Wellesley could make it a fortress. Look at the problems we had in friendly territory. We could not get supplies and our men went hungry. We are marching an army of skeletons back to Portugal. There, at least, they will be well fed. We build up the army and when we are stronger then Sir Arthur is the man to defeat the French." I shook my head, "That is unless he has accidents like the ravine which destroyed his cavalry or reckless charges such as those made by the Guards."

"Aye, you are right there. But for those two mishaps, we would have lost few men! That is our task, Matthews. The senior officers must impress upon this army that discipline will win the war!"

We rested for two days when we reached Badajoz. Sir Arthur invited me to dine with his senior officers in the fortress. It was cooler in the thick-walled castle, after the heat of the road and we ate at a table with a cloth laid upon it. We had well-prepared food served upon fine plates. It felt like a different world from the one we had endured for most of the summer.

Sir Arthur pointed at me while we waited for the main course to be served, "I hear, Matthews, that you have an idea how we can stop Boney!"

I glanced at Sir Rowland, who shrugged, "Sir, I am a lowly Major. What do I know?"

"A damn sight more than some officers who bought regiments." I saw some of the senior officers squirm uncomfortably. The comment was too close to home. "Out with it. I am in need of a diversion!"

"Well sir, we do not have enough men to guard the borders of Portugal. By the time the French are ready to come once more, it will be winter. Those of us who retreated, just a year ago, to Corunna, know that the roads in Portugal can be almost impassable. There are two places to hold up the French, at the Douro and north of Lisbon. The problem with the Douro is that the French could take the route we are taking and simply outflank us and our troops would be thinly spread. The land north of Lisbon is mountainous and full of passes. A small number of troops could block those passes. Frontal assaults are hard. The French would have no fodder for their horses. As a cavalryman, I can tell you, sir, that seeking fodder constantly occupies our minds."

The main course arrived and it was as though the General had not heard a word I had said. He ate silently while his senior officers discussed my idea. When the plates were taken away he leaned forward and pointed at me again, "And have you a particular place in mind, Matthews?"

I sighed. I had hoped my interrogation was at an end. "There is a fortress at Torres Vedras. It has proved crucial before. It dominates the main road to Lisbon, sir. I know it is a starting point. I am no engineer. I am a cavalryman and I have to tell you that cavalry would be stopped by the fortress and if there were smaller fortresses alongside then we might be able to slow down the French."

"Hmn. Then let us hope that Colonel Selkirk can discover who the French will send and when."

Sir John Sherbrooke said, "Just as we have to rebuild, Sir Arthur, so will the French. If they had not had to fight in Austria then I would have feared that Bonaparte would be here sooner rather than later. I believe we have a good six months to recover."

"And I believe you are right." He stood, "Gentlemen I give you a toast, the King and confusion to his enemies!"

"The King and confusion to his enemies."

The next day Sir Arthur detached a squadron of the 16th Light Dragoons and with his senior engineer, Colonel Richard Fletcher, he took Sharp and I away from the army to the fortress of Torres Vedras. It took some time to reach the fortress and we spent four days assessing the potential of the site. You have a good eye, Matthews but, as you said the other night, you are a cavalryman. Colonel Fletcher, what can you do with it?"

"It strikes me, Sir Arthur, that we could build a string of small forts radiating to the coast and to the mountains. With a garrison of, say two hundred men to each fort and a pair of guns then an enemy would bleed to death on the defences."

"Good, then you and your engineers remain here and draw up plans. Bring them to Lisbon when you are done."

With that, we left with our escort. Riding south Sir Arthur confided in me that he hoped the French would give him time to build his defences. "It will take us at least six months, Matthews, to build a half decent line of defence and bring more men over from England. In a perfect world, we would have nine months. It all depends upon Bonaparte. How quickly will he react?"

"I concur with Sir Rowland, sir. The Emperor will enjoy the pomp and ceremony of conquering Austria. By the time he has done, it will be winter and Paris is a long way from Lisbon. I believe that you will have your six months."

"And you, Matthews? What of you? Would you go back to your regiment?"

"I confess that I miss them but I suspect they are more likely to be sent here, to Portugal, than I am to be sent home."

"Very astute of you. And now we await Colonel Selkirk. I will be happier when I receive his intelligence."

"If you do not mind me asking, Sir Arthur, where exactly is he?"

He laughed, "You, of all people should know the answer to that! He is behind enemy lines. Perhaps he is even in Paris. He is a gifted actor, you know. Another David Garrick perhaps."

I had never seen the famous actor. He was dead before I was born but I knew he cast a long shadow and was the standard by which all actors were measured.

"Colonel Selkirk will wheedle out the information I need to know. Knowing what your enemy is thinking is most of the battle. The rest is largely luck."

"And the very last part, Sir Arthur?"

"Why skill, Matthews. Boney has it and so do I."

When we reached Lisbon Sharp and I were dismissed. The town was packed. There were ships arriving with the materiel of war and the very same ships were being used to take the wounded home. I discovered that the three from the 23rd had all returned to England and for that I was happy. I met Colonel Hawker and it was he who gave me the good news. The 23rd had been billeted outside of the city with the rest of the cavalry. Soon they would be taken to winter quarters further north where there was grazing. He was busy going over lists of casualties with his adjutant and the Regimental Sergeant Major. I saw that his arm was still in a sling. He had been wounded by a shell in the charge but his rank meant that he did not have to return to England to prove that he was still fit for duty. He saw my arrival as a welcome diversion from paperwork.

"Matthews, let us take a walk by the horse lines."

I turned to my sergeant, "Sergeant Sharp, you may return to our quarters. I shall be safe enough."

"Are you certain, sir? You tend to have mishaps when I am not there to watch you."

Colonel Hawker laughed, "Impertinent fellow, what?"

I laughed, "But truthful, sir. I will be fine, Sharp. We are in Lisbon and not in the mountains of Spain."

When we reached the horse lines, he took an apple from his jacket for his horse, "It was deeply upsetting to see so many horses destroyed, Matthews."

"And the men too, sir."

"True and I not denigrating the sacrifice those chaps made but they chose the life of a soldier. These poor beasts did not." He waved a hand down the line of horses. "We have less than two hundred and twenty horses fit for duty. When the new draft reaches us from home then the troopers and officers will bring over more horses than the men to ride them. A sobering thought."

"Can you fill the ranks, sir?"

"Not sure! We can replace the officers. There is a line of chaps desperate to buy a commission in a light dragoon regiment. The ladies love the dash and uniform. The non-commissioned officers we can promote. That Sergeant Parkinson will be the new Troop Sergeant when he and Captain Minchin return to active duty. It is a nonsense that they have to return to England to prove themselves to a bunch of civilians who wouldn't know one end of a sword from the other but that is how it works." He leaned over, "You are a chap in the know. Are we likely to fight again soon?"

I did not like to be indiscreet but it would soon be common knowledge that we were building defences. There seemed no harm in allaying the Colonel's fears. "I believe that you will have the winter to bring the regiment up to full strength and to train them for Iberian warfare." In truth, the 23rd was in no condition to do anything other than escort a convoy. It had lost many officers and the heart of its NCO's.

My answer seemed to reassure the Colonel, "Good. When we get to our new quarters you and your fellow must dine with us. The survivors of the charge at Talavera hold you in high regard, Major."

"And I them!"

Mounting Donna, I decided to go the mare's namesake, Donna Maria d'Alvarez. I knew that the Portuguese noblewoman would watch over the royal palace until the King and Queen returned. She was a lady who understood duty. When I arrived, despite the heat, she, her women and her gardeners were toiling in the gardens. The hot weather had burned some leaves and they were busy tidying the plants. I saw that her man Giorgio still kept a watch with his musket. It was reassuring. She beamed when she saw me, "Robbie! What a delight!" She clapped her hands. She turned to her ladies, "You have all been complaining of the heat. Thanks to this fine cavalier we will go indoors and enjoy the cool of the palace. Juanita, chilled wine, if you please. Come, Robbie, I need to know all. Lisbon is now a backwater!"

There was a bowl of water and a towel incongruously placed on a magnificent table in the entrance to the royal palace. Donna

Maria smiled when she saw my reaction, "A necessity, Robbie. We have few gardeners and this means we do not carry dirt through the palace. We can ill afford the cleaners we use as it is."

After we had washed, she led me outside to an enclosed courtyard which was shaded by the palace. There were lemon trees as well as pots of rosemary and thyme. It was fragrant and cool. I saw that there was a fountain but it was not working. We sat in two wicker chairs and Juanita brought the wine. "Major, will you be staying for dinner?"

I had not planned on doing so but I enjoyed the mature lady's company. "If it is not too much trouble."

She laughed, "Having a handsome young cavalier at my table is no trouble I can assure you of that." She waved a hand at Juanita, "Tell the cook I want to be impressed!"

The afternoon and early evening raced by as I recounted the campaign. She was engrossed. I had still not finished when I went to wash for dinner. Donna Maria d'Alvarez went to change and her chief lady, Juanita, entertained me. "You know, Major, my lady sees you as a surrogate son. She lives the war through your exploits. We entertain little these days but, when we do, she regales her guests with tales of your adventures."

"I am flattered. She is a delightful lady and I am happy that she considers me her friend."

Juanita lowered her voice, "And as her friend can I ask that you ask her to rest more and work less. Her doctor fears that she toils too hard and it is not good for her heart."

"She has been unwell?"

"She is a lady of a certain age, Major, what do you think?"

"Then I will ask her although why she should heed me, I do not know."

Donna Maria had made a real effort and she had dressed as though I was important. The cook, too, had worked hard to produce a magnificent meal. I chose the interlude between the main course and the dessert to broach the subject of her health.

"I understand that you have been unwell, Donna Maria?"

She scowled in the direction of the kitchen, "That Juanita has been indiscreet. It is nothing. I blame the summer heat which was followed by two days of fog. I am well now."

"You need not work so hard to maintain the grounds. I can have some of Sir Arthur's men come to work for you. They would be happy to do so."

"Really? They would do that?"

"My lady, they are rough soldiers and the opportunity to work in such a palace and be close to a lady like you and your ladies would not be onerous." I was thinking of the 23rd. If I was held in such high regard then why not use that to the advantage of my friend?

"Then I will take you up on your offer."

The dessert arrived. It was a wonderfully decorated cake. When I tasted it, I knew that it had been expensive to make for it had more sugar than I had tasted in a single dish before. Sugar was expensive! While we ate our cheese and sipped port, she confided more in me.

"I confess that I have found this year difficult. One of my dearest friends, one of King Pedro's officials who remained behind, died." She shook her head, "He was killed, murdered!"

The cheese and the port were delicious and I was somewhat distracted. I merely nodded.

"Don Pedro de Costa was a fine gentleman but he was foolish. He took up with a stunning beauty and it was she did for him."

The Black Widow. I remembered now Colonel Selkirk had told me that it had been a Portuguese official who had been killed. I could not help my reaction. I paused with a piece of cheese in mid-air.

"Robbie, what do you know of this? It happened while you were in Spain and it was not reported in the newspapers."

I put down the cheese and emptied the port. Her manservant refilled it and Donna Maria said, "Leave us, Giorgio. We will serve ourselves." He stared at Donna Maria, "Go, I am more than capable of pouring the wine." When he had left us, she said, "Speak. We are alone."

I owed it to her to speak the truth but it was a somewhat sanitized truth. I kept the more carnal aspects from her. When I had finished and emptied my glass, she came over to refill it. She kissed the top of my head, "There is more than you are telling me for you fear offending an old lady. I can fill in the gaps. I was young once." She sat down. "Then this is more serious than I thought. Don Pedro had valuable items stolen and I had this Black Widow down as an opportunist thief who happened to murder. Now I can see that the theft was to disguise her true purpose."

"Or perhaps to continue to fund her activities."

"Perhaps. So, the French are behind this. Suddenly, this all makes sense and certain events become clearer. I had a reason to hate this woman and now it is doubled. You must be careful Robbie. From what you say, your life is now in danger too."

"She has fled Lisbon. She will be far from here. It is other men's lives which will be in danger."

"Nonetheless you must be careful."

"As should you. You met this woman?"

"Three times," she nodded.

"And you knew her victim. Do others know it was she who did the deed?"

"They did but…"

"Go on…"

"I was the only one invited to dine with them. He kept her hidden; he told me that she requested that he do so for her reputation." She shook her head, "Reputation! Now I see why. I believe I was invited to dine with them because I keep watch on the royal palace. Don Pedro wrote regular reports for the King and Queen. Our dinners were a way of keeping them informed."

"Then you are in danger. It is a good job you have a bodyguard, Giorgio looks to be handy."

"He is. He has shown himself to be resourceful and he is like a rock."

"Then use him!"

She nodded, "I will and now you must leave. It is late and you are alone. You have not your Sergeant Sharp with you."

"No, I have not. I will return, my lady, for I am here with Sir Arthur. I am part of the army which will keep Portugal safe."

"Good! Then I feel safer already!"

When I left, I knew that I was being followed. The last two glasses of port had dulled my senses and it took me a few streets to realise it, however. Our quarters were in a quiet area and the last thing I needed to do was to put myself somewhere quiet. Instead of turning left I turned right and headed down to the livelier area in the centre. I was sobering up rapidly. I would head for the places people drank. There were more than ten thousand British soldiers in Lisbon at the moment. Soon they would be dispersed to winter camps but, for the moment, the presence of so many British soldiers might be my salvation. Whoever followed me was good. I knew they were there but when I turned, I saw no one behind out of the ordinary. I did not have my sword but, in my boots, I had a stiletto and a dagger.

Chapter 20

I hurried as I saw lights ahead. Those following me were still keeping a discreet distance. As I neared the bars and eating houses, I heard the noise of soldiers drinking. Unfortunately, the first ones I saw were Portuguese. Soldiers tended to drink by nationality. One area of bars would cater to one nationality. It seemed to me that this was a Portuguese quarter. I knew there was another section with bars but it was through an alley. I would have a hundred paces to negotiate before I reached another brightly lit area. A gaggle of Portuguese light horsemen rose as I neared them and I used the fact that they filled the space behind me to hurry on and duck down the alleyway. I ran. Most of the alleyways backed on to businesses. They had a habit of discarding their detritus in the alley. Some broken furniture was my undoing.

I tripped over a damaged chair and fell sprawling to the cobbles and, although I rose quickly, I heard footsteps pounding behind me. From the sound, there was more than one of them and that explained how they had been able to follow me. I had hurt my knee and while I could run it off until I did it would slow me. I saw the end of the alleyway and hope rose. Then something hit me on the back of the head. I fell once more. Even as I fell, I knew that they had thrown something at me. My guess was a marlin spike. I was slower to rise. The feet closed and I smelled the sweat and stink of my would-be killers. I felt a blade tear through my uniform and into my left shoulder. It was a hurried blow and the killer had acted too hastily; it was not a mortal strike. I drew my dagger, as I rose, and slashed before me. The dagger connected with the hand of one of them.

Pressing my back into the alley wall I viewed my two assailants. Both were swarthy and had the look of sailors. That explained the marlin spike. The one with the bloodied left hand held a short sailor's sword in his right. That was what had stabbed me. The other had a wickedly curved dagger. I was lucky in that the strike from behind had not touched a bone nor struck an artery. I was bleeding but it was not a flood. I risked reaching down for my stiletto. The one with the sword lunged. I was a swordsman and whilst I only held a dagger, I would use it like a sword. I flicked the blade away and drew my stiletto. It was little enough but I had no choice. The two men were here to kill me.

The one with the curved dagger slashed at me. It was how you used such a blade. I could not get out of the way fast enough for my back was against a wall and although I stopped it cutting deeply, the edge slashed across my chest. My uniform bore the brunt of the attack but the razor-sharp weapon scored a line across my flesh. I knew the longer we fought the more chance they had of killing me. I had to take a risk. I lunged at the knife man's eye. The stiletto was such a narrow blade, almost like a sailor's bodkin, that he must have thought it was just my hand which came towards him for I was fast and it would have been a blur. The point went into his eye and then his skull. He sank at my feet. The man with the sword was already lunging at me and I tried to deflect it. The sword did not tear into my guts as the killer intended but it did pierce my right side and this time, I felt blood gush. I was a dead man.

"Oy, what is going on?" A shadow appeared at the end of the alley. "Hey lads, there is an officer here being robbed. Let's get the bastard!"

The would-be killer ran. I lunged with my stiletto as he passed me and was rewarded by a shout as I stabbed him in the side. I sank to the floor and closed my eyes.

"It's Major Matthews! Quick, get him into the light!" Opening my eyes, I saw that it was Trooper Harris of the 23rd. With him were two other troopers. They carried me into the light. Harris shouted, "Go and fetch the regimental doctor. I saw him in the bar around the corner with Lieutenant Frayn."

"Right. Is he dead?"

"You dozy bugger! Would I need a doctor if he had croaked? Sorry, sir. Grab me a cloth. Use the shirt off that other murdering bastard!"

I could feel myself losing consciousness but I could do little about it.

"Sir, stay with me. Joe fetch me the brandy off the table! It is rough as but it might help until the sawbones gets here!"

When the brandy was poured over the wound, I felt such excruciating pain that I opened my eyes and shouted out. Harris laughed, "Well it is good for something." I felt him press material against my most serious wound, the one in my side.

My voice was weak, "Harris, I have also been stabbed in the back and the shoulder. Not as bad as this one but the doctor ought to know."

He shook his head, "Sir, you are a wonder. Don't you worry. We won't let the hero of the ravine die in a Lisbon back alley."

I was about to answer when everything went black. I passed out.

When I awoke, I was in hospital. I saw the doctor from the 23rd standing above me. "Ah, you are awake. You lost a considerable amount of blood. I think you will survive, Major, but you have been lucky."

My eyes adjusted to the dim lighting. "Harris?"

"Trooper Harris and the rest of the men from the 23rd did not wish to risk the wrath of Sir Arthur. There is a curfew for enlisted men you know. They have returned to the encampment."

I nodded and my head hurt. I must have banged it when I passed out.

I heard a voice from behind me, "Don't worry, sir. I will keep my eye on you."

"Sergeant Sharp!"

He appeared from the shadows, "Aye sir. I was right. I can't let you out alone. Tonight, was the last time I do so!"

I nodded, weakly. "You may be right, Sharp. Any clues about my killer?"

"English, sir."

"How do you know?"

"Tattoos, sir. He was a sailor and the tattoos are in English." Sharp rubbed his chin, "I suppose he could have been American but Harris reckoned he was English."

I nodded, "They did well."

"I slipped them a guinea each, sir. I thought you would have wanted me to."

"Of course."

The doctor put on his tunic, "Now Sergeant, your officer needs to have some rest. If he continues to improve then he can be allowed home in a day or so."

"Right sir, I will be happier when I have him under our roof. It is safer that way."

The doctor must have realised that Sharp wished to speak with me and stood, "Ten more minutes, Sergeant, and then he sleeps."

"Yes, sir, you have my word."

When we were alone, he said, "This has all the hallmarks of the Black Widow, sir."

"But she must have left Portugal!"

"I don't think so. When you didn't return, I went to the harbour and asked questions. She is an attractive woman and people would remember her. She didn't take ship after the murder of that official. If she didn't leave by sea how did she get out of Portugal? I think she has gone to ground here in Lisbon. After we spoke to Colonel Selkirk and Lieutenant Frayn she has been on my mind. I sort of obsessed about her. She nearly did for you, sir, in London, and there are few men got as close as she did. The way I thought about it was this. She is the best at what she does and she failed with you. It wouldn't sit right with her, would it, sir? I thought I bet she hasn't left and I was right. I would have told you when you came home but you didn't." I heard the underlying criticism, "No-one remembered her boarding ship. I met some lads just back from Oporto and none of them recollected her being there and then one lad, a young sailor off the *'Maid of Harwich'* said he had seen her two days ago up near the palace. He remembered her as being pretty. No ships have left since then. The bitch, pardon my French sir, is still here,"

Sharp had done well. He had done better than I had. Had she been scouting out the palace to see if I was there? That would explain the two killers she had left there. Whatever the doctor had given me affected my judgement. I could not think clearly.

Sharp recognised it and said, "You get your head down, sir. I will sleep here, by the door. If anyone wants to get in, they will have to go over me."

"Sharp, I ..."

"No arguments, sir. From what I have seen so far in Spain, Sir Arthur and the army needs you. A couple of nights on the floor will do me no harm."

I could not argue for fatigue defeated me and I fell asleep. I slept well, considering the wounds I had suffered. The one in my side had missed vital organs by a finger. The doctor, who was a good surgeon, had stitched the wound but, when he visited the next morning, he counselled me against violent movements.

"I have sent word to Sir Arthur that you need a month of bed rest. If I had my way then you would stay here in the hospital but beds are at a premium and the 23rd is moving up country. You are a brave man and a tough man, Major, but do not push your luck. A man is only born with so much of it and it seems to me that last night you used more than your fair share."

"I promise you, sir, that I will rest. I have Sharp as my nurse," I laughed, "and, apparently, as my mother too. I will obey him."

"Good! I will tell Colonel Hawker. He will be pleased to hear it."

Sharp brought my best uniform and arranged for four men to carry me to our home in a sedan chair. Dressing was hard and I was unable to do so without assistance. It told me how close I had come to death. It was embarrassing but necessary. Sharp had Harris and a couple of the troopers to act as my escort. The house we had taken was in a quieter area of Lisbon. The family had gone to Brazil with the royal family and the agent had been more than happy to rent it for a peppercorn rent to an English officer. Now, as we approached it, I wondered if this had been a mistake. It was a quiet area; perhaps too quiet!

Once inside the three troopers checked the grounds and secured the rear gate. Someone could climb in but it would not be easy. Once inside Sharp locked and barred the back door. He gave them a bottle of brandy each for their trouble and they headed back to the camp. Sharp seated me in a comfortable chair.

"Now then, sir, we can't have you traipsing up and down the stairs. The doctor was quite clear about movement. You move as little as possible."

"At the moment, Sharp, I feel as weak as a baby and could not stir even if I wished to."

"Good. Then I will make you up a bed here, sir." He pointed to the sofa which looked comfortable enough. Heaven knows I had slept on rocks before now.

I sat in the chair and I dozed. I was not sure if the doctor had given me a draught of something or if I was just weak from the wounds. I knew that the food I had eaten in the hospital had been poor even by the standards of the army. My eyes closed involuntarily.

As he made up the bed Sharp hummed a song. I knew that I was lucky to have him as my sergeant servant. When he had done, he stepped back to admire his handiwork. "There, my old mother would be proud of that."

His words made me open my eyes. "A fine piece of work. I believe I am ready to test it."

"Not yet, sir. The doctor is a fine surgeon but he does not know much about recovering from wounds. You need to build up your strength. On my way to pick you up today, I called at the butchers in the town. My Portuguese is getting better although it helped that I could just point at things I didn't know the name for. I bought some beef as well as heart, liver and kidneys. They have a proper marble slab in the pantry. It will keep the meat for a day or so, even in this heat. We have enough food to last for three days and then I will have to go shopping again."

"I am not sure I could eat, Sharp. I feel so sleepy."

"You will eat sir and that is your nurse's orders! The matron in the hospital might have been a dragon but she is nothing compared with me. I will talk to you while I am cooking, you need to stay awake."

His voice came in drifts as he went, first to the pantry, to bring the kidneys, liver, ham and eggs and then to the kitchen to cook. After each action, he came to the door of my room, which lay off the dining room, to talk.

"I had one of the troopers call at Donna Maria's. He told her what had happened."

"You should not have worried her."

"I did not wish to risk her wrath, sir. She would have fretted when you didn't call to see her. Hang on, sir, there is a pan needs my attention." He scurried off.

He was right of course. She would have wondered why I had not called upon her again.

"Anyhow, she seemed agitated according to Ralph Wilson. She said to tell you not to worry. She would sort things out. Almost ready!" He disappeared again and I became worried. What did she mean, 'sort things out'? I should never have told her about the Black Widow. That she was behind this was crystal clear to me. Hiring English sailors was something that she would do. She seemed to have the ability to hide in plain sight.

Sharp returned a short while later with a tray laden with food. There were strips of fried ham, fried liver and devilled kidneys. There were two fried eggs and fresh bread. He put the tray on a small table. "There, you are, sir. You tuck into that. I will make you a pot of coffee. There was no tea in the pantry and I can't leave you to find some in Lisbon. I am afraid it will be coffee for a while."

The smell of the fried ham was enough to whet my appetite and despite my misgivings, I was able to wolf it all down and then wash it down with coffee. The coffee woke me and I decided to confide in Sharp about my fears for Donna Maria.

"I fear that this is the work of the Black Widow, Sharp. Donna Maria knows the woman and she may try to seek her out."

"I agree that it seems like the work of that black-hearted murderess but how can Donna Maria find her? She is an old lady."

"And a resourceful one. Her chap, Giorgio, is my only hope. He is a big strong chap. Donna Maria is not reckless. She would have taken him with her. Still, I would be happier if she was warned to steer clear of our nemesis."

"Well, I am not leaving you, sir. As much as I like the old lady, you are my officer and I am not having you killed on my watch."

"We are safe enough, Sharp. The door can be locked from the inside. If you went out, I could lock it behind you."

"You are not strong enough, sir. No arguments. Until I have to go out, for food and the like, we are prisoners here. Colonel Hawker was insistent. He spoke with Sir Arthur who was also most concerned. The General has given you a month off to recuperate. So, you see, sir, this is an order!"

I was too weak to argue. Sharp put me on my temporary bed and soon I succumbed to sleep. I must have slept until the late afternoon. Sharp had closed the curtains which kept the room cooler. I awoke and I was stiff. Despite the chair's padding the wound in my back, although minor, was painful. I groaned as I rose. Sharp appeared from the dining room.

"Sir?"

"Just a little stiff, Sharp, and I need to use the toilet. I shall use the outhouse." His face told me he was not happy. "If you think I am going to use that," I pointed to the china pot, "then I have to say I would reduce you to the ranks as a punishment."

He grinned, "Right then sir, lean on me. I have been making you a walking stick but it is not finished yet. Until it is you will have to use me."

Pain coursed through my body as I stood. Whichever arm I used would cause me pain, I had been stabbed in the left shoulder as well as my right side. The act of raising my right arm was impossible and so I used my left. I prayed I would not rip out stitches. Sharp had to lean me against the passageway wall as he unbarred and locked the back door. I went to the outhouse. Even though it was early evening, after the cool of the house the wall of heat hit me like a sledgehammer. I was sweating by the time I had finished and returned to my bed. That simple act told me that Sharp was right. I could not fend for myself. Time had no meaning in our little fortress. We ate late and then slept. When I awoke it was almost ten o'clock in the morning. I had never slept so late in my life but I felt better. Sharp examined my dressings and seemed satisfied. He sniffed them, "No smell of badness, sir. That is good!" He allowed me to leave my bed and sit on my chair. It was more comfortable.

In the middle of the afternoon, there was a knock on the door. Sharp took no chances. He cocked a pistol. I smiled. A killer would not announce himself. It was Colonel Hawker, Captain Minchin and Troop Sergeant Parkinson who presented themselves. I heard Colonel Hawker say, "A fine welcome, Sergeant. Do you always greet guests with a loaded pistol?"

"Sorry, sir. Can't take chances. Sir, it is Colonel Hawker with Captain Minchin and Troop Sergeant Parkinson."

I saw that the Colonel was now without a sling. I tried to stand to salute, "None of that nonsense, Matthews. These two chaps have just returned from England and they are keen to see you. I also have news for you."

I nodded, "You are all welcome and are you both recovered?"

Captain Minchin nodded, "Yes sir. We both have a limp but it does not impair us. There was no reason for us to sail all the way to England to be told we were fit for duty!"

Colonel Hawker shook his head, "There was, Captain Minchin, for you were able to acquire some fine remounts. You are a senior captain now."

The Troop Sergeant said, "Aye sir and it meant we could take Joe Fenwick to your estate. Rafe Jenkins is a good man. He made Joe welcome. He set him up in the new stable. Your builder had just finished it. You will have a fine home when it is all done. Joe wanted us to tell you how much he appreciates what you have done for him. You saved his life and then gave him a new life. That is very Christian."

"You two saved his life."

The Colonel said, "Let us not get bogged down in the past. As I said, Major, I have news. I think, thanks to the fiasco at Walcheren, the King has decided to make much of the battle of Talavera. The Gazette now lauds it as the beginning of the end for Bonaparte."

"We know that is not true, sir."

"Quite but it makes those at home feel better and Parliament has agreed for more men to be sent to us. Sir Arthur is now Viscount Wellington of Talavera and of Wellington, in the County of Somerset, with the subsidiary title of Baron Douro of Wellesley. Quite a mouthful eh?"

"He deserves the title, sir. We both know that he has the beating of the French."

"Quite. And there is something else, a little closer to home, as you might say. Your friend, Donna Maria and her servant chap, George or something, have disappeared."

I looked at Sharp. He shrugged, "If she is with Giorgio, she will be alright, sir. Besides there wasn't much you could have done about it was there?"

The Colonel said, "Am I missing something here?"

I nodded, "You remember that party where we first met?"

He laughed and said, "A little but they had a damned fine Madeira as I recall."

"Do you remember a Mrs Turner? She was a stunning beauty."

"By George, I do."

I said, flatly, "She is a murderess. You remember, Captain Minchin, that Lieutenant Frayn spoke of such a woman?"

"I do recall the conversation. He was quite taken with her."

"She murdered a Portuguese official. Donna Maria was trying to find her. I was in my cups and my tongue was too loose. I fear I may have doomed that poor woman."

Colonel Hawker could see that I was becoming agitated, "Major, your task is to get well. The regiment does not move out for three days. We have a regiment which owes a great deal to you. They can search Lisbon for this woman and for Donna Maria d'Alvarez. You can leave it with me! Come, gentlemen. We have work to do."

When they had gone, I said, "They can do no good, Sharp. We both know that."

"True, sir, but you are not fit enough and if she is loose in Lisbon then I am not leaving you alone. Besides if there are troopers searching for her she will have to go to ground, at the very least." He hesitated, "Sir, I know the Colonel meant well but if anyone was looking for you then all they had to do was to follow them here. The house may now be watched."

"And I had already thought of that, Sergeant. Don't you think that a sedan chair would be easier to follow? If the Black Widow had men watching for me then they know where I am."

He stood, "Right then, sir. Let's do something about it." He disappeared and returned with an arsenal. He handed me my stiletto, dagger and sword. "You can keep these about you, sir." He placed a primed pistol on the table next to my bed and a second one on the side table close to my chair. "They are for you." He disappeared and returned with the Baker rifles. He placed one by the front door and hurried up the stairs. Finally, he put two pistols in holsters about his waist. After clipping on his sword, he smiled, "Anyone who breaks in is going to get a rude shock, sir."

I could not settle for the rest of the day. Donna Maria was in danger and it was my fault. I did not sleep well that night. My repose was not helped by the itch in the wound across my chest. I knew that scratching would not help. I was awake early. Sharp, despite my pleas, refused to leave the house to search for Donna Maria. When there was a knock on the door, late in the afternoon, Sharp admitted Lieutenant Frayn and a newly promoted Corporal Harris.

"The colonel sent us, sir, to reassure you that we have not left a stone unturned. The regiment is combing Lisbon. He has posted four men to watch the palace, sir. That lady, Juanita, she is really upset. We have seen no sign of Donna Maria d'Alvarez nor Mrs Castle." He suddenly stopped, "That is not her name is it, sir?"

"No one knows her real name, Lieutenant. You had a lucky escape."

"I can see that now, sir."

I turned to Corporal Harris, "And I never got the opportunity to thank you properly, Harris."

"No need to, sir. You are a good officer." He tapped his stripes, "Besides, sir, the Colonel promoted me for what I did. Never thought that having to take a leak might result in promotion!"

We all laughed.

The Lieutenant stood. "Anyway, sir, we just thought we would come and tell you that we are all doing what we can. You rest. The doctor told me that you came within the width of a blade of death!"

"Thank you, Lieutenant."

Sharp seemed reassured, "There you are, sir. The lads will find her."

"Yes, Sergeant, but will it be dead or alive?"

We ate although the food tasted like sawdust. I had been the cause of Donna Maria's disappearance and I was the one who could do nothing about it. Sharp cleared away the dishes and washed them up. I drank a port fortified with brandy. It eased the pain and was less likely to make me sleep than the doctor's draughts which knocked me out almost instantly. The last thing I needed was to descend into the land of dreams. It had become a world of nightmares.

Suddenly there was an urgent rattle on the door. Sharp ran through to answer it and he was holding a loaded and primed pistol. The door was down a passageway and I could not see it but I heard voices. They were indistinct. One was Portuguese and I heard Sharp's reply. Then he shouted, in English, "Sir, there is someone who calls himself Giorgio. He says he has to speak with you."

"Fetch him in," I lifted and cocked a pistol, "I am armed. If he is an assassin the two of us should be able to deal with him." I levelled my pistol at the passageway. When they emerged into the light, Sharp's pistol in his back, I saw that it was, indeed, Giorgio. He looked to have been in the wars. I lowered the pistol.

He dropped to his knees, "Major, thank God I have found you. Donna Maria is in grave danger. She is hiding. She asked me to get you to come to her."

Sharp said, "The Major is wounded. He is going nowhere!"

"What happened to her, Giorgio? Where have you been?"

"We sought the woman who had the minister killed. There were men waiting. We fought and I killed one. We ran to the house of my brother. It is by the port. They were watching it and I only managed to slip out a short while ago. I ran here. I think I lost them. I beg of you to come."

Sharp spoke in English. "I don't like this, sir. It does not smell right."

"Please Major, a lady's life is at stake!"

His words pricked my guilt, "Sharp, go with him. Lock the door and take the key with you. That way you know that the door cannot be opened. Bar the shutters if you must. You must get to the lady."

He was not convinced but he was an English soldier and knew the lady. The thought of her being in need was the deciding factor. "Very well, sir, but I bar the door and you keep a loaded pistol" He turned to Giorgio and spoke in Portuguese, "And if this is a trick then you will die!"

"I swear on my mother's life that I have been sent by the lady!"

When the door was locked the click sounded ominously like the crack of doom. The house suddenly seemed to be filled with shadows which threatened my very existence. I put my watch on the table. I knew it would take up to thirty minutes to reach the Tagus and the port area. I would allow Sharp an hour, perhaps a little longer to get there and back. If he was not back by then I would know that this was a trick. Sharp was taking a bigger risk than I was. A thought suddenly filled my head. Giorgio had found the house. How? I had not told Donna Maria where we were staying. What was it the lady had told me? He had been with her for just a few months. It came to me with sudden clarity. Giorgio had been planted in the household by the Black Widow. She was a patient woman and had known that I would surface there, eventually.

I stood. It hurt but I knew that my life was in peril. I went upstairs. There were no shutters there. It took me an age and I was sweating when I reached the upstairs bedroom I had used before my wound. I peered out into the street beyond the small formal garden. The street was empty. That did not mean there was no one there. I knew how to hide in plain sight. I made my way downstairs. We had kept the back door locked and barred but what of the shutters? Had Sharp fitted them? Perhaps not for they made the kitchen dark. Once in the kitchen, I saw that he had fitted them and the door was still barred. The pistol before me, I turned. As I neared the dining room, I heard a key in the front door. My watch was still on the table. I had no way of gauging the time. However, a key had been used.

"Sharp?"

There was no answer and I entered, cautiously, first the dining room and then my sick quarters. The lights had been doused. The room was in total darkness. The primed pistol was in my hand and, as I moved towards the Baker rifle, a figure stepped out. I fired and the ball pulverised the assassin's head. I stayed stock still. If there were two of them the other would move. My hearing had been affected by the blast. If another was going to act then this would be the time to do so. I waited and I heard nothing. I moved to the body. He had used a key. Perhaps this was Giorgio and he had slain Sharp and taken his key. As I knelt over the body, I realised it was not Giorgio. This one wore the clothes of a gentleman.

Suddenly a weight fell upon my back. Even as I fell, I felt some stitches burst. The pistol tumbled from my hand. I could smell a familiar perfume. I was rolled over and the Black Widow sat on my chest. She had a stiletto in her hand. She pricked my throat with it. I saw that she had a veil across her face.

She lifted it. I saw that there were long scratch marks down her face. That explained the veil. "Robbie, you are a hard man to kill!" She leaned over and before I could do anything, she had kissed me and then bitten my lips so hard that they bled. In the scheme of things, it was nothing but it angered me and I tried to move her. Blood trickled down my neck as the tip broke the skin. "Do not struggle, Robbie, you are going to die but in my time. By now your Sergeant Sharp will have joined that Portuguese bitch in the Tagus." She stroked her scarred cheek. "I made her suffer. Who would have thought an old crone could fight so hard? She must have loved you too, but as a son, eh Robbie? Not as a lover."

"You will rot in hell, you harridan!"

"Rot in hell? Such a quaint concept for someone who has seen the horrors of war."

"Then kill me and get it over with!"

She laughed and it was the most evil sound I had ever heard, "Kill you quickly? I think not. I have all the time in the world. Your friends search the city for me, Sharp is dead and I will enjoy making you suffer. I shall mark you a little first. A cut here, a slice there. Take an eye, your nose, your ears, I..."

Two enormous hands appeared from out of the dark and, gripping her, lifted her bodily into the air. Her feet kicked and she tried to stab her assailant. It was to no avail. I heard a voice from behind me, "You are lucky, Robbie, that she took so long to do that which she intended. We would not have reached you in time otherwise." It was Colonel Selkirk!

The feet stopped moving and Angus laid down the body. "Aye, she was a tough one alright. Come, sir, let me lift you up."

His ham-like fist pulled me to my feet. The Colonel had lit the candle once more and was now using it to light his cigar. "You are a lucky fellow. Damned lucky! Angus, see to the Major's wound." The Scottish soldier ripped part of the Widow's dress and pressed it to the wound.

Just then the door burst open and Corporal Harris and Trooper Mulhern carried an obviously wounded Sharp down the passage and into the room. My trusty Sergeant looked up, "Colonel Selkirk, I never thought I would be so glad to see you. So, the bitch is dead?"

Angus said, "Aye, Sergeant, I broke her bloody neck!"

"And you, Sergeant?"

"I didn't trust that Giorgio. He led me down an alley and I remembered that was how they got you. He was quick and he managed to stab my left arm. I gutted him. These two lads found me."

"Aye, sir, the colonel kept the patrols going. We still haven't found the lady."

"Nor will you. Tell the Colonel to call off his search. She was thrown into the river. The Black Widow had her killed."

The Colonel said, "Well you two lads take Sergeant Sharp to the doctor. Angus and I will wait with the Major until you return."

"But, sir…"

"An order, Sergeant Sharp!"

Alan reluctantly left us. When they had gone the Colonel said, "Get rid of the bodies, eh Angus."

"Right sir."

After he had gone, I said, "Well out with it, Colonel."

I saw the wry smile as he said, "Impertinent, Major. You are a clever laddie and I am guessing you can work most of this out."

"You staked me out like a goat!"

"Aye, but it was the only way to draw her out. She failed with you and that hurt her professional pride. She planted Giorgio with the lady. I am sorry about that. We did not know that she knew the Black Widow. When the Portuguese chap was killed, we came back here and tried to find her. She remained hidden. She had gold and she used it to buy mercenaries. We have been watching your house since you arrived. She was a damned clever woman. The key we found on her dead man was what they call a skeleton key. It would open any door. I think you came within a whisker of death. We heard the pistol and came as quickly as we could. Like I said, her gloating saved you."

The Colonel had saved my life but that had not been important to him. He had eliminated one of Britain's enemies. Donna Maria was just collateral damage. For me, it was a loss I would bear until the end of my days. She had died because of me and I would never forget that. I would obey orders but that night changed me forever.

The End

Glossary
Fictional characters are in italics

Boots and Saddles- a bugle call sounded for mounted troops to mount and take their place in line. It has been derived from neither boots, nor from saddles, but from the French boute-selle, "put on saddle"

Brigadier- in the French cavalry he would be the equivalent of a corporal. In all other references, he is the commander of a brigade of either horse or foot

Cesar Alpini- Robbie's cousin and the head of the Sicilian branch of the family

Sergeant Alan Sharp- Robbie's servant and companion

Caçadores- Portuguese light infantry

Major Robbie (Macgregor) Matthews-illegitimate son of the *Count of Breteuil*

Colonel James Selkirk- War department

Colpack-fur hat worn by the guards and elite companies

Crack- from the Irish 'craich', good fun, enjoyable

David Hudson- The Alpini agent in London

Joe Seymour- Corporal and then Sergeant 11th Light Dragoons

Joseph Fouché- Napoleon's Chief of Police and Spy catcher

Lieutenant Commander Jonathan Teer- Captain of the Black Prince

Le Casse-Poitrine -Rot gut (strong drink-slang)

Les Goddams- the English (slang)

Marche a terre- foot slogger (slang)

Middy- Midshipman (slang)

musketoon- Cavalry musket

Paget Carbine- Light Cavalry weapon

pichet- a small jug for wine in France

Pompey- naval slang for Portsmouth

Prefeito – Portuguese official

Roast Beef- French slang for British soldiers

Rooking- cheating a customer

Snotty- naval slang for a raw lieutenant

Tarleton Helmet- Headgear worn by light cavalry until 1812

Vrai Bougre -old campaigner (slang) It means true fellow

Windage- the gap between the ball and the wall of the cannon which means the ball does not fire true.

Historical note

For the London Street maps, I used
http://mapco.net/anon/anon01.htm

Battle of Oporto

This battle happened almost exactly the way I wrote. I have used Major Matthews to represent the actions of a number of people. There was a damaged ferry found. The sources vary in its position. One source has it 3 Km from Oporto and the other 4 miles. I split the difference. Sir John Murray ferried two regiments of horse and a battery of horse artillery across to cut the road.

The bridge was blown leaving Soult confident that he had held Wellesley. It was a barber who rowed across the river and told Wellesley that there were four barges hidden under the cliffs. They sailed back and forth landing three battalions. Amazingly the French mistook the red coats for Swiss mercenaries. It took an hour for the French to realise that they had the British north of the river. With a screen of tirailleurs before them, three battalions of infantry tried to shift the brigade of infantry, British howitzers silenced the batteries brought into action. With the populace raised Soult abandoned Oporto. 300 French were killed and the 1500 in Oporto hospital were taken prisoner. Only 123 British and Portuguese troops were lost. It was a remarkable victory!

Colonel Rufane Shaw Donkin was the brigade commander of the two Irish regiments. He played an important part in the battle of Talavera too. The names of the leading characters and the role they played have been taken from the events. I have fictionalised their conversations.

For the voyage to and from Spain, I used the Stanford University resource http:orbis.stanford.edu

The books I used for reference were:

- Napoleon's Line Chasseurs- Bukhari/MacBride
- Napoleon's War in Spain- Lachouque, Tranie, Carmigniani

- The Napoleonic Source Book- Philip J Haythornthwaite,
- Wellington's Military Machine- Philip J Haythornthwaite
- The Peninsular War- Roger Parkinson
- Military Dress of the Peninsular War 1808-1814
- The History of the Napoleonic Wars-Richard Holmes,
- The Greenhill Napoleonic Wars Data book- Digby Smith,
- The Napoleonic Wars Vol 1 & 2- Liliane and Fred Funcken
- The Napoleonic Wars- Michael Glover
- Talavera 1809-Chartrand and Turner
- Wellington's Regiments- Ian Fletcher.
- Wellington's Light Cavalry- Bryan Fosten
- Wellington's Heavy Cavalry- Bryan Fosten

Griff Hosker
April 2019

Other books
by
Griff Hosker

If you enjoyed reading this book, then why not read another one by the author?

Ancient History

The Sword of Cartimandua Series (Germania and Britannia 50 A.D. – 128 A.D.)
Ulpius Felix- Roman Warrior (prequel)
Book 1 The Sword of Cartimandua
Book 2 The Horse Warriors
Book 3 Invasion Caledonia
Book 4 Roman Retreat
Book 5 Revolt of the Red Witch
Book 6 Druid's Gold
Book 7 Trajan's Hunters
Book 8 The Last Frontier
Book 9 Hero of Rome
Book 10 Roman Hawk
Book 11 Roman Treachery
Book 12 Roman Wall
Book 13 Roman Courage

The Aelfraed Series
(Britain and Byzantium 1050 A.D. - 1085 A.D.)
Book 1 Housecarl
Book 2 Outlaw
Book 3 Varangian

The Wolf Warrior series
(Britain in the late 6th Century)
Book 1 Saxon Dawn
Book 2 Saxon Revenge
Book 3 Saxon England
Book 4 Saxon Blood

Book 5 Saxon Slayer
Book 6 Saxon Slaughter
Book 7 Saxon Bane
Book 8 Saxon Fall: Rise of the Warlord
Book 9 Saxon Throne
Book 10 Saxon Sword

The Dragon Heart Series
Book 1 Viking Slave
Book 2 Viking Warrior
Book 3 Viking Jarl
Book 4 Viking Kingdom
Book 5 Viking Wolf
Book 6 Viking War
Book 7 Viking Sword
Book 8 Viking Wrath
Book 9 Viking Raid
Book 10 Viking Legend
Book 11 Viking Vengeance
Book 12 Viking Dragon
Book 13 Viking Treasure
Book 14 Viking Enemy
Book 15 Viking Witch
Book 16 Viking Blood
Book 17 Viking Weregeld
Book 18 Viking Storm
Book 19 Viking Warband
Book 20 Viking Shadow
Book 21 Viking Legacy
Book 22 Viking Clan

The Norman Genesis Series
Hrolf the Viking
Horseman
The Battle for a Home
Revenge of the Franks
The Land of the Northmen
Ragnvald Hrolfsson
Brothers in Blood

Lord of Rouen
Drekar in the Seine
Duke of Normandy
The Duke and the King

New World Series
Blood on the Blade
Across the Seas

**The Anarchy Series England
1120-1180**
English Knight
Knight of the Empress
Northern Knight
Baron of the North
Earl
King Henry's Champion
The King is Dead
Warlord of the North
Enemy at the Gate
The Fallen Crown
Warlord's War
Kingmaker
Henry II
Crusader
The Welsh Marches
Irish War
Poisonous Plots
The Princes' Revolt
Earl Marshal

**Border Knight
1182-1300**
Sword for Hire
Return of the Knight
Baron's War
Magna Carta
Welsh Wars
Henry III

The Bloody Border

Lord Edward's Archer
Lord Edward's Archer

Struggle for a Crown
1360- 1485
Blood on the Crown
To Murder A King
The Throne

Modern History

The Napoleonic Horseman Series
Book 1 Chasseur a Cheval
Book 2 Napoleon's Guard
Book 3 British Light Dragoon
Book 4 Soldier Spy
Book 5 1808: The Road to Coruña
Book 6 Talavera
Waterloo

The Lucky Jack American Civil War series
Rebel Raiders
Confederate Rangers
The Road to Gettysburg

The British Ace Series
1914
1915 Fokker Scourge
1916 Angels over the Somme
1917 Eagles Fall
1918 We will remember them
From Arctic Snow to Desert Sand
Wings over Persia

Combined Operations series
1940-1945
Commando

Raider
Behind Enemy Lines
Dieppe
Toehold in Europe
Sword Beach
Breakout
The Battle for Antwerp
King Tiger
Beyond the Rhine
Korea

Other Books
Carnage at Cannes (a thriller)
Great Granny's Ghost (Aimed at 9-14-year-old young people)
Adventure at 63-Backpacking to Istanbul

For more information on all of the books then please visit the author's web site at www.griffhosker.com where there is a link to contact him.